the rogue's princess

Also by Eve Edwards

The Lacey Chronicles I: *The Other Countess*
The Lacey Chronicles II: *The Queen's Lady*

the rogue's princess

EVE EDWARDS

DELACORTE PRESS

Text copyright © 2011 by Eve Edwards
Jacket photograph copyright © 2012 by Lara Jade

Visit us on the Web! randomhouse.com/teens

Educators and librarians, for a variety of teaching tools, visit us at RHTeachersLibrarians.com

Library of Congress Cataloging-in-Publication Data
Edwards, Eve.
The rogue's princess / Eve Edwards. — 1st U.S. ed.
p. cm. — ([The Lacey chronicles ; 3])
Summary: In 1586 England, sixteen-year-old Mercy Hart, daughter of one of London's wealthiest and most devout merchants, considers renouncing her family for love of Kit, a lowly actor and playboy, until Kit is accused of treason, testing Mercy's resolve.
ISBN 978-0-385-74093-7 (hc) — ISBN 978-0-375-98339-9 (ebook) — ISBN 978-0-375-98976-6 (glb) [1. Love—Fiction. 2. Social classes—Fiction. 3. Family life—England—Fiction. 4. Great Britain—History—Elizabeth, 1558–1603—Fiction.] I. Title.
PZ7.E25252Rog 2013
[Fic]—dc23
2012035754

The text of this book is set in 11-point Adobe Caslon.
Book design by Stephanie Moss

Printed in the United States of America
10 9 8 7 6 5 4 3 2 1

First U.S. Edition

For Dr. Liz Clark,
with thanks for her years of friendship as well as her
expert knowledge of English Puritanism!

the rogue's princess

Prologue

6 April 1580

THE MOMENT THE EARTHQUAKE STRUCK, Mercy Hart knew it was her fault. God had sent it upon London because she had not been paying attention to her father's prayers as she ought. How many times had she been warned that the good Christian child bent all her thoughts on Heaven, else the Devil would find entry to her soul? From the day she had been weaned, she had been schooled to obey this teaching and, yet, had she listened? No. Instead, she had been peeking between her fingers out of the window, watching the seagulls circling the masts of the ships moored at Rotherhithe, wondering when it would be time for supper.

The room shuddered; dust rained on their heads like marks of Ash Wednesday penitence; the collection of family plates in the cupboard rattled then tumbled to the floor, a stark reminder of the fate of damned souls that would fall into the yawning pit of Hell. Outside, the crowds crossing London Bridge shrieked and cried for God's mercy until it sounded as if they were echoing her name to the skies, blaming her for the calamity. Unable to master her terror, Mercy reached out and clung to her older sister, Faith, hoping that God would take into account that Faith at least was sinless and so decide, in His infinite wisdom, not to bring the roof down on their heads. Mercy breathed a quick prayer, reminding Him that Faith had had her eyes demurely bent on the rush matting, her thoughts turned only on pure objects of contemplation. Mercy added in for good measure her brother, Edwin, who was kneeling straight-backed in front of the girls with hands clasped firmly at his chest like a tomb effigy; he had been mouthing the words, practicing for the day when the family prayers would be his responsibility. Mercy would wager her best cambric apron that neither of them had allowed their mind to stray to supper, a new dress, and what the kitchen cat was doing with that ball of thread, not like her hurdy-gurdy of a brain that was unable to settle to one tune.

Oh, stars! *Your pardon, Lord, I didn't mean to think of wagers.* Mercy quickly took her words back, hoping He hadn't noticed this further lapse. She decided she had best hold her tongue before she dug herself a deeper hole with the Almighty.

"O Lord, defend us from the perils of this night," implored her father, hardly breaking step in his prayer as the world trembled around them. The Final Judgment could be coming at any moment and he was determined to be found ready, torch trimmed, floor swept. There would be no sleeping bridesmaids in his house, none who would miss the arrival of the heavenly groom through lack of vigilance! "Protect and defend the faithful remnant," he cried. The chestnut curls that circled his balding pate shone with holy light, like in those paintings in the bad sort of churches.

Oh, dear, she mustn't think of heretics either! How her sins were breeding like rabbits! She really was a terrible child, just the kind who would be one of those bridesmaids in the Bible who fell asleep and missed the wedding feast.

After another strong shudder, the kitchen maid whimpered and threw herself into the arms of the eldest apprentice. "Sweet body of Christ, we're all going to die!" she wailed.

Mercy's father hitched his voice a notch louder to drown out the maid's panic. "When mountains fall and the seas rise, You, O Lord, will save the righteous!"

Mercy could barely refrain from following the maid's example, wishing her sister would hug her close and make her feel safe. The joists in the floor groaned like a ship's timbers in a storm.

"The ground shakes with Your anger against this godless generation. Have mercy on us, we implore you, O Lord!"

And God must have been listening out for His special servant, John Hart, because at that moment the tremor ceased and a strange hush fell over London, even outside their home, one of the finest houses on the busy bridge over the Thames. Mercy felt faint with relief.

"Praise be to the Lord!" cried Master Hart, rising from his knees, flinging his hands to the ceiling in celebration. "He has seen fit to remove the hand of retribution from us for this time and give us a pause to correct our errors. Children, thank Him for His grace with all your heart. You have a loving God."

On the bridge, the people began cheering. Mercy screwed her eyes tight and muttered fervent words of gratitude with all her ten-year-old soul.

"I will be good," she promised. "I won't neglect to pray, or fast, or read my Bible. I won't hanker after worldly things, like blue dresses with silk trimming, or sweetmeats, particularly not the marchpane ones, neither will I run to hear the street musicians like the wonderful group I heard yesterday outside the city gates. No, no, I absolutely will not. You have spared London to give Mercy Hart another chance. O Lord, I will not let You down." She glanced sideways at the serene face of her sister, admiring how not a scrap of her wispy fair hair showed beneath her coif despite the trauma of the past few minutes. Mercy then noticed that her own riot of brown corkscrew curls had come loose again. "At least, I'll try not to let You down much, I hope," she added, scrupulously honest.

The earthquake had shaken the Theatre at the very moment the players took their bow after the performance of *The Merchant's Daughter*. The audience didn't wait to applaud, but ran from the building screaming, scrambling over benches, spilling nuts like an autumn gale as they shoved past the hawkers. Soon the circular auditorium was as empty as a husk, leaving the players with a barren harvest of praise.

Terrified by this strange shaking of the earth, Kit Turner almost joined the audience in fleeing the stage until he felt a heavy hand on his shoulder. It was James Burbage, joint owner of the company. A stout man of middling stature, rust-colored hair and brown eyes, he was unremarkable until he began to act: then he was transformed into king or cobbler thanks to the astonishing skill with which he performed his part. Despite his artist's soul, he nonetheless kept strict discipline in the ranks worthy of a general, ably supported by his talented son and second-in-command, Richard.

"Stand fast, Kit. You can be in no safer place at present." Burbage gestured to the open air above the stage canopy.

Kit gulped and stood his ground, following his master's orders to bow as if all hell had not broken loose outside. Though the pillars creaked, the stars on the canopy stayed in their places; the sky did not fall. Master Burbage had been right. Feeling a little smug to have been braver than the majority of men that day, Kit swished aside the skirts of his costume and retreated to the tiring-house in his correct place with the other boys, following the leading men.

All restraint gave way once out of the public eye.

"What in the name of all the saints was that?" asked Tom Saxon, another of the boys in Burbage's company. "I saw my life pass before me like . . . like pages in a book flicking in the wind."

Richard Appleyard, an older actor now playing the father or aged statesmen roles, snorted and lightly boxed Tom's ears. "Well, that wouldn't take long, would it, shrimp? You can't be more than fourteen. Not many chapters yet in that story."

"That, gentlemen, was an earth tremor," declared Richard Burbage, as he stripped off his costume. Kit thought him a younger version of his father, being of similar stature with a plain face enlivened by humor and wit. "As men of learning and reason will tell us, a shaking of the ground by natural causes unknown."

"Or"—here Richard's father stepped in and gestured to Kit—"some could say it was the world applauding the debut of our newest member of the cast, Master Christopher Turner, the best merchant's daughter this side of Prato."

The men laughed and cheered, their thoughts deftly turned by their leader to their stage business rather than the perils of Nature. Only Tom Saxon scowled, jealous of the new recruit stealing his place as youngest in the cast, taking the plum roles from under his less than prepossessing nose. The last year had brought a crop of spots to his face that spoiled him for the most elegant parts.

When normal conversation resumed, Tom jostled Kit into a corner and whispered, "Aye, you make a good sort of girl—all that pretty-pretty black hair and big eyes. Take care they don't try to see what you've got under your skirts."

Tall and lean for his twelve years, Kit was no weakling and used to fending off bullies. He didn't bother with a war of words and retaliated with a swift punch to Tom's gut. Kit then carried on undressing as if nothing had happened, though he could feel the elder Burbage's eyes boring into his back for evidence as to why his second boy was now doubled over, trying to catch his breath.

Costumes folded carefully away in their chests, Kit lingered for the final instructions from Master Burbage—reminders to be prompt for rehearsal the next day at ten, warnings to cast members who had not yet perfected their lines in the new play, advice to younger players not to get caught up in bad company in the taverns. Unlike the others, who had heard it all before, Kit drank in every word with the same respect he would give the priest on Sunday—more, if truth be told. This world of the Theatre was so new to him—the shine still on the penny, not worn by use or soiled by passage through many hands. Until recently a pupil at Maidenhead Grammar School, Kit had been thrown on his own resources after the death of his father, the Earl of Dorset. In life, the earl had taken scant notice of his bastard son, providing only a small stipend to pay for Kit's education; after his demise, even that interest appeared to have died with him. Funds dried up, but Kit had hung on at school for a year, taking on menial tasks for the master to pay his way, wondering if anyone was going to come for him. Months ticked by and the Lacey family, his legitimate relations, did not stir themselves to help him; he had been forgotten.

And then the players had rolled into town in their wagons, bringing an explosion of color, music and wonderful words. This was the world as it should be, not as Kit knew it: laughter, courage, wit and passion. Watching the Burbages perform, Kit realized what he wanted to do with his life. Using all the arts of rhetoric drummed into him in the classroom through mind-numbing hours of Horace and Cicero, he had talked his way into the company. He was helped by the fact that the voice of one of the boys had just broken. That made a space for a new recruit to play the female roles, which were by custom given to boys of Kit's age as no women were allowed on the English stage. Burbage senior had been impressed by Kit's silver tongue and offered him a trial, first as the troupe's boy-of-all-work, and now, for the first time, on the stage. Kit knew he was fortunate to have snatched up this means of earning a living in the face of many rivals, and meant not to waste a second of it. It was no small thing to be part of the only company to have a license to present plays from the Queen herself and to be listed as retainers of the chief man of the realm, Lord Leicester, for this made them—in a very distant fashion admittedly—royal servants.

The company dismissed, Burbage and son off to meet the Master of Revels to gain permission for a new play, Kit readied himself to go home, tucking his earnings in the toe of his left shoe to beat cutpurses, and checking his knife was on his belt. He lodged on Throgmorton Street, which meant a good ten minutes' walk down a rutted track so he couldn't be too careful with his riches. The Theatre had been built to the north beyond the city walls in the tanners' fields an arrow shot from Bedlam asylum. As Master Burbage was fond of saying with a nicely judged pinch of irony, all the undesirables were excluded from London itself: the mad, the foul-smelling and the players. Kit couldn't understand why actors were held in such low esteem; to him, they seemed the noblest of fellows.

As Kit stepped out of the tiring-house, he was startled to find a crowd of protestors in the yard. They must have gathered in haste after the quake for some bore signs on rough wood, words scrawled in charcoal: *The earth shakes—God hates players* and *Salvation or the stage.* They were already haranguing Master Appleyard, led at the front by a flush-faced preacher from one of the stricter parish churches in Bishopsgate ward. Kit had always made it a rule to steer clear of men like him. It had been his experience that they showed no mercy to bastards such as he. These churchmen had evidently been in the back of the line when God ladled out the milk of human kindness.

"You players are an abomination, an offense to God!" the preacher yelled over the hoots and jeers of the crowd. "Your plays have drawn down His wrath on this city!"

Appleyard, as peaceable a fellow as one could wish to meet, looked rather surprised by this accusation. His round-cheeked face wanted to smile, but he sensed the crowd would not react well to his usual charm. He held out his hands in supplication.

"Good my masters, calm yourselves. God does not worry about our little plays; He has the whole of Nature to order. Go from this place in peace."

But the preacher was not to be silenced. "You dare to interpret

God's word to me, old man? You play lewdness on the stage and then talk of our Lord's ways as if you know them? Repent ye before devils drag you off to Hell!"

Appleyard shrugged, seeing that this crowd was beyond reason. "Then let me through so I can go and contemplate my doubtless manifold sins in the privacy of my own chamber."

The priest was not sure what to make of so placid a response. The merry-natured player looked as if he were going to make good his escape. To do justice to the momentous occasion of an earthquake, the Puritan preacher needed another flint to ignite his followers, one with more of an edge to strike his wit upon. Inadvertently, Kit provided him with his tinderbox.

"Look, my brothers, here is a young man they have already corrupted—dressing him in women's clothing and getting him to simper and preen on the stage like a courtesan!" The priest stabbed Kit in the chest with a bony forefinger before he could slide away in Appleyard's wake.

"Leave me alone." Kit brushed him off, anger building. He had never simpered, not now, nor would he ever. He'd played his role as true to life as he could, giving his character spirit and dignity. There was nothing lewd about the merchant's daughter; she was as witty a daughter of Eve as any yet seen onstage. "I wager you didn't even attend the play, so how can you judge its merits?"

The priest vengefully twisted Kit's ear. "Oh, listen, my brothers! Listen to the boy-whore preach to his betters! Not attend the play! Why, we don't need to sniff brimstone to know Hell is here!"

"Get off me! I'm not a whore!" Kit tried to squirm free, looking for a way through the crowd, but the men were tightly pressed

9

together. No stranger to the ways of the London mob, he began to feel truly alarmed for his safety. Their faces had become indistinguishable from each other: a thick crop of tawny circles, mouths opened in howls, pebble-hard eyes glaring at him; they were like nightmare scarecrows lined up against him, and he the poor crow about to be strung up by the farmer in warning to other scavenging birds.

"On the very day God sends the warning of the earthquake, this creature dares correct me!" The priest seized Kit by the hair and dragged him round to face his congregation. "Is it too late for him? Is he lost from the paths of righteousness?"

"Now see here, sir: that's enough!" Appleyard tried to push through to rescue Kit, but ended up fluttering ineffectually on the edge of the crowd. "Have pity. Let the child go."

"What! Let him back into the clutches of evildoers?" The priest swung Kit this way and that so all could see him. "This boy wallows in sin, wearing skirts and piping like a girl to entice good men from the paths of duty! His every sigh onstage promotes unnatural practices, sins of the flesh too heinous to be named. His masters: procurers, not players! He must be cleansed—purified before God!"

Kit shuddered at the hatred directed at him, but kept his teeth clamped together, determined not to plead for mercy. His life had been one long struggle to keep his pride and he wasn't letting it go now, even though, like the mouse under the cat's paw, he could feel the hot breath of the preacher on his neck, the clutch of hands on his clothing as the crowd bore him along.

"Cleanse him! Cleanse him!" chanted the crowd. A wild holiday mood was upon them as the priest played them skillfully, like a flautist playing his pipe.

They dragged Kit to a horse trough outside an inn, lifted him high and dumped him in. Kit gasped with shock as water soaked through his clothes, cheap dye running out and staining the water brackish brown as it leaked from his jerkin. The preacher pushed him under, harsh fist on his chest.

"Wash away his sins, O Lord!" he bellowed, thoroughly enjoying the performance he was giving at Kit's expense. He pulled Kit up by the hair. "Do you repent?"

Kit gasped for breath, but refused to speak.

"He still spurns the light," crowed the priest.

Hands pushed him back down, holding him under longer this time. Kit took a mouthful of water and came up choking, nose stinging, eyes streaming.

"The Devil claims him—see how he squirms in the fires of Hell!"

Kit was fighting for his life now; another dowsing like that and he feared he would drown. He scratched and kicked, but nothing he did made his captors release their hold on him. Under again and no relief—all he could hear were the muffled sounds of his attackers, rough hands forcing him where he did not want to go. Hauled up a final time, Kit was dumped beside the trough facedown, his vision narrowing as though he were being dragged backwards down a dark tunnel.

"See, God's judgment on a sinner!" bellowed the priest.

When Kit did not move, the preacher realized his victim was barely breathing. He shuffled back, at a loss how to complete the scene. He had been hoping for some grand finale, weeping and wailing from the player, begging their forgiveness, but a silent, broken boy did not make for a very good ending. Some in the crowd began to murmur against the priest.

"Oi, you! What you doing to that lad?" A new voice broke into Kit's confusion. "Damn it, man, you've killed the poor sprat!"

"No, no, Goodman Ostler, he feigns, he feigns." The priest gathered his robes about him, trying to regain some respect. Like any seasoned performer, he knew when he was losing his audience and this was one such moment. "And don't you use such ungodly language in my hearing!"

"Ungodly? I'll give you ungodly!" The ostler pushed up his sleeves.

"Now, now, there's no call for that sort of . . . Help!" Panicked that he might be charged with murder, or thumped by the irate ostler, the preacher fled the scene, taking his flock with him.

"Good riddance to poxy rubbish," muttered Kit's rescuer, kneeling down in the mud to check the boy over. It took a hefty thump on the back from the kindly ostler to push the water from Kit's lungs, leaving him coughing and retching in the mire.

"All right now, lad?" the man asked, his smiling brown eyes a stark contrast to his beaten face. Nose off-center, he looked as though he had come out the worst in a kicking contest with a horse. Not that Kit felt his appearance was any better at that moment.

"Thanks." Kit got gingerly onto his knees then sank back to rest against the trough. His jerkin was ruined—and he'd loved that garment.

"Damned bloodsucking Puritans, pardon my French." The

man helped Kit to his feet. "Want to dress the rest of the world in their colors and leech away the fun."

Master Appleyard appeared at Kit's side. "Got our boy for us, then?"

"Aye, but not before they half killed him. He's one of Burbage's lads?"

"Aye. First day acting for the troupe at that."

"Oh rare, there's a famous beginning! I predict he'll go far, this one."

"Are you well, Kit?" Appleyard patted his arm awkwardly. "I beg your forgiveness that I couldn't separate you from the mob earlier. Two of them had me by the neck."

Kit hugged himself, shivering in the chill evening air. "No matter, master. You couldn't have stopped them. They would've just ducked you too."

"Marry, but I would've tried and then I wouldn't feel so cowardly now. What's the good of playing heroes onstage if you fail at the first sign of trouble, eh, my lad? You'd best skip along. Get yourself to your lodgings and change before you take ill." Appleyard was still looking fearfully around, afraid that the preacher would return with reinforcements to finish the job.

"I'll see him home," offered the ostler.

"Thank you, John. I would be most obliged to you. I fear I wouldn't be much protection for him on the streets this night, not with the citizens acting as mad as rutting bucks trying to spear us on their horns."

The ostler settled a paternal hand on Kit's shoulder. "Come on, lad. You have nothing to fear from me. We'd best take it at the double: you're squelching in your shoes."

Reminded of his precious earnings, Kit wriggled his toes, relieved to find his money still where he had put it.

"Thank you, sir."

"Apace, apace, Kit, before they rise again like the dead at the last trump!" Appleyard waved and hurried off for his own lodgings.

Delivered to his landlady like a cat fished from the Thames, Kit hurried to his attic room to change. Neither of the apprentices with whom he shared the chamber was home, so he could change into dry clothes without smart remarks from them. Indentured to a coffin maker and a butcher respectively, his roommates scorned, as well as envied, Kit his employment, a confused state of affairs that had them insult then flatter him like changeable winds battering a weather vane—the southerly breeze of warm flattery when they were after free entry to a new play, the cold shoulder of a north wind when jealousy gripped them. This would only get worse now that he had been made a proper member of the company and given an acting role: he'd be spinning like the cock atop Bowe Church with their contrary moods.

His landlady took his wet things to hang over the fireplace in the kitchen. She promised she would see what she could do for his poor jerkin, but neither of them held out much hope for it. Mumbling good-natured complaints about boys and their mischief, she creaked her way down the narrow stairs. The ostler had spared Kit the humiliation of explaining to the goodwife exactly what had happened. Kit preferred to keep it that way.

Alone again, Kit huddled on the bed in the gloomy chamber and hugged his long legs to his chest, trying to clamp down on the shivering wracking his body. Left completely on his own in the world, he refused to regret his decision to come to London and take to the stage even if it brought such punishments upon him. Onstage, he could be princes and queens, people of importance. When he was older, he would be able to act heroes, warriors and kings—he couldn't wait for that. He needed this escape because, offstage, he was plain Kit Turner, an earl's bastard, forgotten by his family, and loved by no one since his mother's death when he was but seven years old.

Kit pulled a splinter from a finger then sucked the wound, wondering what his mother would say to see him here. An optimistic woman with an exotic dark beauty quite out of the common sort for Berkshire, she'd had such hopes for him, thinking his father would set him up in some honorable profession, such as a soldier or man of law. When the other boys at the grammar school had teased him for his birth, she'd always said: "Just you wait, Kit, they'll be laughing on the other side of their faces when your father takes you into his household. You'll be sharing tutors with earls and gentlemen!"

But his father had never taken in the stray son and Kit's mother had died bearing another unwanted babe, the child surviving only a few hours after her. He couldn't tarnish his memories of her and blame her for being a nobleman's mistress—he had never been old enough to ask the whys and wherefores of the relationship, but he guessed it would have been hard for a woman of humble birth to refuse such a man as an earl. No, the fault was in the father who neglected the son that he knew he had been responsible for siring.

Staring defiantly into the gathering dark, Kit refused to get down on his knees for his nightly prayer, sick of all that worship business after the "purifying" he had received in the horse trough. If God was going to send an earthquake just because Kit had finally found a place he could be happy, then He wasn't much of a god and Kit renounced Him as he had his father and his negligent family. Bitter experience had taught him that if you were going to be rejected it was as well to beat them to the punch and get your own rejection in first.

chapter 1

1586

"ARE YOU SURE, ABSOLUTELY AND utterly certain, that there is nothing ungodly about this feast for your father's fellow trades-men?" Mercy asked her best friend, Ann Belknap, as the two sat in her little bedchamber watching the boats take the perilous passage under the arches of the bridge.

The goldsmith's daughter, her hair the hue of her father's wares, eyes a clear gray-blue, smothered a smile. Mercy knew that Ann understood how seriously she took such matters—and how she felt she had to report any little infraction to her sober-minded father as if she had some huge debt to pay and he was in charge of the tally.

"No, Mercy, my father's friends are all respectable men and their wives are above reproach. I have asked you to bear me company for a family supper, not to dance with the Devil on the steps of St. Paul's in naught but your shift."

Mercy blushed at the thought, but couldn't stifle a giggle. When it was just the two of them, Ann was far more outspoken than she dared be, saying the most outrageous things. Mercy loved her all the more for it as it gave her an outlet for her own rebellious thoughts to hear them in someone else's mouth. Mercy had, of course, given up her childish notions that she had personally caused the earthquake all those years ago, and now was embarrassed by the self-regard that had thought such a thing possible, but she still labored under the belief she owed God for everything and had to live up to His exacting standards as befitted a child of John Hart.

And yet an evening at her friend's should be permissible, surely? Before she knew it, she heard herself saying: "I would be delighted to come. Thank you for the invitation."

"Good, then you must stay for the night, as you will not be back before curfew." Ann tweaked Mercy's drab skirt. "And you must let me dress you too—I've a kirtle in a pretty color that would become you and two glorious new bodices just come from the tailor—you can wear one of them." Daughter of one of the City's richest men, Ann's wardrobe had more clothes than most court ladies. She was so generous with her father's riches that she had probably ordered the extra bodice with Mercy in mind. "My father would not approve of you coming to a merry feast looking as though you are in deep mourning."

Mercy felt she had just been made to agree to something, but she wasn't sure what.

"Did I tell you Master Fletcher called on Father to ask for Catherine's hand?" On impulse, Ann leant out of the window and threw a straw into the water below to watch it be carried away on the hungry tide.

"Nay. What happened?" Mercy perched beside her, sniffing with relish the fresh air of a stiff breeze off the sea.

"He was sent away with a flea in his ear. None of us will marry anyone less than a guildsman if my father has his way. Catherine was relieved: Fletcher's breath smelt of onions."

The gust of wind sent Mercy's ruff into a flutter, pins from where she had not anchored it securely scattering into the water below. She hastily grabbed the loose end before it too went sailing.

"Here, let me do that." Ann clucked her tongue. "You have a mighty skill at striking wide with the pins, like a half-blind archer shooting at the butts on Finsbury Fields."

"I know. I'm hopelessly untidy even though I try not to be." Mercy gestured to the room she shared with her sister. It was a case in point. Her trundle bed was a tumble of sheets; Faith's made right and tight as if she had never slept in it. Their belongings were in a similar state: Mercy's trunk a jumble, Faith's neat as if for military inspection.

"I don't understand it," continued Ann as she worked her way round Mercy's collar, "neither your brother nor your sister wear such plain, dull clothes, and your father is the biggest importer of cloth in London! I noticed that Faith is wearing a lovely russet kirtle and white sleeves today, so clearly this is none of her doing."

Mercy made no comment. It was a matter between her and God, and Ann would just laugh if she told her. Besides, she was used to being the less-regarded sister in the shadow of Faith's shining reputation.

"My friend." Ann had nearly reached the end of her task, tipping Mercy's head sideways to ease in the last fastening. "I think you must be a fool for wasting your position; you could have your pick of the shipments. It's as though you don't like being a girl."

Mercy hummed in a noncommittal manner.

"You must admit that choosing pretty clothes is part of the fun of belonging to our sex. Lord knows, we have few other advantages."

Mercy smoothed her gray skirts, secretly agreeing that they were dreadful, but she had made a bargain with God when she was little and she meant to keep it. "I like being this way."

Ann turned away to gather a few things for Mercy, putting them in a little leather bag. "No, you don't. I see you eyeing my orange kirtle. You, Mercy Hart, are a counterfeit good girl. There is a merry maid just wanting to burst out."

Wasn't that the truth? Mercy was beginning to regret her decision to go; she knew her weaknesses well enough to realize she should resist putting herself in the path of temptation.

"Please, Ann, I've said I'd come to your feast. Let that be enough."

Ann shoved a nightgown and clean shift into Mercy's arms and held the bag open to receive them. "Then we shall make our escape. Supper is at seven."

In the family parlor downstairs, Faith was sewing on the bench seat by the riverside window. The light fell across her face, making her look like the painting of the Madonna in St. Mary Overie, the one that had survived the reformers' whitewash. Faith would not welcome the comparison as such depictions were suspect, so Mercy kept that thought private. Mercy's grandmother, Mary Isham, sat bundled in blankets by the fire, her chin wagging in the way of the very old as she stroked the tabby cat curled on her knee. Her white hair was bizarrely decked with ribbons like that of a girl on May Day.

"I'm going to Ann's, Gran," Mercy bellowed into her ear.

Grandmother Isham smiled up at her granddaughter and cupped her cheek. "That's good, dear. France is said to be very pleasant."

Ann giggled.

Mercy didn't bother to correct her grandmother's mistake; she trusted Faith to convey the message to her father on his return.

"Do you mind if I go?" Mercy asked her sister.

Faith looked up and smiled serenely. As ever when seeing that expression on her sister's face, Mercy was reminded of the Thames, far upstream in its placid course, winding through meadows near Windsor; and, if anyone cared to ask her opinion, Mercy thought herself more akin to the turbulent tidal reaches outside their front door.

"Of course not, dearest." Faith's voice was melodious and soft, hardly impacting on the quiet of the parlor. "What time will you be home?"

Mercy felt her tones were like an untuned viol in her sister's presence. "About nine tomorrow morning?"

Faith threaded a needle with blue silk. "Then I hope you enjoy yourself."

As the two friends turned to leave, the front door banged opened and Aunt Rose came in from the street, a basket on her arm loaded with vegetables. A tall woman with handsome features, something of a warrior-queen in the way she battled through life, she was already talking as she entered. "I swear it is madness out there. The bridge is packed with pilgrims going south and Kentish men going north; you have to be as thin as a fillet to get through."

Grandmother Isham perked up when she saw her favorite daughter come in. "Ah, sweet, come sit by the fire, warm yourself."

Rose looked outside at the sunny winter day and smiled. "Thank you, Ma. I'll be with you anon when I've put this lot away. The market was like a cockfight. You would've thought there were no more carrots to be had in Christendom the way the goodwives were pulling caps askew to get at them."

Grandmother Isham caught Mercy's hand. "Rosie put my hair up." She turned her head for them to admire. "She said I looked as pretty as a picture when she'd finished."

Mercy leant down and kissed the old lady's wrinkled cheek. "And so you do, Gran."

"My Ben will be tickled when he sees me." She patted her hair, pushing one ribbon astray.

Mercy tied it back into place. "That he will." Sadly, Grandfather Ben Isham had been dead these ten years and would never see anything again.

"He always likes me in ribbons and nothing else," the old lady said proudly, tugging at her shawl.

Alarmed that they were about to be treated to a display of rather more aged flesh than they had bargained for, Faith got up from her seat and put her sewing aside. "Now, now, Gran, you know Grandfather Ben is not here." She knelt by the old lady, holding her hands to stop her from unlacing her bodice.

Grandmother shook her head. "Of course he is, you silly goose. Faith, you are such a giddy girl sometimes! He went out but a few minutes ago."

"Leave her be, Faith," warned Rose softly. "Let her keep her beliefs."

Faith pursed her lips. "But it is a lie."

Rose put her hands on her hips, the dispute an old one. "So to live up to your strict interpretation of the truth, she must learn of his passing daily and grieve afresh?"

Mercy hated the tension that bristled between the two women, both mothers to her when she had never known her own. Since Rose Isham's disgrace had forced her to come to live in their household, she had always been at odds with her perfect niece. At twenty, Faith was an impeccable daughter who had not put so much as one slippered foot wrong, the belle of the bridge, her hand sought by guildsmen across London. A spinster in her thirties, Rose had blotted her reputation ten years ago by daring to love a worthless but smooth-talking man, living with him until he abandoned her five years later when a richer prospect for a wife came into view. Shamed, but spirit not broken. Rose appeared to have far more time for Mercy, the awkward sixteen-year-old who tried so hard, but never achieved her aim of matching her sister. With Faith, Rose always acted as if talking to her were as welcome as sucking lemons.

"Ann, tell Rose about my trip," Mercy declared a touch too brightly, forcing a turn of subject.

Ann rose to the occasion. "Mistress Isham, according to your mother, I am taking your niece to France. Can you believe it?" Ann laughed merrily at the absurdity of the idea.

Rose dropped her gaze from the silent battle of wills with Faith and shook her head. She began unpacking her purchases. "Aye, of you, I can believe anything, Mistress Ann. Next port of call the moon. But what's all this about France?"

Mercy held out her hands to squeeze her aunt's fingers. "Gran misheard. I'm going to *Ann's* to a fine supper. We shall have, oh, I don't know, at least ten dishes, all superior to those on the Queen's table!"

"And I'm to dress Mercy like a duchess." Ann smiled conspiratorially at Rose.

"Pray do so. We are tired of seeing her in these hedge-sparrow clothes." Rose hugged her niece—Mercy was still the baby of the family with no younger children coming along behind her. John Hart had not remarried after his wife, Rose's sister, died giving birth to Mercy. "Go enjoy yourself, sweet."

"I'll be good," Mercy promised solemnly.

"We know you will, love." Rose ushered her to the door, wrapping her niece's cloak about her shoulders. "On occasion, I would wish you to be just the tiniest bit bad."

Mercy felt a twinge of guilt leaving Faith, Rose and Gran in each other's company. Without her presence to smooth the way, the younger two were prone to fall into bickering and that upset Grandmother Isham. She prayed Edwin and her father would return soon to dilute the combustible mix.

Ann hooked her arm through Mercy's. "Don't worry about Rose and Faith. They are not your burden to bear."

Mercy smiled at her friend even though she didn't agree. They were family—and family was everything. After God, that is.

Kit wondered what on earth had possessed him to agree to dine at Alderman Jerome Belknap's house that evening. True, Belknap was a particular friend of James Burbage and had floated the company many a loan when they'd hit lean times. He was also said to have a brood of fine-looking girls, all heiresses if the rumor about his will was to be believed. Even without that promise of future wealth, their dowries had to be substantial. Pretty faces would alleviate what would otherwise inevitably prove to be a deadly dull occasion. Kit, if pressed, couldn't imagine more tedious company than a pack of City merchants all discussing percentages, or whatever it was these men talked about when they could be torn away from totting up their gains in the counting houses.

Primping his ruff and combing his hair in a tiny hand mirror, Kit had to own up to the fact that the real reason he had agreed to come was that he wished to please Burbage. He owed more to the man than any other alive, even his own family, with whom he had recently been partially reconciled. He had met his half-brothers during the summer two years back when one of their servants had courted his friend, Milly Porter. He had learnt then that ignorance of his existence rather than neglect had lain behind his abandonment at the tender age of ten. He had given them a grudging acquittal. But his ties to them were nothing compared to those linking him to Burbage. The manager had taken him on when others had abandoned him, paid him well while he played boy roles and then crowned all these obligations by giving him the chance to graduate to the hero roles he had always hankered after. If Burbage said jump, then Kit would have great difficulty not leaping.

Still, he would much prefer to be spending the evening down at the Two Necks with Tom Saxon and Guy Warrender. Kit took a swig of sack from a bottle by his bedside and let out a heartfelt sigh. He had been promised an introduction to Anthony Babing-ton and his set—noisy young gentlemen who lived life with a flash and flare that Kit wouldn't mind emulating.

Burbage collected Kit from his lodgings on Silver Street shortly before seven. The actor-manager raised an eyebrow at his leading man's attire.

"Really, Turner, do you have to so blatantly break the rules under my very nose?"

Kit brushed down the sober black doublet and hose he had "borrowed" from the tiring-house. Normally he would be facing a hefty fine, but both he and Burbage knew he was only following orders to come dressed as if for church. None of Kit's usual clothes, with his exuberant taste for color and fashion, fit the bill.

"Come now, sir, at least I won't disgrace you at Alderman Soberside's table."

Burbage gestured to the torch-carrying linkboy to precede them to Cheapside. "True, you look very fine, exactly as I wished."

Kit tugged at the tight white ruff under his chin. He preferred to go clean-shaven, and without the protection of whiskers, the starched cambric itched like fury. His hand brushed his pearl ear-ring, and he thought better of it so removed it from the lobe. Why spoil his disguise with something that so loudly proclaimed his aspiration to keep at the cutting edge of fashion?

"And why do you want to parade you newest leading man be-fore the city worthies, sir? Or is the plot too secret to share with a lowly mechanical such as I?" Kit asked.

Burbage clapped him on the back. "Business. Richard pleaded a prior engagement, so you are to show them the youthful vigor in my company, the crowd-pulling power of a handsome face. When

26

they look at you, they will be costing out how many ladies will be paying for the best seats to admire your . . . um . . . fine acting."

"You mean legs."

Burbage didn't even blush. "Aye, I mean legs. Not that you aren't a fine actor too, but you have that little extra that young men like Tom Saxon and Will Shakespeare can't aspire to. You know well enough they are only ever going to be walk-ons with a line or two. You, like Richard, are the ones who have to carry the play."

"Well, thanks, I think." Kit was secretly very pleased to find the elder Burbage mentioning him in the same company as his talented son—there was no better young actor in London in Kit's opinion.

Alderman Belknap's house did not disappoint Kit's expectations of City opulence. With a frontage on Goldsmith's Row, the house stretched back far from the street, opening out onto a garden, which even in this wintry season was pleasing to the eye, with clever intertwining paths and low box hedges framing the beds. At the far end, set up on an artificial mound, was a summerhouse, like a miniature castle. He could imagine it a very pleasant place to spend a July evening with the roses blooming and birds singing in the twilight. Only banking wealth could have purchased such a little patch of heaven right in the center of one of the biggest cities in the world. Kit tried not to feel envious, or give away, by gawking, how impressed he was.

The house itself was decorated in modern style: in one room the plaster was painted with the family crest, fruit trees and mythical beasts; in the next the walls were paneled with oak. A fine carpet lay on a side table, showing off the jewel-bright colors that must have been woven in some Arabian city. Kit's stomach rumbled just imagining what wonders the kitchens of this alder-man would produce. It was a well-known fact that many City men dined far better than the court, having first call on the most exotic imports arriving in the bellies of the merchant ships.

Their host greeted them in the family parlor, his back to a roaring fire, not that the day was that cold for February, more a statement of how much money he had to burn if measured in coals or faggots of wood. Kit had prepared himself for a butterball of a man rolling in his riches; instead he was introduced to a tall, daddy-longlegged gentleman who would not have looked out of place in a pulpit, gray hair clipped close, face almost gaunt, clothes fine, but restrained with only a modicum of fur lining and very little gold flashing on fingers. How such a Spartan fellow could run a prestigious business as a purveyor of golden luxury and loans was a puzzle. Perhaps the fact that he looked unlikely to be se-duced by lucre himself was the very reason for his success. Suspi-cious of religious types, Kit stood back, watching for any sign of the manic gleam in the eye that he'd seen all those years ago in the preacher that had dunked him in the horse trough, but Jerome Belknap seemed quite sane and happy to reconcile his devotion to God with a love of the theater.

"And you, Master Turner, I saw you in *The Knights of Malta*—excellently done, i'faith." Belknap appeared to have genuinely en-joyed the play—Kit thought it an indifferent piece, enlivened only by lots of crowd-pleasing sword fighting. His side still bore the bruise from a mistimed swipe by Saxon.

"Thank you, sir." Kit amused himself by acting the modest man of sober opinions to match his host and his garb. "I am flat-tered by your high opinion."

"I'm glad to see you are taking after your master and his son rather than those wild fellows that run riot in the taverns giving the stage a bad reputation, what's-his-name Marlowe, Saxon and the like."

Burbage coughed, warning Kit to behave.

"Indeed, sir, I have no desire to squander my time in low company." Kit wagered his expression could have charmed the sternest of puritans.

"Good, good. My family have been eager to meet you ever since I announced you were coming to supper—and my business partners, of course. We may be serious fellows in Cheapside, but never let it be said we have forgotten how to make merry!"

Kit had an image of himself as a lion in the Queen's menagerie in the Tower, being poked at for the amusement of the city populace. He wasn't sure he relished this role that Burbage had foisted on him.

"Ah, here are my girls. Mistress Belknap, my wife."

A smiling lady with a fair complexion and slight frame curtsied to the company. She was gaily dressed in a light blue damask kirtle and bodice with white sleeves. Gold embroidery glittered discreetly on seam and forepart. Kit wondered if his friend Milly Porter, who owned a fine finishing business on Silver Street, had had the task of creating the detailing. She would have been the one who could get right the balance between a suggestion of opulence and tasteful restraint.

"And my daughters, Catherine, Alice and Ann."

Three of the four girls clustered behind Mistress Belknap curtsied. They were little blond copies of their parent, dressed like a rainbow, one in orange, another in green, the third in violet. Kit had no idea which was which. They were pretty enough; rumor had not lied on that account.

"And last, but not least, little Mercy Hart, a good friend of my daughter Ann." The fourth girl, hidden at the back of the group, bobbed a hasty curtsy, preventing Kit from getting a clear sight of her. Belknap turned to Burbage. "You must know of her father, John Hart?"

Burbage nodded. "Ah, yes, he has cornered the market in silk I hear, but not likely to be interested in my business unfortunately."

Belknap smiled ruefully. "Aye, that is so or I would have invited him tonight. Girls, look after Master Turner here. I'm going to introduce Master Burbage to my other guests and I'm sure our business talk will bore him."

Kit watched cynically as Belknap took Burbage over to the city merchants gathered at the other end of the chamber. So this was the part of the evening where he was supposed to prove his power to charm the ladies, was it? With an internal shrug, he steeled himself to begin, deciding that he would prove Burbage's trust in him by impressing the hardest challenge in the room. It was clear that this Hart fellow was an important connection that had so far eluded Burbage. A friendly cloth importer would be invaluable to the costume makers at the Theatre. Kit would see what he could do to turn this Mercy Hart to their side.

chapter 2

"Master Turner, have you been with Master Burbage long?" asked Mistress Belknap, signaling for her servants to begin serving the welcome cup of mulled wine.

Kit seized a drink from the tray, remembering just in time to take prudent sips, rather than downing it in one. "Indeed, ma'am, since I was a boy. He taught me everything I know about the business."

"And a better teacher you could not hope for."

"You echo my thoughts exactly." Kit almost yawned. The strain of keeping back his usual flowery style of address was as tiring as holding the reins on a team of spirited horses. And he still hadn't caught a clear look at the shortest of the girls, his quarry for the evening. It was time for him to cut her from the herd. "Mistress Hart, tell me, do you enjoy hearing a play?"

The sea of rainbow skirts parted as the Belknap girls turned to their guest, granting him his first clear sight of her. Kit felt as if he had just been thrown from the saddle. He had not been expecting to encounter such a creature in an alderman's parlor. She was stunning: more curves packed into her five feet two inches than many a ship's figurehead, a sweet heart-shaped face and the most earnest pair of green eyes he had ever seen. As he watched, a faint blush rose over her strawberries-and-cream skin, making him even hungrier, though this time not for food. He couldn't help letting his gaze drop to her chest, where small fingers played nervously with the laces on her modest peach-colored bodice.

Peaches—that was absolutely the last image he needed right now when he was trying his utmost to behave.

"I've never heard a play, sir," the girl said shyly.

So she didn't attend the theater. For the moment that did not matter to Kit; he was willing to be anything she wanted as long as he could get her talking.

"What about music? Do you like Byrd's madrigals or do you prefer Tallis?"

The girl shuttered her eyes with a sweep of her long dark lashes. "You must think me very ignorant, sir, but I am not familiar with the latest music. My father does not approve of anything but psalms sung at home."

The Belknap daughter in orange was watching the interchange with amusement, her squirrel-bright eyes leaping between them. Kit guessed that meant she knew that he was not quite as he appeared this night, an easy deduction if she had last seen him skewering Saracens onstage.

"Mercy has a lovely voice, Master Turner," the Belknap chit said. "Perhaps later you could teach her one of Lyly's songs?" She turned to her friend. "They are very good, Mercy, nothing unsuitable about them, you'll see. Even the Queen asks for them to be played—Lyly's her favored poet and he trains the boys of St. Paul's to be excellent performers."

The girl appeared to be struggling against a desire to prod her friend in the ribs for making the suggestion. "What's right at court is not necessarily welcomed under my father's roof, as you well know, Ann."

So that was Ann. Kit sensed an ally in the orange-garbed maiden. "And you, Mistress Ann, how like you the fashion for madrigals? I see they have even begun to print the sheet music so that each singer has his stave facing the right way when a quartet gathers around a table—a welcome innovation."

"Marry, sir, that is very convenient in a house that has a tuneful family, but ours is sadly lacking in that respect." Ann's eyes twinkled with merriment. "My sisters and I are most politely asked not to sing the responses at church for fear of throwing the others off key."

"But do you play?"

"The lute, but badly. Mercy here is far more accomplished than I, even though she pretends not to excel at anything so worldly."

Ann staggered, but continued smiling as if nothing had happened. If Kit was not mistaken, the little daughter of the cloth merchant had just kicked her friend in the calf—well padded by layers of skirts from any true injury. This parading of Mercy's skills was proving a very entertaining subject, confirming his suspicion that she was eminently easy to tease. He always appreciated that in a girl, not having a very serious approach to life himself.

He placed his hand on his breast and bowed. "Then, Mistress Hart, I would be desolate to leave this night without hearing your voice or enjoying a few melodies from your accomplished fingers."

'Swounds, he wished he hadn't created that image as his mind was now full of entirely inappropriate images of her wandering hands and his all too willing flesh. She was a decent girl, far too modest for such sport, and he shamed her by even entertaining such ideas in private. *Behave, Kit, behave.*

"I'm sure she will be more than happy to oblige," Ann replied, prudently moving out of kicking distance. "Oh, Mother? Do you know where we put the lute after Mercy's last visit?"

Mistress Belknap beamed her approval. "Oh, Mercy, are you going to play for us? You know how I love to hear it after years of being tortured by music lessons for my own daughters." She leaned confidentially towards Kit. "Sadly, sir, they all make the lute sound like the strings are still attached to the gut of some unfortunate creature."

"To sound so awful must be a skill of sorts," suggested Kit gallantly.

"One of use to bird-scarers perhaps," muttered Mercy, thinking only Ann would hear her little commentary.

Happily, Kit caught her words and laughed out loud. His damsel had a sharp sense of humor. Until today, he had never believed in that nonsense about falling in love on first meeting, but he was reacting to this girl as he had to no other. The fact that she was completely oblivious to her effect on men was all part of her charm and he felt quite drunk in her presence. He was wracking his brains to think how he could get her on her own for a few minutes to further their acquaintance.

Mistress Belknap took Mercy's hand. "Will you play for us, love?"

"Have mercy on us, Mercy!" chorused the three daughters— then fell into giggles, telling Kit this was all part of an old familiar joke, playing on her name.

Mercy buckled under the combined pressure, as Kit anticipated she would. Already he was certain that his maiden had not a selfish bone in her very comely body. "To please you, ma'am, I will." She took a worried glance around the room. "But only if all the company are happy to hear me. I would not want to put myself forward and seem a proud sort of girl wanting all the attention for herself."

"I know, Mother!" exclaimed Ann, acting as if the idea had only just struck when doubtless the lovely little Machiavelli had been busy plotting. "Why not persuade Master Turner to join her? All of London knows he's a fine performer. Your guests would be *desolate* not to hear him before they leave." She smiled broadly at Kit as she parroted his words back at him.

He bowed to kiss Ann's hand. "It would be an honor."

"Oh, Master Turner, is it not very rude of us as to ask you to sing for your supper?" cried Mistress Belknap, looking thoroughly delighted by the idea. Her feast was about to become a famous success if they could get London's brightest star to shine for them in private.

"Ma'am, I have been singing for my supper since I was a little lad, so I have no qualms about adding another to the count." Kit decided there and then that he was also falling in love with the Belknap family as they were allowing his plan to be apart with the maiden to tumble so perfectly into place.

"Then it is agreed. After supper you must have a place to rehearse. The closet off the parlor should suit. I will ask the servants to set candles, lute and music in it ready for you. Ann will help you select the songs." *And act as guard on her young guest's virtue,* Mistress Belknap's eyes warned Kit.

Kit thought Ann would make a wonderful third to their party.

"I can hardly wait to get started. There are several love songs that I am sure Mistress Hart will enjoy learning and I am a most willing tutor."

Mercy could barely eat a thing. How had this happened? She had come in all innocence to a family supper and ended up agreeing to entertain the entire company of aldermen and their wives with secular songs, accompanying the handsomest man in London. There was no way in Christendom that word of this would not get back to her father and she hated to anticipate his reaction. He wouldn't shout at her, or scold her as such, but she knew he would be so disappointed. The heaviness of that would weigh round her neck like a milkmaid's yoke for weeks, if not months. Faith would give her that sad look, the one she reserved for serious breaches of decorum. Edwin would splutter something about the wild company she kept and the well-known liberality of the goldsmiths. All three of them liked Ann, but none entirely approved of Jerome Belknap as, among God-fearing folk, he was known to be very free-thinking. To hear that Mercy had taken part in such a frivolous gathering would be the proof they had been waiting for that all was not as it should be under Belknap's roof. There would be a sermon in it at least.

"More marchpane, Mistress Hart?" Master Turner offered her a plate of her favorite sweetmeats, but the sight of them turned her stomach. She was too nervous to eat.

"No thank you, sir."

Mistress Belknap had placed the pair of them side by side at the board in order for them to "discuss music." Mercy had decided

36

the lady was as bad as her daughter when it came to encouraging flirtations. For the Belknap ladies, it was all a piece of harmless fun, not meant to go beyond the bounds of decent behavior, but for her, it was a torment. It would have been bearable if every smile on the young man's face had not made her heart flutter. She was feeling by turns hot and cold in her borrowed clothes, wishing that Ann's peach camlet bodice was not so tight around the bust and the ruff was not so frothy. She had no clue how to behave with the man's unguarded looks of admiration. He had not been offensive—far from it, he had been nothing but polite. She reassured herself that he appeared a sober-enough fellow in his black doublet, a wealthy senior apprentice, perhaps, to the Master Burbage Ann's father so liked. Mercy wondered what line of business they were in to make his voice so famous. Were they makers of musical instruments? That would explain his expectation that she had frequented places of entertainment; doubtless he had to risk going to them himself for the sake of his craft. The Hart family stood apart from the current fashion for the stage. Though Ann had never said as much to her, Mercy suspected the Belknaps even went to the Theatre—that was how liberal the father was. Some churchmen said it was the very nest of the Devil's brood, but Mercy had a sinful hankering to see what it would be like.

"Why do I get the impression, mistress, that I make you very nervous?" her dining companion asked in a low voice. "Or is it the prospect of our performance?"

"Yes," whispered Mercy, chasing a piece of piecrust around her plate with her spoon to avoid looking at him.

"Yes to what? Yes, I make you nervous or, yes, you are worried about playing with me later?"

Mercy flicked her eyes to his face, wondering if the double meaning had been intentional, but he was studying her expression without so much as a glint of a naughty smile. He had to be honest or a very good actor. She decided the lascivious thoughts had been entirely of her own creation and begged God's pardon for them.

"Yes to both. I am . . . um . . . not accustomed to dining in such company. I live a very quiet life at home."

"I had guessed as much. And earlier you said you had never heard a play: why is that? I thought almost all of London went."

Mercy glanced around her, checking that they were not over-heard. "I have been told the stage is given over to very dangerous spectacles, plays that teach immoral behavior and drive the watch-ers to"—she lowered her voice—"acts of lewdness."

He brushed a hand across his mouth, hiding his expression momentarily. "But you have not attended a performance to judge for yourself?" His note of disapproval was plain in his voice; this was clearly a sore point with him.

"I doubt it would be allowed." Even as she spoke, Mercy won-dered if that was the truth. Her father had never banned her from going, merely made his own thoughts on the subject clear to his children. She knew Aunt Rose had slipped away to see the occa-sional play without making a great announcement of it to the fam-ily. These absences had been handled by everyone ignoring the subject on the principle that if they weren't acknowledged no one would have to take offense.

"That is a shame, for how else can you make up your own mind? I would argue that the play is the very place to teach moral-ity, on occasion far more successfully than from the pulpit." As he gestured vigorously to emphasize his argument, a lock of his wavy black hair fell forward, teasing the solid line of his jaw. Mercy squeezed her fingers round her knife and spoon to stop herself from reaching out to brush it back. "By seeing vice punished and virtue rewarded, would you not be improved by the experience?" he continued. "It is a perverse mind that takes away evil lessons from the plays put on the London stage, all of which are first approved by the Queen's own servant, the Lord Chamberlain."

"You make many good points, sir," Mercy said soberly, not wanting to anger the young man. "I have much to learn, it seems."

"And I would be more than happy to teach you." His dark eyes held hers for a thrilling few moments before he blinked and turned away, breaking the spell. "Come now, Mistress Hart, you must eat something. One of these custards, perhaps?"

Mercy nodded dumbly, wondering where her wits had fled to when she most needed them about her. He broke off a corner of the creamy tart on his plate and placed it on her spoon, then watched as she nibbled it, his eyes fixed on her lips. To her mortification, Mercy felt her cheeks blush. She had been right in her first suspicions: he was attracted to her and, Lord help her, she was horribly drawn to him. But, then again, was it so bad if he liked her? She was of marriageable age. As a respectable apprentice invited to dine with aldermen, would he not be a suitable husband for her? Ann would say so. She was forever reeling off the selling points of the potential spouses among the young men of Cheapside like so many bullocks going under the hammer at Smithfield. Was it not Mercy's duty now that she was grown up to turn her thoughts to a future beyond her family if she were not to be an unmarried burden on her brother?

Suddenly the prospect of leaving her home did not seem as

terrifying when she had a young man looking at her with such devotion. And he seemed so kind and concerned about her feelings. So quiet and respectful.

She swallowed her mouthful and gave him a blinding smile. "Thank you, sir. That was delicious."

"Hmmm." He seemed quite lost in the contemplation of her mouth. She licked her lips self-consciously. He shifted uneasily in his seat, rearranging his long legs under the board.

She looked behind them at the roaring hearth. "Are you uncomfortable, sir? Is the fire too hot?"

"Not the fire." He cleared his throat. "Mistress Hart, I believe our hosts have finished. What say you that we retire to practice our songs together?"

After their host gave the prayer of thanks for the meal, Mercy got swiftly to her feet, eager now to be apart with the young man. She tried to ignore the fact that she had rashly convinced herself on little evidence that this flirtation could be the prelude to true love. Instead, she caught Ann's eye, signaling that they were ready to go. "Yes, let's do that. I am ready to learn a new song if you will teach me."

chapter 3

KIT WASN'T SURE HE WAS going to survive the experience of being in the little closet off the parlor almost alone with Mercy Hart. She seemed oblivious that she was within a hair's breadth of being backed up against the wall and kissed most soundly. Instead she chattered on about music as if her earlier reticence was all quite forgotten. Ann Belknap was a hopeless guard, sitting by the door with her back to them, reading from a manuscript collection of sonnets as if there was nothing in the world for her but poetry at that moment. Kit wondered idly if any of his sonnets had made it into the sheaf; they were enjoying not a little popularity at court and he had even heard one set to music. He had a profitable side-line in writing verses for unpoetical gentlemen courting romantic ladies.

"Play me something, mistress, so I may judge your skill for myself," he asked Mercy, to stop himself doing something he would regret.

She went pink with shy pleasure as she settled the lute on her lap. Kit tried not to imagine putting her in the same position on his.

"You are a musician, sir?"

"Among other things," he said modestly.

"I guessed as much. Is Master Burbage a maker of musical instruments?"

What was this? How could she not know to whom she was talking? Was it possible that she had missed hearing of Kit's reputation? Perhaps there were those who would say it was not for him to boast, but he had gained a certain fame in London for his role in *The Knights*. And Burbage, elder and younger, were names known in almost every household.

"Not exactly, mistress. Are you not acquainted with him, or maybe his son?"

She strummed the lute, bending her cheek to the board to hear if it was in tune. The position did most interesting things to her bodice. "Your pardon, sir, but no. As I said, I live a very quiet life and rarely go out in London society." She looked up, eyes sparkling. "This is the most exciting evening's entertainment I have ever attended."

'Twas wondrous strange! Had she not been to the play, a bear baiting or even a fair? The Belknap supper was the tamest event Kit had attended in many a year; it was hard to imagine that anyone would consider it daring. He realized he had lost the thread of the conversation in his preoccupation with the maiden's artless innocence and, um, other blessings. Oh, yes, Burbage.

"Master Burbage is . . ." He wondered what he could say. He suspected that owning up to being one of the players she was so suspicious of would send her running from the closet as if he carried the plague. "Is a noted purveyor of entertainments to court and elsewhere." There, that was suitably vague. Not a lie, but it could mean anything from a provider of musicians to an owner of trained horses. "Come, play for me."

He listened with real enjoyment as she plucked her way through a sweet fantasy for lute that he recognized from hearing a time or two at the Theatre. He applauded when she let the last note hum to a close.

"Beautiful. You make the lute sing like the dying swan, saving her best notes for the end."

She looked up, startled by his lapse into flowery compliments. Kit kicked himself mentally. *Sober citizen, remember!*

"Thank you, sir. It was but a trifle."

"Where did you learn it, if you are not encouraged to study such music at home?"

She looked down, hiding her jade-colored eyes from him, embarrassed by her confession. "I . . . I . . . heard it played at the barber shop near my home. It has been very popular of late."

Kit smiled in understanding. He, like many young men, had often taken up the lute left out by his local barber, an amusement to pass the time while waiting for a shave. Men of talent were encouraged to entertain the queue while they tarried, to the point that barbers across London had become the best places for the exchange of the most fashionable songs and various regular customers had gathered their own followings to hear them perform.

"You must have a very good ear, Mistress Mercy." Indeed, she did: a delicate pink whorl like the inner parts of a shell just showing under the flap of her coif. He wondered what color her hair was; dark if her eyebrows were a reliable guide. There seemed to be a promising amount from the heavy mass caught up at the back by the modest coif.

"Thank you, sir. I am never quite sure if I should."

"Should what?" He wished he could pay more attention to her

words, but his mind kept wandering in the most damnable directions.

"Copy the music like that. I never quite know what I am playing, not even the title or composer."

"Any musician worth his salt would be flattered to have such a fair interpreter of his work."

She lowered her voice to barely a whisper. "But what if the music is not decent?"

Catching himself before he laughed, Kit realized she was being serious. His little maid was one very staunch moralist, which didn't bode well for his hopes of stealing a kiss. But how could he lift her from this hook of a spiritual dilemma on which she had hung her enjoyment?

"I defy you to find an indecent piece of music, mistress. Words, it is true, can lead astray, but music is the language of angels, above reproach."

She looked very relieved to hear this explanation, giving her the excuse she needed not to feel guilty about her attraction to such worldly things. "That is true. I can see I have been getting myself in a fearful muddle over nothing. It is not as if I'm about to march out of my door and make my living playing for the crowd now, is it? Entertaining my family at home is surely a safe and respectable pastime."

"Indubitably." While his sober outside nodded gravely to Mercy, the real Kit was chuckling at her sweet confusion. She was quick to take correction; perhaps his hopes were not in vain? A kiss could be innocent too, if presented in the right light under the most promising circumstances. "Now what shall we play together?

I would suggest Lord Cumberland's 'My thoughts are wing'd with hopes,' a very pretty air for tenor and lute. Lyly has had it performed before the Queen with great success." And it had also been a favorite at the Theatre, but she did not have to know that. He passed the music to her.

Mercy worried her bottom lip as she scanned her part. "Yes, I think I am familiar with some of this already. The chorus is fairly simple to play." She deftly plucked the part.

"Then shall we take it for a gallop?"

She nodded, her poise all musician as if a mantle had dropped on her from above, covering the shy girl.

Kit took a breath and began singing the love song to the moon, which, in the lyrics of the piece, was entitled Cynthia, a well-known code denoting the Queen. On this performance, he was quietly changing the subject from Cynthia to Mercy in his mind.

"My thoughts are wing'd with hopes,
My hopes with love."

Mercy glanced up once or twice to catch him gazing at her, sensing the passion beneath his words if not understanding she was the cause. Indeed, he had to be moonstruck to take so to this girl on first meeting, but he was a hopeless captive to his emotions. There was nothing rational about what he felt, and yet he wanted to throw himself into the flood like a leaf in the millrace, letting it toss and turn him as it would. The voyage downstream might be perilous but, oh, it would be glorious.

"Thoughts, hopes and love return to me no more,
Until Cynthia shine as she hath done before."

"That was . . . that was wonderful," Mercy said as he finished the final phrase, her dreamy gaze still lost in the song's spell. "You are truly gifted, sir."

He seized her hand where it rested on the strings and raised it to his lips. "And you, mistress, have played your way into my soul. What enchantment do you use when you pluck the strings, for my heart echoes the very notes?"

Mercy did not pull away, but neither could she bring herself to meet his intense gaze. "No enchantments, sir."

"Ah, but you do, though you know it not. You cast the spell of the beautiful soul, bringing this unworthy mortal in helpless thrall to your feet."

Too much? Kit hid his grimace. He knew his language was ornate at the best of times, a hopeless habit caught from prolonged exposure to the stage. His best friend, Milly Porter, would mock him unmercifully for it if she were here, but happily his little maiden was listening wide-eyed as if it were the first time she had ever heard such compliments.

Then he realized it was exactly so. She was the girl that poets sung about: the bud with the dew of innocence still on the petals. It was her debut on this stage of love. He must be very careful with her, for it would be sacrilege to disturb so perfect a bloom; he must use no debased coinage of words.

Mercy's eyes were round with wonder, dark pupils rimmed with the hint of green fire. "No, sir, it is I who am not worthy. I play very ill compared to your mastery of the music."

He kissed each finger in gentle worship. "Nay, mistress, your touch is exquisite." He turned her hand to place a kiss in the center of her palm. "And from this moment on I will not stand for there to be another opinion on the matter." He cupped her soft hand to his cheek, letting her feel the strength of his jaw, the rough texture of the skin.

Mercy's lips parted, but she clearly could not think of anything to say, caught up in the enchantment woven between them. Checking they were unobserved by their lax guard, Kit quickly dipped forward and pressed his mouth to hers, stealing the kiss he had been promising himself since he first saw her.

"Will you let me call on you?" he whispered. "Tell me where you live, sweetheart."

Mercy seemed dazed, unsure of her next move.

"Tell me, please, or I will have to go knocking on all the doors of London and make myself a notorious nuisance. 'There goes that lovesick Turner!' the city men will cry. 'Pray take him to the doctor for his lady has smitten his heart with Cupid's arrow.'"

She smiled at that. "Well, we can't have you risking a visit to the doctor. On London Bridge, at the sign of the bolt of cloth. Southwark end."

"Southwark end," he repeated, letting his breath stir the curl of dark hair that had come loose by her ear after his kiss. "Bolt of cloth."

"You . . . you will call on my father? Request permission?"

He almost asked "Permission for what?" before he realized she thought he meant courting in preparation for marriage. The unlikely thought danced across his mind that maybe he did want to woo her as a decent apprentice would a merchant's daughter. It would be a beautiful dream for a bastard player to hold for a time. "Aye, I'd do that and more for you." If he was allowed.

She closed her eyes and rested her head briefly on his shoulder. "Master Turner." Just that, nothing more.

"I'm known as Kit to my very good friends."

"Kit."

Ann suddenly broke into a paroxysm of coughing, giving due warning that their sweet interlude was about to be disturbed. Mistress Belknap appeared in the door.

"Master Turner, Mercy, are you ready?" Her shrewd eyes flicked to the curl bouncing on Mercy's shoulder. "Mercy, tidy yourself, girl. I swear you can't move a pace without losing pins in your wake like a cart with a badly packed load."

Mercy groped for the betraying lock and stuffed it under her coif, but not before Kit had time to see that his damsel rejoiced in the most wonderful wine-dark hair, the very red-satin brown of an autumn chestnut fresh from the husk.

"You have picked a song for us?" Mistress Belknap continued smoothly, stoically ignoring Mercy's fluster.

"Aye, a song of hopeful love," replied Kit.

"As long as it doesn't get its hopes up too high," Mistress Belknap warned, giving him a pointed look.

Leaving the Belknap supper at eleven, Kit floated back to his lodgings, barely aware as Burbage bribed the watch to let them pass after curfew.

"Enjoyed yourself, lad?" Burbage asked jovially, a little deep in his cups.

"It was a very pleasant evening." That was an understatement: he was still spinning with joy inside like a child's top.

"Aye. You and that little maid entertained us most sweetly.

You swayed at least three merchants to our side by your talents." Burbage yawned. "Shame we couldn't put you both onstage. They do in France, you know."

"Do what?" Kit dug in the pouch at his belt and replaced the pearl in his ear.

"Let women play women onstage."

Kit snorted. "We can't be having that here. It would give the Lord Chamberlain an apoplexy and be very bad for the boys. As a former company boy, I am against it." He raised his hand as if voting "Nay."

Burbage chuckled. "Never fear, Turner, I am not about to set such fires in our theater. They would close us down within a week. Here we are—your lodgings."

Kit paused outside the door, too excited to settle for the night. Candles were still lit a few doors down in the narrow canyon of the street: Milly must be working late. "I bid you good night, sir."

Burbage saluted as he walked on, a link boy going ahead to light his path, stout cudgel in hand to deter thieves lurking in dark alleys. Kit knocked softly on Milly's door, hoping she would be welcoming of visitors, even this late. The door opened a crack, a dark face appearing warily, before the gap widened. Milly's husband, Diego, stood in the entrance. Of middling stature, and of an age with Kit, the blackamoor had once been in service to the Lacey family. Since his marriage, he had become quite a famous personage in his own right in London, managing a successful business teaching riding skills and fencing to gentlemen at a house in Southwark owned by his father-in-law. Unfortunately, he was a cool friend to Kit.

"Turner, what brings you here so late?"

Kit stepped inside so Diego could shut out the night. "I hope you don't mind, but I wanted to talk to your wife. Is she awake?"

"Aye, finishing an order for Lady Jane. She stubbornly refuses to let her down by being tardy with the new livery."

"Then may I go up?"

Diego shrugged. "I do not stand in your way, Master Player."

That was invitation enough for Kit. He took the stairs two at a time, familiar with the route even though it was unlit. The rest of the family must have retired already. He found Milly, as he expected, seated on a stool by the fire, a candle on a low table to light her work on an embroidered stomacher. She looked up and gave him her warm smile. A slightly built redhead, Milly was a person whose character was far more formidable than her frame.

"Kit, you stranger, this is a surprise! You've not called round so late for months!"

Diego sauntered in behind him. "That's because he knows I like to have you all to myself after business hours."

Kit rolled his eyes at the young moor's territorial speech. "God save us from the newly wedded! Gilding not yet off the lily, Diego?"

Diego touched his wife's neck with a gentle brush of blunt fingertips. "Nay, and it never will be."

Kit was glad to hear it. He had had doubts about the wisdom of their unorthodox match, but London seemed to have taken it in its stride. The patronage of his noble legitimate brothers, Will and James, and their wives, had helped in this.

He wandered about the room, disturbing embroidered frill and bejeweled hatband in his aimless perusal.

"What has set your hose in a twist, Kit?" Milly asked as she snipped a thread. "Did the laundress forget to shake out the ants after hedge-drying your clothes?"

Kit wasn't sure he could pour out his heart before the disapproving Diego, but he was unlikely these days to catch Milly alone. Her husband did not trust him enough to leave them in peace and, to be sure, Kit had offered him enough provocation over the years to earn the suspicion. No other thing for it: he threw himself into the confession like a man jumping overboard with the ship on fire about him.

"I met the most beautiful creature in the whole of the world tonight."

Milly tried to thread her needle, but missed. Diego stepped in to do it for her, giving her eyes a rest. "By *creature*," she asked, "do I take it we are talking about a girl?"

Kit paced to and fro in the space between the window and her stool. "Aye. Mercy Hart, daughter of a cloth merchant and City worthy."

"And where did you meet this paragon? Surely not in your usual evening's haunts?"

Kit smiled at the thought. "Nay, she would not know what the inside of a tavern looked like. She is from a very strict family, God-fearing folk all of them. I met her at Alderman Belknap's supper."

Milly frowned. "The Belknaps? Oh yes, I remember them: a very kind family, rich as a fleet of treasure-filled Spanish galleons, and prompt to settle their accounts. But I do not think I know your lady."

"I want to court her." Kit said it as if issuing a challenge.

Milly did not pick up the gauntlet. "I see." She bent her head over her work, her method of ducking an argument with her friend.

Diego was not so reticent. "You wish to wed this merchant's daughter after one evening's acquaintance?"

"Aye." Kit's eyes blazed.

"Is she wealthy and particularly gullible?"

Milly placed a restraining hand on her husband's arm.

"This is not about money!" Kit protested. "Nor is she gullible— just innocent!"

"So it is love?" Diego smiled at his wife. "See how the arch-cynic has fallen."

"I want you to meet her, Milly." Kit ignored Diego's evident enjoyment of his predicament. "She is so unworldly, unspoilt, and has the most amazing eyes that speak with every glance. And she plays the lute like an angel."

Milly put the finished piece aside and stretched her weary arms. "Why do I think there is a 'but' in all this?"

Kit hung his head. Milly was always as damnably sharp as one of her needles. "She doesn't know I'm an actor. She thinks the stage is most like to be the work of the Devil."

Milly gave him an exasperated look. "Oh, Kit, why ever did you hide the truth from her? If you are serious about the girl, she will have to know what you do and not be ashamed of you."

He held up empty hands. "I know I'm not worthy of her, but I didn't want to end our conversation before it had even started. I wanted a chance to convince her that I was what she wanted."

"You can't do that by not being yourself!"

Kit didn't like the track this discussion was taking. He just wanted to share his excitement with her, not hear all the drawbacks. "I was myself."

"Then why are you dressed like a preacher?"

"Orders. From Burbage." He tugged the dreary doublet straight.

"And would she still look on you with favor if you were not in your borrowed weeds?"

Would she? "Of course," Kit replied staunchly, though he was far from sure.

"Then next time you see her you must not feign to be ought else than you are."

Diego shook his head. "My love, you have the player wrong. Being all these people and many others *is* his true self. He has the nature of taffeta, changeable with each light upon it." He held up a scrap of the same offending material, shifting its colors in the candlelight.

Kit didn't like this portrait, for in part it held much truth. "You charge me with inconstancy, sir?"

Diego shrugged, throwing the scrap into the workbasket. "Is that so bad a quality? You Englishmen seem to think oak the only wood, where others may say a more pliable tree has virtues in other circumstances. Do we not prize the yew to make the bending bow?"

Milly patted her husband's arm as a gentle prompt to give over the argument, which he gave every sign of enjoying far too much— it was seldom Kit laid his heart open to anyone. She stood up and took Kit's hands. "This is deep matter for such hours. I'm pleased you've found her, Kit. And, as for constancy, you are as firm a friend as any in all England."

He smiled into her upturned face with its bright hazel eyes and dash of freckles. "Thank you."

"Bring her to meet us when you can."

"I will."

"And"—here she squeezed his fingers painfully to make her point—"do not hide who you are. She may reject a player, but you have noble connections now that her family will doubtless value."

"I don't want her on such terms." Kit had spent most of his last few years being fiercely independent of the Laceys.

"Oh, Kit, be practical: that is how the world works."

Diego tugged her away from Kit, brushing her neck with his lips. "You waste your words, my love. Never try to speak sense to a lover: it is as welcome as talk of the succession to our Queen."

Aware he had outstayed his time, Kit turned to go.

"Oh, I forgot!" Milly called him back. "Tobias came by earlier. He went to find you."

Kit groaned. This was all he needed. His half-brother Tobias Lacey, the youngest of the legitimate Lacey boys, had fallen into the habit of seeking sanctuary with him whenever he was in disgrace with their eldest brother, the earl.

"What is it this time?"

"Could he not be here just to pay you a visit?"

Diego snorted and resumed dotting nibbling kisses along his wife's collarbone.

"Unlikely." Kit folded his arms.

"He did mention something about a horse race to me," Diego offered, looking up momentarily. "Nothing too serious."

"God's nails, that means the jackanapes will be snoring in my bed, hiding from Will until someone settles his debts."

"Surely not. The earl is a reasonable fellow," said Milly.

"Exactly. But Tobias drives all of us beyond reason."

Despite his disapproving words, Kit privately relished feeling responsible for someone, for family, having been without such connections for so long. Not that he was going to confess that to anyone; he enjoyed playing the part of wearied older brother. "Oh, well," he sighed. "I had better go back and see what he's done now."

chapter 4

ROSE GOT UP EARLY HOPING to be first in the kitchen, but Faith was there before her, stirring a pot of oatmeal while the maid bustled about tidying the place.

"Good morrow, Aunt." Faith lifted the spoon to test the porridge.

"Good morrow." Rose saw there was nothing for her to do. A newly laid fire glowed in the hearth, a fine set of polished firedogs standing guard on the flames. Curls of smoke rose up the brick-lined chimney, the scent mingling with that of the fresh manchets the maid had fetched from the bakers, already placed on the table for breakfast. It was a carefully arranged scene of domestic efficiency that all but shouted that Rose was not required. It was a difficult situation, to be sure: Faith as oldest daughter wished to stamp her command on the household, but Rose had fifteen years and much experience on her and in other circumstances would have expected to run things. She was too often left feeling the unwanted guest in her brother-in-law's home.

"The cabbage you bought yesterday is touched with blight." Faith nodded to the net in the pantry where Rose had hung the vegetables.

"I pray your pardon. It was the pick of those available."

Faith gave her that infuriatingly gentle smile she was so skilled in, doling it out like alms to all petitioners. It would have been easier for Rose if it had not been sincere. "I do not mean to criticize, Aunt. I bring it to your attention in case you wish to try elsewhere next market day. That stallholder clearly carries inferior goods."

Rose squeezed her temper into a corner of her heart. She wanted to shake her niece, mess up her appearance until her fine blond hair looked a bird's nest and her prim ruff wilted, bring her down into the dirt with the rest of humanity. No wonder poor Mercy spent all her time trying to curb her natural spiritedness; her sister was as perfect and heavy as a marble angel hovering over the family. Faith was so utterly good and patient that Rose could not endure being in her presence for long.

"I think I'll walk to meet Mercy." Rose plucked a wrinkled apple from the pantry to make a portable breakfast.

"It's a long walk, Aunt. I'm sure the Belknaps will send a servant to accompany her home." Faith gathered the utensils for the family breakfast while the maid set the board on the trestles in the parlor.

"All the same, I wish to go. Will you see to my mother when she wakes?"

"But of course. I have the porridge ready for her."

Rose had to allow that Faith was unflagging in tending Mother Isham, her only failing there being her strict adherence to truth. But what could Rose's poor distracted mother do with "truth" when her mind had become a ragbag of snippets, the past far more real to her than the present?

Stepping outside the Harts' house felt like escaping a prison. Rose wrapped her cloak about her, this day considerably colder. February had snapped icy jaws again after the sunny yawn of yesterday. She liked living on the bridge: it was neither one thing nor another—not serious-minded, money-orientated City; not pleasure-seeking, immoral Southwark—suspended between the two like a maiden unable to choose between two suitors. Houses covered the entirety of the bridge, leaving only a narrow street down the center. This passage was thronged with people crossing into the City, lingering to buy goods in the many shops. You could get everything from a pair of fine leather boots to a fashionable plumed cap within a short walk: all you need do was look overhead for the sign denoting each craftsman. Here the sober guildsman could head south, shedding his respectability for a scarlet cloak and dive into the Southwark stews; traveling the other way, the drab could spend her earnings on a prim bodice and petticoat and fool the folk of the City that she was an irreproachable goodwife.

Rose paused outside her favorite shoemakers. She had a weakness for elaborate footwear and recently she had fallen into the habit of admiring a pair of red pointed slippers that sat in the window awaiting collection. Not that she wanted to buy them, for they reminded her too much of her own shame. After her lover Henry Talbot had cast her over five years ago without making good his promise of marriage, she had plucked all her own plumage, got rid of her gaily embroidered petticoats, gaudy shoes, jaunty caps and even cut her blond hair off at the neck in a fit of self-punishment. These gewgaws had become a symbol of her stupidity to have fallen into the pattern of the silly maiden gulled by the handsome but selfish man who cared for none but himself.

Rose wiped the fog of her breath from the pane, thinking it an apt image of how blind she had been. She hadn't even had the excuse of youth. She had been twenty-five when Talbot had swept into her life in her hometown of Norwich and waited until she was thirty, still thinking they would be married when he got round to it. Oh, his excuses had been plausible enough, and she had thought herself in love. First he had told her that they had to move so could not stay long enough to have the banns read; next he could not afford the special license; then the priest in their parish was too disapproving; and so the excuses went on. It had taken Henry no more than three weeks to meet, woo and wed the woman who now called herself Mistress Talbot, the final stab in Rose's dying love for him.

She could have sued him for breach of promise, of course—they had been handfasted when she first left her parents' house to move in with him, which for the common people was almost as good as a wedding—but the humiliation of a trial was not to be borne. After fleeing to London, it hadn't taken her long to realize she had loved an idea of the man, not the reality, but the return to earth from her make-believe heaven had not been any less painful as a result. Swallowing her pride to ask if she might live with her brother-in-law, John Hart, had not been the softest of landings as, without him saying anything, she had felt judged and condemned for her weakness.

"Back again, mistress?"

A handsome but tough-looking older man with pepper-and-salt hair stood at her shoulder sharing her view of the shoes. She judged him fairly wealthy from the quality of his clothes. This was no importuning beggar wheedling a penny from her.

"I beg your pardon?" Rose was convinced she did not know the man and he certainly didn't look like a shoemaker with his blacksmith's build.

"I've seen you here every morning at about this time as I go to buy my bread. Curiosity is one of my sins and I had to know what it is that holds your attention." He peered in at the little window. "Shoes, is it?"

"Aye, sir." Rose smiled at her folly. The man did not seem dangerous, and she could afford a moment of neighborly conversation.

"For me it is swords. I own far too many—more than I can use." The man leant against the window frame and crossed his arms. "My son-in-law says I have no more sense than a salmon."

"We are all apt to swim upstream into the net of foolishness over some matter or other. I imagine your son-in-law has his faults."

The man chuckled. "Aye, he does—and I enjoy telling him about them." He straightened and bowed to her. "Silas Porter, mistress. I own the fencing school by the Southwark gate."

Rose dipped a curtsy. "Rose Isham." She waited nervously to see if her reputation had preceded her, but the man gave no sign. "My brother-in-law is John Hart."

"Ah, then my son-in-law has had the pleasure of teaching your nephew, Edwin, to ride and I instruct him in the blade."

"Aye, John thinks the skills will be of use to Edwin in his travels."

Silas raised an encouraging eyebrow, prompting her to continue. "Edwin is likely to go to many foreign places in the pursuit of business, and John does not want to send him out unprepared."

"Sound reasoning, though I pray Edwin never needs to draw a sword in defense of his life." Silas's gray-green eyes shone with amusement. "He's a peace-loving fellow, your nephew, and has not the thirst for blood of many rapscallions who come through my doors. With them, I spend all my time urging restraint; with Edwin, it has all been about summoning up the appetite for violence."

Rose found it almost impossible to think of her quiet, sober nephew calling up a bloodcurdling yell and driving a sword through any man's guts. "Aye, I imagine he must be a most reluctant pupil."

"But the better man for it. I've seen too many lives wasted for little cause due to a hasty recourse to the blade."

Rose judged she had been talking more than was decent for a first meeting of a neighbor. Regretfully, she curtsied again. "I am running an errand, sir. I must bid you good day."

Silas saluted her in military fashion, betraying his former profession. "I hope to see you again. I pray the shoemaker keeps his window full of such flies to draw the salmon each morning."

Rose laughed. "Indeed. Or need I linger outside an armorer to find you?"

He shook his head. "Nay, I'll be fishing here, never you doubt it."

Somehow the pleasant discussion had taken a sharp turn onto the path of flirtation and Rose was not certain if she welcomed the direction even if she had unwittingly encouraged it with her jest. Friendship with men was all she aspired to now. She had shed tears and sighed enough over the perfidy of lovers. No longer at ease with him, she moved to win through to a new road, one she could walk alone and gather her thoughts.

"Well, then. Good day, sir."

"Good day, Mistress Isham."

Weaving quickly through the crowds, Rose hurried to put a distance between herself and the distracting master swordsman. She didn't need to look: her instincts told her that he was watching her swim away.

"Aunt Rose, you need not have bothered to come fetch me!" exclaimed Mercy on seeing her outside the Belknaps' house.

Rose waved up to her niece, who was hanging out of the upper casement, wild curly hair falling around her face betraying that she had still been abed at nine with half the day already over. "Get within, sluggard. Make yourself decent so we can go home. I'm sure Mistress Belknap wants her house back to herself."

The mistress in question was standing at the door. "Nay, Mistress Isham, Mercy is always welcome here. I think of her as an honorary daughter."

Rose accepted the invitation to step inside for a moment. "How was yester eve?"

Mistress Belknap beamed. "A wondrous success thanks to your niece and another guest. They entertained us most charmingly with madrigals after supper."

"*Mercy* did that?" marveled Rose.

Mistress Belknap took alarm at her scandalized tone, knowing how strict the Harts were about such matters. "I pray your pardon if you think it wrong of us to encourage her."

"Nay, you mistake me. I'm pleased she's not hiding her light under a bushel as she does at home. I am just surprised you persuaded her to do so."

"I think we have our other guest to thank for that."

Mercy clattered down the stairs to hug her aunt. "Good morrow!"

Rose squeezed her in return, wondering what had prompted this gush of high spirits. Mercy was like the gargoyles on Westminster Abbey after a downpour. "Good morrow to you. But have you not forgotten something?" She tapped her niece's head.

"Oops, my coif. Back in a minute." Mercy bounded back up the staircase, taking the steps an indecorous two at a time. She reappeared with her corkscrew curls now decently hidden. "I'm ready to go."

"Bag?"

Mercy huffed a sigh at her own forgetfulness. "*Almost* ready to go."

Before she could return upstairs, Ann appeared at the stair door and threw the bag to her. "Here it is, Mistress Leave-her-own-head-if-it-wasn't-attached-to-her-shoulders."

"I'm a hopeless case," Mercy admitted, rubbing her eyes.

Rose looked between the yawning Ann and Mercy suspiciously. "When exactly did you two go to sleep?"

"They were gossiping until the small hours, I'm afraid." Mistress Belknap gave her daughter an indulgent smile. "They had lots to discuss. We'll see you soon, I hope, love?" She kissed Mercy on the top of her head.

"Aye, mistress, and thank you for having me to stay."

63

"You are welcome under this roof at any time—particularly when we have guests we want to impress!" Mistress Belknap called after her as they stepped out into Goldsmith's Row.

Waving farewell, Rose linked her arm with her niece. "I hear you were a success."

Mercy looked abashed. "Do you mind?"

"Mind that you played the lute? Of course not. I love to hear you." Rose shook her head at her niece's ability to put so many barriers up between herself and honest enjoyment of life's few pleasures. There was enough suffering in the world without subtracting the things that made it bearable.

They walked on in silence awhile until Mercy spoke. "I was wondering, Aunt: would it be possible to go with you to the Theatre when you next attend a play?"

Rose would not have been more surprised if Queen Elizabeth had popped out from Watling Street and knighted them both on the spot. "Did I hear you right? You want to go to a play?"

Mercy fumbled with her cloak. "Not if it is wrong to wish to do so."

Some would say it was, but they were the kind of men who had been most cruel to Rose after her disgrace, so she had little time for their opinions. Her brother-in-law, Mercy's father, would frown, but he was not a rash man, suspending judgment until he saw proof that his fears were founded.

"I do not think it wrong," Rose replied honestly. "I enjoy a good play."

Mercy smiled at her. "Then I do not either. Indeed, I have been told that the stage has the power to sway men to correct their faults when they see vice punished and virtue rewarded."

"Indeed." And since when had her niece started arguing like a university man?

"And I thought that it was best to judge for myself. I have been taught to be responsible for my own salvation, weighing each sin I commit and confessing it to God alone. I think I should therefore decide if the stage is good or bad in the same way."

"Or you could just go and enjoy it, you goose," Rose teased, tweaking her niece's sweetly serious nose.

Mercy struggled with this unlikely idea. "I suppose I could. But is it right to do so?"

"Oh, Mercy, when are you going to realize that God rejoices in our happiness and shares our sorrows? A little laughter at a play is not going to send you to the Devil, no matter what some say."

"But should I tell Father?"

"I can't see why you should keep it from him, for that would make something innocent suspect. I will choose the play with care, make sure it is one he will approve. You should ask him when you get home at dinner."

"Yes, yes, I'll do that." Mercy bit her lip. "And should I tell him about my playing the lute yester eve?"

Rose laughed. "Of course, Mistress Goose, he will be proud of you. An accomplished daughter who can offer music in a man's house is something to cherish and set in plain sight, not stuff under a pillow."

Mercy skipped with excitement. Rose had to pull her back before she scattered a flock of sheep being driven across the bridge by a sour-faced shepherd.

"Good." Mercy laughed, spinning on the spot, forcing even the herder to smile. "That's settled, then. I'm going to a play!"

After greeting Faith and Gran, Mercy took herself off to the bed-chamber she shared with her sister to read her daily portion of the scriptures as set out for her by her father. It was a particularly enjoyable sequence about Daniel in the lions' den, so it was no hardship. She then took out her journal to make note of her spiritual thoughts—the problem was she didn't have any. She chewed the end of the quill.

Almighty God, thank you for granting me a splendid evening at Ann's. I pray I did not fall into the sin of the proud by taking too much pleasure in the applause for my playing.

She let her pen rest too long, making a blot. Did she have to record the kiss? She still wasn't sure if that had been right or wrong. At the time it had felt so very, very right, but now she wondered.

Pray keep my heart from evil thoughts.

There, that ought to do it—a general catch-all for any sins that might creep up on her when she thought about Kit. It was difficult to confess all in a journal that she knew her father might read one day when he asked to see the progress of her journey in faith. She realized people, Kit included, thought her naive—and perhaps she was—but she tried not to be so gullible, she really did. Men often stole kisses from maidens, making promises they meant not to keep, but her heart told her that Kit was different. Love of man for woman was a godly thing when blessed by the church. The kiss could be but a prelude to so much more, and she couldn't wait to find out what that might be.

Unable to pursue such heated thoughts without straying into sin, she flicked back to her previous jottings to see how she was doing then added on this day's tally:

Scripture verses read: 40.

Prayers said: at least 5.

Sinful thoughts: 6 and a half (if thinking about the kiss was a bit of a mixed bag).

She scratched down her usual conclusion:

Lord, I offer you this record of a poor servant and pray you pardon my trespasses.

With a sigh of relief at having unburdened herself of this, she tucked the journal back in its hiding place under her mattress and then flopped on the bed. While exhausted from having gossiped with Ann until the early hours, she was strangely abuzz with excitement. Poor Ann must have tired of her "will he, won't he?" ramblings about Kit. Her friend had, unusually for her, kept her counsel, saying she would not give an opinion on the matter as she thought it would do Mercy good to find out all there was to know about him for herself. For some reason, Ann believed Mercy needed her horizons expanded, whatever that meant. Ann had agreed unreservedly, however, that Kit was the handsomest man in the whole of London—not that Christian girls should judge their future partners by such worldly measures, of course.

Mercy rolled onto her side and hugged herself, aware of her body in ways that she had never been before. It was as though she were the lute and meeting Kit had plucked her strings for the first time. Twelve hours later she was still humming. She couldn't wait for him to call. Perhaps he would come this very day? The next at the latest. And she had a play to look forward to, something to share with him when he did visit her. Wouldn't he be surprised to find that she had so swiftly taken his advice and gone to judge for herself?

Sometimes, life was just too, too sweet.

chapter 5

TOBIAS LACEY WOKE TO FIND his half-brother snoring gently beside him. He smiled up at the ceiling. His guess had proved correct: Kit had not been so hard-hearted as to turn him out in the middle of the night and had left him to sleep on. He slipped out of the bed, careful not to wake him, and pulled on his hose and boots to go in search of breakfast. Dame Prewet, Kit's landlady, was already preparing dinner, so his hopes were somewhat dented that he was in time for the earlier meal.

Happily, she understood the appetite of the shaggy-haired seventeen-year-old. "Good morrow, young sir. There's bread in the pantry, and good butter. Help yourself," she called to him as she rolled the pastry out on the table, elbow-deep in flour.

Tobias bowed. "You, Dame Prewet, are a jewel among women."

The old lady chuckled. "And you are an imp of a noble house. Now make yourself useful—take some up to your brother. He has a rehearsal to attend—it's already close to ten."

Tobias loaded a platter, grabbed two cups of small beer and balanced his tray up the stairs. Kicking the door open, he plonked the lot on the side table.

"Breakfast is served, my lord!" he called merrily, whisking the covers from his brother.

"It can't be time to get up yet," growled Kit, turning to bury his face under the pillows and leaving the rest of himself exposed to the daylight.

Tobias dumped a wet cloth from the ewer onto his bare back. "You don't want another fine for being late. Rise and shine—your public awaits!"

Kit's reply was to throw the rag and pillow in the general direction of Tobias's voice. Tobias caught the pillow and chucked it back, which only gave Kit the excuse to bury his head again.

"Ah me! Sometimes one has to be cruel to be kind." Tobias picked up the ewer and began to drip the icy contents on his brother. It produced the desired result. Kit leapt from the bed and squawked in fury.

"Pestilential whoreson!"

Tobias put the ewer back on its stand. "Now, now, I won't have you slandering my mother like that," he said without rancor.

"Your mother is doubtless beyond reproach; it is you who is the menace!"

"I brought you breakfast."

The peace offering was noted and seized on as Kit began pulling on his clothes: a lace-edged shirt, and a particularly flamboyant doublet of green and yellow, trimmed with silver bonework. Tobias always admired his older brother's flare for fashion; he must spend most of his earnings on his wardrobe to afford such fine stuff, skimming a fraction of an inch below breaking the sumptuary laws that dictated what each class could wear. Nicely judged indeed.

"What brings you to disturb my peace, brother mine?" asked Kit through a mouthful of bread.

"'Swounds. I just wondered how you were—thought it time to call on the more interesting part of the family. Will and Ellie are expecting another happy event; Jamie is insufferably single-minded now that Jane too is increasing; where else can I go where the talk is not all of babies and female stuff?"

"So you came to me for some good sound man-to-man talk, did you? It was nothing to do with the horse race you lost?"

"I did not lose!" Tobias said indignantly. 'Sblood, his plot had been discovered. "I won by a nose, but Kingsthorp reneged on our deal and left me in debt to the stables for the hire of the horse."

"Hmm."

"It's only a small sum."

"But . . . ?"

"But Will told me in no uncertain terms that there was no more money until Lady Day. His cargo from the Indies has still not landed and he's up to his own ears in debt, as usual."

"What about Jamie? Rich wife now: his money problems must be a thing of the past."

Tobias snorted. "He would only laugh and tell me I had made my own bed and should learn the lesson by lying in it. Besides, he has this strange notion that he shouldn't pillage his wife's estate to bail out his impecunious brother—his words, not mine. He says he's waiting until there's something worth spending money on for me—like a position at court."

Kit picked up a bundle of black clothes and tucked them under his arm. "Gods, you have me feeling sorry for you. Come your ways, then: if you're dodging the bailiff after your debt you'd best stick with me like a preacher to his Bible. With my wise words, I'll guide you out of mischief."

Tobias brushed the crumbs off his rumpled clothes. "Excellent. I was hoping you'd let me watch the master at work. What is it today?"

"We're doing *The Merchant's Daughter* again."

"What? That old chestnut?"

"Don't slight the play—I have very fond memories of that one. I had my first role in it as a boy—Clarinda, the daughter."

"Oh, aye, that's a good part. So now you're to be her lover, honest Tom Cobbler, who is in fact"—here Tobias did an ironic roll of the drum on the table top—"Thomas Knightly, the baron's son! Audience gasp and swoon at the happy chance, cue for the jig."

"Aye, that's me."

"Do we get to dance?"

Kit grabbed his plumed cap. "We always dance, as well you know. No play, not even the bloodiest tragedy, would be complete without a merry jig to send all away in good spirits."

"True. Anything to please the crowd."

An amusing day in prospect, Tobias took up an extra chunk of bread to eat on the way and followed his famous brother to the Theatre.

The cast stopped rehearsing shortly after midday to eat a quick dinner at the local tavern. Kit made sure to call into the stables to greet John Ostler, his old friend from the trough incident, and introduce him to his newest hanger-on.

"John, here's my lackwit brother, Tobias Lacey."

John sized up the young nobleman and decided a tug on the cap would suffice as a welcome.

"Do you have time for a play today, John?" Kit brandished a complimentary ticket endorsed by Burbage.

John scratched his head then hitched up his sagging hose, re-tying the points. "Nay, lad, not today. Party of young gentlemen come to see the play want to stable their horses here. That there Tom Saxon of yours invited them, they said."

"Shame. Any chance tomorrow?"

John brightened. "What's it to be?"

"*The Knights of Malta* again."

"Well, that's more to my taste than the tale of love you're serving today. Get ye within, lads, or you'll miss dinner."

Kit and Tobias pushed their way into the busy taproom. The rush before the theater opened was upon the place and they had to squeeze in at the end of the board between a stout farmer's wife and an ill-smelling tanner.

"Lovely company you keep, Kit," Tobias murmured, annoyed that he'd got the tanner rather than the soft cushion of the dame to press against.

Kit waved to the maid to bring them a serving of the day's stew. "Go back to Lacey Hall if you don't like it, sprout."

"Turner, Turner!"

Kit swiveled in his seat to find Tom Saxon waving at him from a private booth on the far side of the room. "I think you've just been rescued." He grinned at Tobias. "Mary, we're taking our fare over there," he called to the maid.

Heaving Tobias up by the elbow, he plowed through the crowd to join Tom and his dining companions.

"Turner, you didn't get a chance to meet us last night. This is Anthony Babington." A young man with tightly curled brown hair and gray eyes nodded to him. "Robert Gage and Charles Pilney." Babington's two companions bowed in their seats, too close to the board to rise.

"Christopher Turner." Kit bowed, delighted he had this chance to meet the set of gentlemen he'd heard much about. They were cutting a dash in the tavern world at present, admired for their swagger and bold talk. "And this is my half-brother, Tobias Lacey."

"Master Lacey," acknowledged Babington. "Your brother is the Earl of Dorset, is he not?"

"Aye, marry, sir, he is." Tobias took a seat next to Babington.

"Interesting: an earl with a player for a half-brother." Babington's eyes flicked between them like a carter's whip urging on the horses.

Tobias shrugged. "I know, terrible embarrassment, is it not? But Kit can't help having an earl in the family. We just don't talk about Will much."

The men hooted with laughter at this. Tom pulled Kit to sit next to him at the same moment the maid arrived with their stew. All eyes immediately went to the girl as she was coming perilously close to spilling from her bodice.

"Do you have everything you need, sirs?" she asked coyly.

"I wouldn't mind a drink from the buttery bar," replied Tom, ogling her cleavage.

"God amercy, sir, you make a dry jest." She cuffed him over the head without too much rancor.

"Nay, Mary, after the play I'll have coins in my pocket that'll jingle like the bells at Bow. Wouldn't you like to hear them peal?" He buried his face in her midriff and took a pretend bite.

This byplay hugely entertained the others. All urged Tom on with his wooing with ribald remarks.

The maid was well used to dealing with over-amorous customers. She took both his ears in her capable hands and twisted them so he had to look up. "Enough of your pishery-pashery, Tom Saxon. I know you theater boys—all talk and no . . . money." Kit spluttered into his ale at this innuendo. "Besides, this maid is not for barter." She leant forward and planted a sound kiss on Tom's lips, then bounced away, giggling.

Tom fell back in a feigned swoon as the others cheered the damsel. "I think I love the wench."

"Hey, Saxon, she almost took your eyes out with her finest points!" crowed Babington.

"For a moment there, I thought I was in heaven!" sighed Tom.

"For a moment there, I'd say that ugly face of yours was," quipped Kit.

The riotous party spilled out of the tavern at a quarter to two, barely enough time for Kit and Tom to change for their first scene. They had had more ale than usual, succumbing to the temptation to keep calling the luscious Mary back to their corner. Tobias was leaning rather heavily against his brother, somewhat the worse for the experience.

"My masters, we must bid you farewell, as we have a play to put on," Tom said, bowing to Babington and his crew with the clumsy exuberance of the half-sotted.

"Shall we meet afterwards—return to see how goes our brave Saxon's wooing of the fair Mary?" suggested Babington, clapping Tom on the back.

Kit grinned. This was going better than he could hope. Tom had gained them entry to the swaggering set with his antics.

"Master Turner?"

He spun round to find Mercy Hart and another woman staring at him in amazement. They had clearly just descended from a pillion saddle as their horse was being led away by John Ostler.

Oh, darkness and devils, this was not how he wanted to meet her again, not standing among this sharp-eyed set of young gentlemen. But it couldn't be helped.

"Mistress Hart." He bowed, trying to prevent the men seeing her by standing directly in her path.

His poor Mercy was looking in some confusion at his bright clothing, wondering how her black raven had transformed overnight into this peacock.

"I decided to take your advice and go to a play," she said softly, her eyes willing him to return to the man she thought she knew.

Kit tugged at his ruff awkwardly. "That is very good, mistress." Oh, hell. He'd not even had a chance to explain to her and now it was too late.

Babington jostled Tobias aside to stand next to Kit. "What's this? Another sweet plum! Is London not stocked with the most tasty morsels at present? Will she come join our party after the play? I wouldn't mind a closer acquaintance with her wares."

Kit felt a surge of anger against the man's crude language—and against himself for putting Mercy in this position. Such talk had seemed apt in the tavern, but not in the cold light of day.

"No, Mistress Hart will not be joining us," he said stiffly, hoping to signal that they were dealing with a very different sort of girl here.

Too tipsy to notice, Babington had the effrontery to seize Mercy's hand, as if she were a common serving maid, and devour her arm with kisses. "Can I not change your mind, sweetness? I am the helpless suitor for your charms: let the sun of your approval shine on this poor man."

"Make that twin suns," sniggered Saxon.

Kit had to restrain himself from giving in to his urge to punch both men; only Mercy's shocked expression gave him strength to pause before he made a bad situation worse. But he couldn't let her be pawed like that. Swiftly, he moved forward to make Babington unhand his lady, knowing it would likely lead to a quarrel later with the hot-tempered gentleman.

Fortunately, the older woman beside Mercy stepped in at this point and smacked Babington away.

"Fie on you, sir! Have you no shame?"

Babington swung round to the angry lady and clasped her round the waist. "What's this? A fiery matron? And a handsome one too! Gads, I love a lively armful. Come kiss me, sweet and thirty!"

His wooing was brought to an abrupt stop by a well-placed

knee, fresh cause for hilarity among his peers. They gathered round him, making jests at his expense. Kit however was desperate to mend things with his damsel, who was rapidly marching away with her defender.

"Mistress Hart, Mercy, please!" He caught up with her. "I pray you pardon him—he is not himself: he's had too much to drink."

Mercy looked at his hand on her arm as if it had metamorphosed into a scorpion. His heart turned over: yester eve she had regarded him so lovingly—now he was as desirable as a chamber pot. "And this is an excuse for accosting my aunt and me?"

Aunt? Hellfire. How was that for a first introduction to her family? Kit was aware that he was perilously close to losing his position at the theater for tardiness, his damsel for the insult and his new friends for appearing such a killjoy. Mayhap the last was no loss, but the other two he refused to give up.

"Give me a chance to explain—after the play." The trumpets were about to be sounded to signal the opening scene and he still had his cobbler garb to put on. "Please, Mercy, I cry your mercy."

With a huff of a sigh, a softening of her stance, she glanced sideways at her aunt, who had stood a curious spectator to this conversation. "After the performance, then."

Kit reluctantly released her hand. "Meet me here and introduce me to your aunt?"

"Aye, sir." Mercy's face dimpled as she once again graced him with her smile.

After dropping the fee in the box at the entrance, Aunt Rose showed Mercy to a seat on one of the benches set back from the stage, safely out of the reach of the heaving mass of groundlings that had paid a penny for the privilege of standing next the stage. Looking around her, taking in every fascinating detail of this dangerous place, Mercy noticed that Kit's friends had made themselves unpopular by taking stools on the very edge of the raised performance area, a place reserved for gentlemen of means. She couldn't see him among them, something for which she was grateful: it suggested he had more taste than to thrust himself into the public gaze as they did. This confirmed her suspicion that she had had the misfortune to interrupt him when he was conversing with distant acquaintances—customers, perhaps, whom he could not slight. She wasn't quite sure how to explain his clothes, but perhaps he would settle that to her satisfaction when they met later.

"Mercy, how do you know that young man?" her aunt asked stiffly.

"I met him last night at Ann's house." Mercy smoothed out the playbill. *The Merchant's Daughter*—that sounded an innocent enough piece. "He sang while I played for him."

Rose held her hands knotted tightly in her lap. "And you do not mind his reputation?"

Mercy supposed that his fame for being a fine singer was a drawback for any modest young man. "I know he is very talented, but he seems not to worry about it, so I suppose I should not either." Oh, stars, she was blushing again. "I have hopes he will call on Father—he said he would."

"Call on your father? Whatever for?" Rose's face was strangely pale.

"To court me, of course." Mercy huddled forward on her bench. "We must hush now, Aunt, I think it's about to begin." She didn't want to miss a word so that she could judge the piece fairly as she had promised Kit.

"Mercy . . ."

An alderman's wife hissed at Rose to hold her tongue as the players had entered, two boys dressed as girls. Ah yes, Mercy had heard of this. Some preachers had claimed it was unnatural, but it did not look that odd to her: both were smooth-cheeked and sweet-looking. They carried themselves gracefully, making the illusion that they were female fairly convincing. Their talk was innocent too: one was beloved of a shoemaker, but feared that her father, an important merchant of the City, would refuse them permission to wed. She was determined not to go against daughterly duty and announced—to the groans of the crowd—that she would reject her true love and marry the elderly man her father had chosen for her.

"Don't do it, love!" shouted a groundling. "That old codger won't keep you warm at night!"

A titter ran through the groundlings at this comment, but the boy-girls carried on as if they hadn't heard. Mercy knew she should be supporting Clarinda's decision, but a rebellious part of her couldn't help thinking the heckler had a point.

The boys left and a party of adult actors entered from stage left: the merchant and his trusty servant, Hasty. There was something about the servant that seemed familiar. Had he not been in the inn yard with those rude men?

"And here comes the dishonest honest shoemaker!" bellowed the merchant. *"Tom Cobbler, I welcomed you into my house to make my daughter's slippers, not to steal her virtue!"*

Mercy watched eagerly for the entrance of the lover, wondering if he would be as fine a man as Clarinda had claimed. He entered stage right, wrapped in a hooded cloak, hobbling as if injured.

"Come, man, your disguise of being a poor lame man, the one you used to win my favor, will serve you no more. Hasty here has exposed your secret."

The lover stood up straight and threw off his cloak. *"You are right, sir. This disguise is not worthy of my feelings for Clarinda, but how else was I to enter her presence when you bar the door to me?"*

It was Kit.

"You are an arrant knave of no place,
Your very presence is an affront to my face!
Get thee gone, and my hatred go with thee."

The lover knelt, overcome with sorrow. *"I leave, but my heart stays with her that loves me."*

"Are you all right, Mercy?" her aunt whispered.

No, she wasn't all right. She would never be all right again. Kit had played her false. Everything had been a lie. "I am well, Aunt. Don't worry about me."

Oh, she felt a fool! There she had been telling her aunt that Kit—a player, of all things—was going to call on her father and ask for her hand in marriage! She wished she could dig a hole and bury herself, but she couldn't, for her pride's sake, let either him or her aunt know how mortified she felt. She had to endure.

She watched the play with growing distaste. Predictably, Clarinda changed her mind about obeying her father and decided instead to elope with Tom Cobbler. It was only the fact that he was an aristocrat in disguise that saved the day, reconciling her father to the match. Hah! Mercy's father would never be swayed by such worldly attractions. He would worry more about the duplicitous nature of the man than the blueness of his blood.

Three painful hours later the play concluded with a silly jig, Kit dancing with the boy-girl while all the other players revolved around them. The groundlings loved the display, clapping in time to the music. Kit's "friends" on the side of the stage shouted lusty advice about the wedding night, laughing at their own blunt wit.

"Let us go, Aunt." Mercy felt she had aged a decade in the time spent watching her dreams of true love turn to farce on the stage.

"Mercy . . ." Rose placed a comforting hand on her arm.

"I know. I was stupid. I should have asked more about him before encouraging him. It was my mistake." Her tone was most unlike her, clipped and bitter. "I don't want to see him again."

Rose followed her out, pushing past the row of applauding spectators. "But you promised to meet him."

"For what purpose? So he can mock my ignorance again?"

"So he can explain. I saw how he looked at you, love. He truly admires you."

"You saw his friends. He probably thinks I'm silly enough to be enticed into their low company. I have sinned enough coming to the theater; I do not want to add my ruin to the tally."

Rose let her hand fall, wrongly thinking Mercy was taking a swipe at her. That was the last thing Mercy intended. She loved her aunt and if any forgiveness for Rose's fault was required from her she had long since granted it.

"I pray your pardon, Aunt. I am not myself. It was . . . it was a shock."

82

Rose smiled grimly. "I can imagine. But it is better for you to find out now than before it was too late. Here speaks bitter experience."

"Exactly." Mercy stamped across the road to the inn, speeding like a runner trying to win the victor's crown, well ahead of the others now pouring out of the Theatre. "But I'm not meeting him. Don't ask me to."

"You gave your word."

"To a man who does not exist. I do not hold myself bound by it."

Rose choked. "You, my so-honest niece, will break your word? What has he done to you?"

Broken my heart, Mercy thought. "Nothing, Aunt. Our acquaintance was so brief that it does not count at all."

But the fact that she harried the ostler to bring their horse round immediately so they could escape without crossing paths with Kit betrayed how agitated she was feeling. Her aunt, however, kept her counsel, wise enough not to try to soften her towards the player while the humiliation of the discovery was still raw.

chapter 6

KIT RUSHED TO CHANGE OUT of his costume. He had tried very hard not to look for Mercy during the performance, knowing that it would throw him into a spin when he should be remembering his lines. Had she realized that he'd said all his speeches of love to her, giving the performance of a lifetime? Everyone else had noticed. Ned Maplestead, the boy playing Clarinda, had been giving him odd looks, having been on the receiving end of such unaccustomed passion. James Burbage had congratulated him afterwards on deepening his range as an actor and promised to look out more such roles as this in future.

"That lad Shakespeare's been saying he wants to write me a play for some time now." Burbage grimaced. "Can't believe he has it in him—he's a Stratford man, nothing but wool to be had there. Still I might give him a try if he can produce something in this vein."

Kit glanced over at the new addition to the company, a plain-looking fellow already losing his hair, but with a pair of keen eyes that never missed a trick. A bit of a mystery so far, keeping himself to himself, was Will Shakespeare; Kit would be intrigued to see what he could come up with when let loose on a play. Not that it mattered that much: playwrights were the hacks on which the actors rode; no one had very high expectations of them. Even a provincial man like Shakespeare might just come up with something that could be trimmed into shape by an experienced cast.

Burbage pressed a small stack of coins in Kit's palm. "I see you're in a hurry. Here're your earnings—and a bit extra for last night."

Kit grinned and shoved it in his money pouch. "Thank you, sir." Excellent: he had enough to treat Mercy and her aunt to supper, the first step in his campaign to win his way back into her favor.

The crowds were thinning by the time he was able to leave the tiring-house. A few persistent admirers had hung on, hoping to catch a glimpse of the leading man.

"There he is!" called one goodwife, dragging her friend with her. "Master Turner!"

Kit pasted on a smile to meet his followers, all the while scanning the departing crowd to spot his little lady. She'd been dressed in a plain dark blue cloak, had she not?

"We thought you were wonderful today. When will you next be acting Tom Cobbler?" the goodwife asked, uncertain what to say now she had her idol before her. She twisted the playbill in her hands.

"I am not sure. We change back to *The Knights* tomorrow."

"I like that one too. You are so gallant in the lead." The goodwife fanned herself with the rumpled bill.

"You are too kind." Kit wanted to cut this short so he could search for his damsel. "I look forward to seeing you here again, then?"

"Oh yes!" The two women hurried off giggling together, quite drunk on the little sip of Kit's presence in their lives.

Not seeing her outside the Theatre, Kit hurried over to the very place where he had last talked to Mercy, deciding she might have interpreted his words literally. The spot stood opposite the tavern, shaded by a holly tree. Kit leant against the trunk, studying all that passed for a glimpse of the short maid with the tall good-wife, but he could not see them. Surely she would come? Perhaps she had mislaid something in the Theatre and gone back to look for it? It was easy for anyone to drop a glove or a handkerchief.

He waited for an hour, finally running out of reasons for her not showing up.

Tobias bobbed out of the tavern where he had resumed drinking with Saxon and his friends.

"Still here, Kit?"

Kit nodded, stamping his chilled feet. Darkness had fallen. He had to admit she had no intention of meeting him.

"So that one left you standing. Hey ho, but there are plenty of comely girls inside. In fact, I've just bought drinks for two lovely creatures, Mab and Bab," drink-sozzled Tobias stuttered. "Or maybe they are Meg and Peg. No matter. Come along with me."

Kit pushed himself upright, feeling like a fighter knocked out in the first bout. She hadn't even wanted an explanation. He'd picked the one girl in London who was ashamed to be seen with him. He could go into the tavern and have them swarming round him like bees to the honeypot. He'd show her.

"Where did you get the money to buy drinks, sprout?" He

threw an arm over his brother's shoulder. He could act the careless lover even if he didn't feel it.

"I said you'd be along. I'll pay you back when Will's ship comes in. Honest."

Dishonest honest maid. She said she'd let him explain, but she'd run at the first opportunity.

"Aye, I'll stand you a drink, little brother—until you no longer can stand." Which wouldn't be long by the looks of things. "Let's go see Meg-Peg and Bab-Mab."

After settling the reckoning with the innkeeper, Kit dragged Tobias from the tavern shortly after nine. There went the money he had meant to spend on Mercy's supper. He was not sorry to say good-bye to their two companions. Predictably, as Tobias had done the choosing, the girls had had more bosom than wit and he had soon tired of their conversation and was in no mood for their advances. He couldn't help but think they seemed so tawdry after Mercy.

Tobias stumbled and groaned. "'Sbones, Kit, I think I'm going to be sick."

As any caring brother would, Kit removed his cap and cloak then stood well back to allow him to relieve his symptoms in an obliging bush. Tobias staggered out, looking a little better.

"Did I charm Peg, Kit?" he asked, having passed into the melancholy stage of drunkenness. "Did I woo her like a very . . ." He paused searching for an appropriate image. "Like a very wooer?"

"Aye, you wooed her bravely, brother."

Tobias swayed to the far side of the road, then managed to

stumble back to Kit, a mariner caught in his own private storm. "Did I kiss her?"

"Aye, that and more," lied Kit, knowing his brother would only ask to go back if he thought he had unfinished business with his ladylove.

"She was a famous wench, was she not?"

"A paragon among tavern maids," agreed Kit solemnly.

"I love you, Kit."

Oh, a fig for alehouses! This was probably the signal for an overflow of brotherly affection followed swiftly by insensibility and they still had quite a way to walk.

Kit sighed and put an arm round his brother's waist to hold the boy up before he toppled over. "I love you too, sprout, but look lively. The watch is on the prowl and we must get you home."

Tobias hiccuped. "If they try to stop you, I'll pistol 'em." He made feeble bang-bang noises with his finger.

"No need for violence, man. Just be quiet."

With no small difficulty, Kit managed to grapple Tobias up to his room and dump him on the bed. He sprawled on his back, one foot on the ground, arms flung out like a starfish. Placing a cup of small beer and a basin beside him for emergencies, Kit retired to the window. He had no desire to sleep.

His earlier anger against Mercy had ebbed away, leaving an awful emptiness inside. He hugged his knees to his chest as he perched on the bench under the casement. Perhaps he was too old to curl up like this, but his childhood habit had never left him; he'd spent more nights than he could count in this hedgehog style— prickles out to fend off the world. Mercy's rejection had scratched at his tender belly and he felt the wound deeply.

Not good enough for her, and she hadn't even stayed to tell him so herself.

He'd left the shutters open so he could see the moon riding among the clouds, lighting the topmost flag of the Theatre beyond the huddle of roofs and trees that separated him from his workplace. For years all he had dreamed of was making a success of his career on the stage; now, abruptly, the source of his happiness had become the obstacle.

Would Mercy have a big enough heart to come to accept him for who he was? Today suggested not. So did he care enough about her to try to be something else? Aye, that was the question.

Before he took any drastic decisions, he would have to try once more to talk to her. After all, seeing him onstage without any warning must have disturbed his little Puritan greatly. Perhaps her aunt had dragged her away, believing him a man of low character? He had not considered that. He could forgive Mercy for leaving him waiting if she could forgive him not telling her the whole truth from the beginning.

His thoughts were interrupted when Tobias turned over and fell off the bed, landing in a heap on the floor. With an exasperated sigh of affection for the idiot, Kit got up and threw a blanket over him. Tobias did not wake.

At least that meant he'd have the bed to himself tonight. Today had not been a total disaster.

Third in line, Mercy knelt at her father's chair to receive his Sabbath blessing.

"How fare you, child?" her father asked kindly, framing her

face with his large hands. He had green eyes like her own, while her brother and sister took after their mother—Mary Hart was said to have had blue eyes, though she had not lived long enough for Mercy to remember them. "I have hardly seen you since you stayed at Ann's."

Mercy knew herself to be such a worthless creature. "I am well, Father."

"I did not realize you played the lute so skilfully. My friends in the City have nothing but praise for your abilities."

"Thank you, Father."

John Hart scratched the side of his nose, senses pricked by a vague threat to his family. "But I am not certain that it is something that you should indulge in too often, Mercy. There is danger you will be led into vanity." He studied her gravely.

"I agree, Father. I did it to oblige Mistress Belknap, but in future I will try to avoid making a display of myself."

He nodded, well pleased with her answer. "You are a good girl, Mercy."

She hung her head. "No, I'm not, Father."

He chuckled. "Well, none of us is perfect. It is unholy to think so. But you do well enough. I was pleased with your thoughts on the play. I am glad you realized for yourself that the pretty packaging concealed traps for the foolish. The Devil makes use of such primrose-strewn paths to draw many to their ruin. I was right to let you go—now you will no longer be tempted by it."

"Aye, sir."

He placed his heavy hand on her head and said his usual prayer over her. He rose, drawing her to her feet. "Let us leave for church. The bell is already tolling."

Faith in arm with her father, Edwin escorting Mercy, the Hart family walked to their church, St. Magnus, at the northern end of the bridge. Rose preferred to attend the service in St. Mary Overie in Southwark, where the priests wore the surplice and clerical cap and used the prayer book. The Hart church, a medieval building with arched windows filled with clear glass, was led by a severe follower of Calvin who rejected all such Romish signs, preferring to cut the liturgy to the minimum so he could expound the word at greater length, his words echoing off the bare walls. Privately, Mercy usually preferred the kindly old priest at St. Mary's, but today she vowed she wouldn't let her mind drift during the hour-long sermon.

Reverend John Field was in fine form this morning. He rattled through the confession and creed to spend a good ninety minutes castigating Londoners for their manifold failings, their lack of attention to the poor coupled with their spiritual poverty. By the time he had finished, Mercy was determined to make sure she gave the pennies she had saved to the first good cause she came across, giving up the treats for herself for six months.

Mercy had almost reached the end of the service with no lapses of attention when she caught the Dodds sisters whispering behind her. They were holding up their shared prayer book to try to hide their secret conversation, but she could hear them very well in the hush.

"Who do you think he is?" asked Humiliation. "I've not seen him at church before, more's the pity."

"Is he not the most . . . most well-made man you've ever seen?" asked Deliverance, all in a flutter. "He doth great credit to our Creator."

The two girls had to stuff their knuckles in their mouths to stifle their scandalized laughter at their own naughty words.

I will not turn and look, Mercy promised herself. *I will not give in to unworthy curiosity.*

"Look, look, he's getting up!" hissed Deliverance as the service concluded. "He's coming this way!"

Mercy couldn't help herself. She half turned on her bench. Sweet Lord above, it was Kit, all dressed up as he had been for the Belknap supper, the only difference being a pearl that swung incongruously in his earlobe. He couldn't possibly be planning to speak to her, could he? That was too much! He'd shame her in front of her entire church and her reputation would never recover. Actors were to her church what the demons were to angels— creatures of the outer darkness that should not venture onto sacred ground. But there was nowhere to hide, no chance of escape.

Kit came to a stop at the Hart family, his gaze skipping from Mercy to each of her relatives in turn. He bowed low to her father.

"Sir."

John Hart, full of Christian good cheer after the improving sermon, returned the gesture. "Have we met, young man?"

"No, sir, but I had the privilege of meeting your daughter at Alderman Belknap's supper party last week."

John Hart thought he now understood. "Ah yes, I hear that was a merry evening. My daughter turned out to be quite the musician."

"Indeed she is. I had the great pleasure of singing to her accompaniment."

Hart wasn't so sure he liked the sound of this. "Indeed, what kind of song was this?"

"A song in praise of Her Majesty, sir, in a setting by the court choirmaster, Lyly."

Mercy looked down at her shaking fingers. He wasn't telling her father lies, but that did not properly describe the charged words of love he had sung to her. Kit was doing it again, hiding behind things that distorted the truth like a mottled mirror.

"I'm pleased you chose a suitable piece, none of these loose songs that I hear about the streets these days. What did you say your name was, sir?"

Kit smiled. "I have not said as yet, sir. My name is Christopher Turner. I am a player at the Theatre and illegitimate half-brother of the Earl of Dorset."

This double serving of truth fell into the quiet conversations in the church like a crack shot on the tennis court. Mercy could swear that half the gossips in the congregation had heard as his words bounced off her father's shocked face. She had just been berating Kit for not telling the whole truth; now she was wishing he had been a bit more circumspect. And what was this—an earl for a brother? It was like a tasteless rerun of *The Merchant's Daughter. Lo, I am not Tom Cobbler, but a baronet's son!*

"A player?" coughed her father.

"Indeed, sir. Mercy, I mean, *Mistress Hart*"—he bowed in her direction—"did not know at the time. For that I have to apologize, for I fear she was offended when she discovered the truth."

"You earn your living in the Theatre?" Her father could not get past the first confession. He probably expected devils to leap out from behind the communion table and drag Kit off to Hell.

Mercy began to worry for Kit. Anger had made her compare him to a demon earlier, but really, her heart prompted, was he not more like Daniel walking into the lions' den? He could not expect any friends in this strict gathering of God-fearing folk and yet he had still done it. For her.

"Aye, marry, sir, I do work there. I always thought it a touch better than stealing from old ladies as a means of putting bread on my table," Kit replied with a self-mocking note in his voice.

Faith pulled Mercy up by the elbow. "Come along, sister, we must talk to Mistress Field."

It was the first time Mercy had ever heard Faith utter anything approaching untruth. They both knew there was no such requirement—that was how serious Faith thought this interruption of their decent family Sabbath. But Mercy was not ready to abandon Kit to her father; though she was angry with him, she was not so uncaring as to leave him to the lions.

"I will be there presently, sister. I believe Master Turner has only called by to offer an apology to me then be on his way. Is that not so, Master Turner?" She offered him the decent chance to take his leave.

"Nay, Mistress Hart, I was hoping to ask permission of your father to court you."

Mercy prayed for a thunderbolt to strike her now, burn her up until all that was left was a pair of smoking shoes. She would never outlive this.

"Mercy!" She had never heard her father use that tone to her before. "What is going on?"

Edwin, until now a bemused spectator to this scene, stepped in to save her from further humiliation. "Father, shall we not take this conversation somewhere a little more private than *the middle of our church?*" Mercy reminded herself to tell him later that he really was her favorite brother of all time.

Recalled to his surroundings, John Hart nodded and briskly beckoned his daughters. "Come, girls, Master Turner here will follow with Edwin. We will talk more at home."

The two young men stood back as the girls followed their father from the church. John Hart offered abbreviated greetings to their friends and neighbors, his daughters trailing along in meek silence. Mercy wished her face was not broadcasting her distress, but she had no control over her flushed cheeks. She was torn between a desire to slap Kit for his boldness and an urge to protect him from her father's coming wrath. Whatever happened at home was going to be ugly, she just knew it.

Tight-lipped, John Hart strode back across the bridge, nodding curtly to those who offered him Sabbath greetings.

"Explain," he snapped.

Mercy ran to keep up with him. "I met Master Turner at Ann's and we played music together as you have already heard. We . . . we had a private conversation at that time, which made me think he would fain woo me as his wife." She swallowed, hoping he did not demand more details.

"And then?"

"We met when I went to the Theatre with Aunt Rose. It was then I realized he was a player. He wanted to explain why he had not told me this before, but I hastened home before he had a chance. I was upset that he was not an apprentice musician as I had thought."

Hart stopped abruptly outside their door and shoved it open.

"And that is all, or do I need question your aunt? No dalliance, no kisses or other lewdness?"

Mercy gaped like a perch netted at Fish Wharf.

Her father pulled her roughly inside and stood her before his chair while he strode the room. "I see there *is* more."

Faith gasped. "Mercy, you haven't . . . ?"

"A kiss. One little kiss. At the Belknap supper." Mercy squeezed her hands together.

Grandmother Isham roused from her bundle of blankets by the fire. "What's this? Someone's been kissing young Mercy?" She reached out to her granddaughter. "That's lovely, dear. Was it a pleasant kiss or all thrusting tongue and whiskers?" Her eyes twinkled, curious to know the answer.

"Mother Isham, will you be quiet!" thundered John Hart, quite unlike his normal forbearing self.

But Grandmother had latched on to a subject in which she had a keen interest. "But girls need kisses, John. Sunshine to flowers, that's what they are! You kissed my Mary often enough, admit it."

"Mary was a woman above reproach. She was my wife!"

"Not when you first kissed her, I wager."

Edwin and Kit entered together at this moment, attracting all eyes.

"Is that him?" whispered Grandmother, none too quietly. She waved Mercy closer. "Oh, very good choice, darling. He is quite the most handsome man I've seen since my Ben came wooing. I wouldn't mind a kiss from him if he were willing. Here, my fine gallant!' She puckered her mouth.

Kit looked most alarmed to be propositioned by the old lady

within seconds of entering. Mercy's heart did a painful flip when she saw that he had quickly surmised the state of Grandmother's mind and took her hand gently in his to offer a respectful kiss. "It is an honor to be allowed to salute you, ma'am, with the worship of my lips."

Grandmother chuckled and patted his cheek. "Oooh, I like this one, Mercy. Do keep him, please. He looks much more fun than your brother."

"Faith!" roared John Hart. "Take your grandmother to the kitchen and close the door!"

Faith hurried to obey, guiding the reluctant lady from the courtroom of the family parlor.

"Don't you scare away this lovely young man, Johnny, or I'll take a rod to your backside!" threatened Grandmother as she went. "And don't blame Mercy for letting him kiss her! No red-blooded girl could resist him."

chapter 7

THE DOOR SHUT ON THAT piece of old wives' wisdom and the silence that then fell was the most uncomfortable one Mercy had ever experienced. Her father paced the room, dominating it with his thunderous mood. Shaking in her shoes as she stood before him, she felt like the church spire about to be struck by lightning.

"Sir, what mean you treating my daughter like a common tavern wench?" asked her father coldly, his ire flashing out to hit his tall target.

Kit turned apologetic eyes on Mercy. "That wasn't me. That was a young man with whom I was standing outside the Theatre."

Oh, he really shouldn't have said that. Mercy shredded the frayed ends of her purse strings nervously.

"What? I was talking about you kissing my daughter at the Belknaps'; what are you talking about?"

Kit had said too much to backtrack. He glanced at Mercy, but seeing she was not going to add anything, he rushed to explain. "An acquaintance approached your daughter and her aunt in an inappropriate fashion outside the Theatre, but the elder lady ended his pretensions swiftly and with great presence of mind. Nothing more passed between them."

Her father turned to Mercy. "You did not tell me of this? Why not tell me the truth about your visit to the Theatre?"

Mercy felt close to tears. "I did not think of it after the event. Aunt Rose stopped the man before he could go too far."

Her father turned away to master his temper. "Edwin, I pray your pardon that you have to hear of such behavior from two that share your blood. I had not realized that Rose had led Mercy so far from the paths of righteousness to think such an approach of no matter."

"Sir, this is not my aunt's fault!" Mercy protested.

"I disagree, but that is for another time. Now we have to deal with this scandalous behavior on your part, Mercy. You let this man kiss you."

Mercy mangled her fingers together. "Aye, sir."

"You did not push him away with objections as any decent maid would."

Hadn't she? All she remembered was a soft touch of lips; it hadn't felt like something that should be rejected at the time. "Nay, sir, I . . . I did not."

"Now look here, Master Hart," interrupted Kit, "I want you to understand that your daughter is entirely blameless. She has done nothing wrong and wrestled only to do what is right."

"Wrestled indeed," muttered Edwin, looking at her with disbelieving eyes. Mercy could tell from the shocked expression on his face that her brother only now realized that his baby sister had grown up without him noticing and he didn't like the change.

Kit held his temper, though the scorching heat in his eyes warned that he was angered by her father and brother's reaction to their brief interlude at the Belknaps'. "I did not approach you today to make it worse for your sweet daughter. I came to ask that you search your Christian charity to find a place for me, aye, marry, a wandering sheep in your eyes, but one who loves Mercy and wishes to be given a chance to prove it to her."

"Wandering sheep? You are more like the thief that climbs o'er the wall of the sheepfold to steal the lamb." John Hart folded his arms. "In what world do you live, Master Player, that you think an actor, and a bastard one at that, worthy of my daughter?"

"Father!" protested Mercy. "His birth is none of his fault. You should not hold that against him." She was now quivering with rage to hear such insults leveled at Kit.

"Immoral women breed immoral children." Kit's eyes flashed with rage at the slur to his mother, but John Hart carried on regardless. "This player is the very proof of this adage, Mercy, by his choice of profession." Her father strode to her and seized her upper arms, giving her a shake. "Open your eyes. Do not believe his soft words of love. What can this man want from you other than your money or your maidenhead?"

"Do you hold me of so little account, Father, that I can have no other attractions for a man?" she asked in a whisper of a voice.

Her father released her and patted her condescendingly on the head. "I know you struggle with carnal appetites, Mercy, as I did in my youth. You have more of my blood than your mother's in you. I've always applauded you for your control until this point. You are too innocent to see yourself as men do. Your form is the kind that tempts the weak and vicious; it reflects well on you that you have so far lived so as to put yourself above reproach. It is my role as your father to stop you tumbling into error merely because a man says he loves you."

So her father was more or less agreeing that he thought her nothing but a ripe body waiting to be plucked as that hateful man had told her outside the tavern.

"I see." She dropped her eyes to her toecaps. She wanted to disappear through the cracks in the floor.

Kit gave a low growl of frustration. "Sir, you do your daughter a disservice if you suggest I cannot love her for herself. Indeed, she is a beauty, but that is nothing to the beautiful soul that resides within." Kit sounded sincere, but he would, wouldn't he? He was a good actor.

"And you discovered all this on an evening's acquaintance?" sneered her father. "That is remarkable. And tell me, did you or did you not know that she was daughter of one of London's richest merchants?"

"Aye, I knew she was your daughter, but that has nothing to do with my feelings for her. I'd love Mercy if she were barefoot and without a penny to her name; and I love her as she is—a princess in this house of a merchant prince."

But his pretty words ran like water off granite as he sprinkled them in her father's hearing. John Hart went to the door. "Barefoot and penniless, you say? Well, that's the only way you would ever touch her again. Go your ways, sir. Scud, scud." He opened the door to throw Kit out like yester eve's ash. "I want no player in my family and, if Mercy wants to see you again, she will have to renounce the name of Hart."

"But, sir!"

"Get thee gone or I'll kick you out like the scurvy dog you are."

John Hart's plan to force Kit to make an ignoble exit was spoiled by the return of Rose from church. She bustled into the house already talking, as was her wont.

"Ah, John, thank you for opening the door for me. Church was so interesting today; I think even you would have approved of the sermon." She took a pin from her hat to loosen it from its anchorage in her braided hair. "And the psalms were beautifully sung. That new choirmaster has quite a skill with the boys." Her words came to a sudden end when she saw the visitor in the parlor and Mercy standing in disgrace before her father's seat of judgment. "Oh."

"Rose, did you know that this player had accosted my daughter?" John Hart said coldly. "Kissed her, pawed her, wooed her with false words of love?"

Through tears, Mercy saw Kit clench his fists at his side.

"When?" gasped Rose, looking in confusion between Kit and Mercy. "Indeed, we met at the Theatre, but there was no opportunity . . . I swear I was with her the whole time, John."

"But you knew they had met before?" he ground out.

"Well, aye, Mercy told me. Surely she's told you the same?"

"Too late to save her reputation. This player"—he spat the word like a curse—"confronted us at church. There will be none ignorant of her shame before the evening service."

"Mercy, is this true?" whispered Rose, hand at her throat.

"For the love of God, sir, I but kissed her—once and most innocently," exploded Kit. "She is untouched, any fool can tell!"

John Hart pointed to the still open door. "Out! Out, you blaspheming wretch!"

"What have I done now?" cried Kit. "I love your daughter, sir. That is my only crime."

"You took Our Lord's name in vain." John Hart cast about him for some way of forcibly ejecting the tall actor. "Edwin, put the man out!"

Edwin paled, but manfully dashed for his rapier that hung by the fireplace. He waggled it in the direction of the door. "Get thee gone, player."

Exasperated beyond what he could bear, Kit threw up two hands in despair. "Peace, peace. I'll go." He clenched a fist, one finger pointing accusingly at Edwin. "But don't you dare blame your sister for any of this. If I hear you've made her cry one tear over this sorry affair, I will demand satisfaction from you!"

Mercy scrubbed a wrist across her eyes. "Kit, please go."

Unable to leave her like this, surrounded by hostile relatives, Kit hastened to her side, ignoring the blade in Edwin's hand. Daring them with a look to stop him, he hugged her to his chest, brushing her tears away with his thumb. "Please believe me when I say I only meant to honor you, to woo you like you should be wooed. Forgive me for bringing trouble upon you—it was not my intent."

She nodded against his chest.

"Unhand my daughter, sir!" spluttered John Hart.

Kit gently set her aside and walked stiffly out of the door without another word.

The family stood in silence for a few awful moments.

"Sister Rose," began John Hart, clearing his throat against the emotion that had lodged there, "I offered you sanctuary after your unfortunate lapse, thinking you genuinely repented of your error, but it seems I was wrong. Your actions took my daughter to a place of dissolute company, exposed her to insults and furthered the pretensions of that . . . that man."

Rose let her hands drop to her side, her smart blue felt hat falling to the floor. "What are you saying, John? You blame me?"

"Perchance you did not intend any of this, nor did I when I gave permission for her to go, but nonetheless your example has weakened my daughter when the Devil came calling. She would not have even thought to venture to such places without you putting the idea in her head. These are dangerous years for girls of her age—a time of temptation and trials of the flesh. I cannot allow her to fall through lack of vigilance. I think it is time you found yourself another lodgings."

"What?" gasped Mercy. How had this become about Rose when it had been her own behavior that brought Kit to their door? Her father couldn't do this to her aunt—not because of her!

"I will give you money, of course," continued John Hart, ignoring his daughter's cry.

Rose swallowed, not having the luxury of being able to refuse his charity. "I see. I will look for a new place immediately."

"Please, Father, it's all my fault!" begged Mercy. "I was the one who encouraged Kit—not her!"

John Hart's face was set. "Do not interfere, child, this is between your aunt and myself. She knows her presence here is a problem for more than just you."

"But you can't . . . Please! I'll be good—so very, very good, I promise!" Tears dampened Mercy's ruff, making the neat folds sag. She sank on her knees to grab the hem of her father's doublet, feeling as if, like a tallow candle, she was melting away in the heat of his anger. "Please don't send her away."

Rose clucked her tongue, knelt beside her and folded her sobbing niece into her arms. "Don't take on so, Mercy. You are not to blame."

"But I am!" Mercy's shoulders heaved in hopeless sobs. She had tried so hard, but as always she had failed and she couldn't even remember why or how. Had it been the kiss? Or the singing? Or her appearance attracting the advances of horrid men? Whatever the cause, she had been found not good enough and now this earthquake had been sent to shake their family apart.

"Mercy, cease this unseemly display and go to your chamber," barked John Hart, his short temper a sign that he was uncomfortable with the harsh judgment he had just passed on his sister-in-law. "I want you to spend the remainder of the day reflecting on your behavior and pray to God that He will save your good name in the eyes of our fellow believers."

"Oh, John, is that all you can think of?" asked Rose mockingly, helping Mercy to her feet. "Her good name when you've broken her heart?"

"To your room, Mercy!" bellowed her father.

Not wishing to anger him further, Mercy nodded and slid from her aunt's embrace, taking the stairs to her room like a thief to the gallows.

Kit stood at the river's edge at the Southwark end of London Bridge looking back at Mercy's house, which, like the others, seemed too heavy for the structure to hold up—a row of fat-bottomed merchants seated on a spindly bench. How had that meeting gone so wrong so quickly? He had convinced himself in the solitary contemplation of his bedchamber that if he approached Hart on the neutral ground of a church, appealed to his Christian charity and found out what he needed to do in order to earn the right to court Mercy, then all would be well. But rash, so rash! Instead he had caused his lady much suffering and been barred from the door.

The rising tide licked at his boots. The evil-smelling shore was undergoing one of its twice-daily scourings. All to the good, for the river was the receptacle of all that was foul in London. Yet for John Hart no amount of washing would make this player clean enough for his daughter. Kit moved back before the leather of his boots was ruined, clambered up the muddy bank and climbed the short flight of steps at the top. A party of card-playing boatmen watched him, wondering if he was a prospective fare, then lost interest when he made no sign of engaging their services.

Should he give up? He was no idealist, having been raised in a hard school where blows had far outnumbered loving touches. The cynical part of his character reminded him that it was foolish to trust powerful feelings created by so brief an acquaintance—they were akin to a violent illness, striking overnight and carrying off the victim by morning. Not used to this sensation of self-doubt, Kit sat on the low wall at the top of the steps, staring at the back of Mercy's house, seeking some sign, some guidance that what he felt was not insane.

A window on the top floor opened and a white-coifed head appeared in the gap, leaning on folded arms, heedless of the cold day. Kit felt a stab in his gut. It was Mercy, still sobbing, but hoping none would hear her if she took her tears outside. Oh, God, this was not fair. He would give his right arm to be allowed to comfort her.

"Oi, master, are you going to sit there all day or leave space for our customers?" challenged one hairy specimen of a boatman, eyebrows like tortoiseshell butterfly caterpillars on his pale cabbage of a face.

Kit offered him in return the traditional finger of a Londoner. Dismissing the men, Kit turned his back on them. He knew what he should do. He jumped down the steps and grabbed a stick from the shore. The tide was not yet so high as to cover the mud—he had canvas enough for what he intended.

"What's the daft gallant doing?" laughed another of the card players, his features resembling one of those mischievous monkeys kept as pets by court ladies.

"Writing something." The boatman threw down his cards to watch.

"What does it say?"

The man shrugged. "Can't read. Can you?"

"Only my name."

The boatman slapped his friend on the back. "Well, mate, I've got news for you: I don't think he's writing your name down there, not with all those curly folderols and hearts."

Kit blocked out the mocking voices of the boatmen to concentrate on his message. There was something soothing about running the stick through the sandy mud, creating perfect patterns.

My thoughts are wing'd with hopes
My hopes with love.

He didn't want to shame her further by writing her name on mud for all London to see, but if she looked up and read it she would know it was for her. Unfortunately the tide was rising, threatening to obliterate his careful pattern, and she still had her head buried in her arms. This wasn't working as well as it would in a play. There the maiden would by chance look up and see the lover's message; today he would have to take more drastic measures.

"Mercy Hart!" he bellowed through cupped hands over the sounds of the city. He was helped by the relative peace of Sabbath, which meant fewer carts were thumping over the bridge.

Mercy sat up and wiped her eyes on a sleeve, looking in every direction but the right one for the source of the cry. He smiled despite himself: someone really needed to look after that girl.

"Mercy Hart!" Kit began jigging on the shore, waving his stick. "Over here!"

Finally his maiden turned the right way, two hands covering her mouth as she gasped with surprise.

He blew her a kiss. "I love you, Mercy Hart!" He stepped aside to point to his message word by word. He could see she was mouthing each word with him. Throwing his arms wide he acted out the sentiment:

"*My thoughts . . .*" He tapped his head.

"Are wing'd..." Here he flapped like a bird, laughing as she began to smile.

"With hopes..." He threw his arms wide and went on one knee, the posture of a supplicant.

"My hopes with love." His laughter died and he clasped his hands to his heart.

The boatman behind him chuckled. "Aye, if the maid don't want him, I think we should put him onstage. He's almost as good as a play."

The other card player squinted at Kit as he picked his nose with a stubby finger. "I'm sure I've seen him there already. My daughter's been in a flutter about a man very like him."

"That'd explain it. Only a theater lad would make such a spectacle of himself."

But they were wrong. To his delight, as he watched, Mercy copied his actions, first touching her head, then fluttering her arms, and finally pressing her hands to her heart. She did not shout that she loved him, but there was no need: he understood what she could not say.

"I will find a way!" he called over the water. "I promise you—I will."

Mercy watched until the very last letter of Kit's message was washed away by the tide. He had long since gone, leaving her with a flock of kisses blown to her window. She had pretended to catch each one and put them to her lips to his cheers of approval.

The tide reached the steps and Mercy closed the window.

Taking out her journal, she made note of the day's events with a single word. *Disaster*. She added her spiritual thought.

Dear God, I love Kit Turner.

Then she tallied up her score for the day.

Scripture verses read: 65 (the lesson at church had been a long one).

Prayers said: 1 (she had been repeating the same one: "Please let me find a way to love Kit and stay a Hart").

Sinful thoughts: too many to count (she had been breaking the commandment to honor thy father and mother with almost every other thought).

Slapping the book shut, she put it back under the mattress, then strode about the room, caged with her turmoil. Maybe she wouldn't keep a journal anymore. There was little point as she could see no improvement, only a record of her continuing failures. Soul-searching may be good for most God-fearing folk, but for her it was an endless spiral down, not the purifying experience she had been promised.

A strange feeling bubbled up inside her. If she had to put a name to it, she would call it "rebellion." Her father was in error. For the first time in her life Mercy questioned his judgment. Oh, he could scold her for her faults—she had too many to enumerate—and she would accept the correction, but he had been plain wrong to eject Kit without a hearing and to tell Aunt Rose she had to find a new home.

"Father is mistaken." She whispered the words daringly, half expecting a bolt of heavenly displeasure to strike her. Nothing happened. She said it a bit louder. "Father is wrong." See, even God agreed, because He had not punished her.

The heavy tread of boots on stairs warned her of her father's approach. She had been expecting his visit for a while now; he would want to make sure she was drawing the right conclusions from her time of spiritual reflection.

He opened the door. Mercy remained standing with her back to the window, holding on to the sill behind her. The full light fell on him, revealing the white hairs threading his chestnut locks, two paler streaks in his beard on either side of his mouth. She had not realized that he was getting old; he had always seemed the still point round which everything else in the family revolved, unchanging and unquestioned.

"Father."

"Mercy, my dear, we need to talk about what passed below."

She nodded.

John Hart closed the door and stood, leaving the expanse of the room between them. "I know you think I am angry with you, but this is not the case."

He could have fooled her.

"You are very young still. You could not be blamed for falling into error. Much more experienced women than you would have done the same, as I think your grandmother, in her own special way, made clear."

This was the problem about crossing her father's will: he always sounded so reasonable. He didn't beat his children or lock them away with only bread and water to eat as other parents did; he heaped his love on them like burning coals. Jesus had had it right when he said the best way to respond to enemies was to forgive them.

John Hart ran his fingers over her writing desk, absentmindedly tracing the outline of the inkstand and pen. "I imagine you have no idea what depths of sin such a one as Turner must have plumbed in his life—I pray you never find out. The only way for a God-fearing girl to behave when confronted by one such as him is to separate yourself from the source of temptation." He pushed the ink further away from the quill, fearing to see the white feather soiled by the contact.

"You say he is a sinner, Father." Mercy began her fight back by being as reasonable as he was. "But did not our Lord spend his days on earth with sinners rather than those who thought them-selves saints?"

"Aye, marry, he did. But you are not He. He is our Good Shepherd, His mission to seek the lost in such places; you are but a lamb that must stay in His sheepfold, not wander off on your own to be picked off in the wilderness by the wolves of this world."

It was pointless arguing scripture with her father. She already knew that on many matters there were points to be found for both sides in the same chapter, if not the very same verse. Still, she had the courage of her convictions; she might be only sixteen, but she believed herself old enough to judge right from wrong in this case.

"I pray your pardon, sir, for any offense I have given you, but I believe you are wrong to dismiss Master Turner without giving him a fair hearing."

Her father shook his head sadly.

"And I also think you are in error putting my aunt from the house. It shows a lack of Christian charity that I am surprised to see in my father, who until now has always told me it is far more blessed to give than receive."

This audacious criticism by a child of her parent sent his dark eyebrows winging upwards. "Mercy, what has come over you? The Devil's rot has taken further hold than I had imagined."

She clenched her fingers on the wooden sill. "May I not express an opinion without sinning?" Reckless words, but they were true and that drove her forward, though each step felt like treading on hot coals. "Is the commandment to honor my father meant to gag my conscience? You taught me that salvation must be of the soul's own working out. I do not mean to show disrespect to you when I try to puzzle my way through life's mazes."

Her father's expression was tenfold more sorrowful than when he had entered. "Ah, Mercy, you know I love you dearly, but I fear you err. I will leave you more time to think upon this matter. You have a good heart; I am sure you will come to see where you have strayed over time." He turned to go. "At least you should be relieved of any further importuning from the player. Now he knows you will bring him no money, his interest will wane and he'll fix on some other prey."

"You don't know the man at all, Father."

"Neither do you, Mercy. Neither do you."

chapter 8

Too old to be banished to her room, Rose made her escape from the house as soon as John Hart went upstairs to browbeat his daughter some more. In many ways, John was a fine man, better than most, but he was making a poor fist of this hand of cards, trumping hearts with heavy spades and thinking he'd won the game. Did he not see the damage he was doing?

Leaving Faith feeding her mother a dinner of broth, Rose turned north on the bridge, thinking to wander to St. Paul's in the hopes the walk would settle her spirits. Oh, it hurt to be cast out, sure enough, and she was worried where she could go now, but she was even more concerned for poor Mercy. In Rose's estimation, a player was not an unfit husband—just so as long as he was faithful and had coin in his pocket. Some men, like Master Burbage and Master Henslowe, made a respectable living from the stage, even owning their theaters. Others, like the court poet, John Lyly, were highly regarded for their theatrical skills. Lyly was invited into the most illustrious homes with his troupe of trained choirboys performing his plays. It was only the Puritans, of whom John Hart was unfortunately one, who confused pleasure with sin.

Kit Turner for lover and husband? Why, at first, Rose had

been astonished at this strange match for her niece, but she could see the attraction of it. With half of London in love with the handsome young player, no wonder Mercy was not immune. On the principle of once bitten, twice shy, Rose had a healthy suspicion of men, but seeing Mercy and Kit together in the parlor had made her believe once again that there might be such a thing as true love. His longing for something good and pure in his life had been palpable, while her desire to protect him had been plain in each word she tried to speak in his defense.

"Back again, Mistress Isham?" Silas Porter overtook her by the shoemaker as she walked slowly north.

"Good morrow, Master Porter. Nay, no shoes for me today. I am walking to St. Paul's."

"Are you now? Well, I am walking to my daughter's to dine. May I share the road with you?" He offered her his arm.

Why not? It was a long time since a man had shown her such courtesies; it was a pleasant change to be treated like a lady rather than an embarrassment.

"Now here's a pleasant Sabbath pastime—a walk with a pretty neighbor. Tell me about yourself, Mistress Isham," Silas encouraged, gallantly steering her round a pile of fresh horse dung.

Not a question she welcomed. "There is not much to tell, sir."

"Hmm." He evidently didn't believe her. "Then perhaps I should go first, to encourage our better acquaintance."

She smiled. "Perhaps you should."

They were just passing a gap in the houses on the north bank of the Thames. Pausing together, they looked back at John Hart's house and, beyond that, the southern gatehouse, which was decorated with the grisly reminders of what happened to those who offended the Queen. Silas pointed over the river to the distant heads. "I'll start with them, then. That could have been me."

"What! Are you serious?" Rose shuddered. She usually avoided looking at the tarred heads of those who'd fallen foul of the law, put up there as a final humiliation after execution.

"Oh aye, deadly serious. I spent many years in the Tower, thanks to a not-so-youthful indiscretion."

"What did you do?" Rose couldn't credit that the happy-looking man at her side should have spent time in London's most feared prison.

"Thought I knew better than the Queen." Silas squeezed her arm. "Never fear: I learnt my lesson. What I considered to be sticking to the principles of my Catholic upbringing, I now think of as stubborn folly. I've seen enough of war to know in my gut that civil war is the worse sin—and that is what will happen if we fall to fighting over church governance. You need not worry that you are walking with a traitor: I left that man behind in the Tower and am now a contented subject of Her Majesty."

"I am glad of it, sir."

"Aye, the wise soldier keeps his head below the parapet when the missiles start to fly: not a bad rule for life." He patted her wrist. "You must not think me entirely ignorant about you, my dear. London is nothing if not a barrel of gossip served on tap. I've supped at the buttery bar like most and heard the stories."

Rose tried to pull her arm free. He thought she was *that* kind of woman, did he? "I see."

"Nay, lass, don't mistake me. Who among us would be the first to cast a stone? I meant only to lay your mind at rest that I am aware of your misfortune. If you give me the man's name, I'll go skewer him for you."

She did not think he was joking. "It is in the past, sir." Aye, Henry Talbot could be riding in a carriage or buried six feet under and she would no longer care.

"Nay, 'tis not. It angers me that you have to walk the bridge each day dragging your reputation with you like a chain. I know how that feels, but at least my manacles were struck from my ankles when they set me loose from jail. I admire you for holding your head high. That was why I approached you, I swear."

"And that is your only motive?" Rose was no innocent to take a man at his word.

His eyes twinkled with humor, winning her over where protests would have failed. "You might be surprised at some of my motives, but, aye, it was the main one, and will do for now."

"Then a fig for all gossips!" She snapped her fingers in the wind, imagining she was stepping out of the chains he had spied at her ankles. He was right: she should be angry that she had been forced to bend in penitence for so long when the truly guilty had gone free of reproach. "And I thank you. It has . . . it has been difficult." Rose realized the confession was a huge relief. For the last five years, she had had no one with whom to share her misery, not wanting to burden Mercy, her mother infirm and the others too righteous to understand. "But I fear it is all about to start again. My brother-in-law has decided I'm a bad influence on his youngest daughter. He has asked me to find somewhere else to live."

Silas's grip tightened on her arm. "He has, has he? Do you want me to skewer him, then?"

She laughed and shook her head. "Is that your answer to all of life's ills, sir?"

He gave her a sheepish grin. "Aye, marry, it is for us old soldiers."

"No, no, that won't be necessary, but if you know of a decent place where I can rent a modest lodgings then I would be grateful."

Silas scratched his beard, considering something. "Look now, Mistress Isham, don't take this wrong, but would you like to come dine with my daughter and son-in-law? I don't mean to rush you into unwanted introductions, but they know many people in this city of ours and might come up with a name for you. And I have a proposition too, but it might be best if I put it to you with others present."

That was all very mysterious, but dinner sounded better than walking hungry around St. Paul's. "Very well, I accept."

Dinner turned out to be a merry affair. Silas's daughter, Milly, was a kind hostess, making Rose feel instantly welcome in her kitchen as she made the final preparations to the meal the maid had got ready before taking the rest of the day off. A sweet-looking girl of no more than nineteen, it was hard to credit that Milly was in charge of a successful finishing business with lords and ladies among her clients.

"How did you say you know my father?" the girl asked cheerfully, snipping rosemary over a dish of mutton and raisins.

"He is a neighbor of a kind. I live on London Bridge."

"Interesting. He has never brought a lady to dine before." The girl's eyes twinkled with calculation that Rose wasn't sure was unwarranted.

"Then I consider myself honored."

"Oh, pish, think nothing of it. I like the old man to have a friend." She winked at her father who was playing with the kitchen cat by the hearth.

"What's all this about old, Milly? I'll have you know I am but forty-one."

Milly swooped on him and kissed his cheek. "As I said, old."

"You won't think it so when you reach my age," he grumbled good-naturedly.

Milly's most unusual husband, Diego, a blackamoor, came in from the garden carrying a load of firewood. Rose was pleased that she hadn't missed a step when they were introduced, but he was the first African she had ever seen and she had to admit his dark skin was a fascinating contrast to his wife's pale complexion.

"Diego, Mistress Isham is aunt to young Edwin," said Silas as he stacked the firewood in the basket.

"Is she?" Diego shook his head and smiled. "Not a natural in the saddle, but he tries hard."

"Yes, that would be Edwin," agreed Rose.

"Her time with Edwin's family is coming to an end and she needs new lodgings. Can you think of any decent place for her?"

Milly stirred the pot. "Do you wish employment too? Do you have a trade?"

Rose shook her head. "Nay, none but housekeeping. I would like to find work eventually, but I am sure John will not leave me penniless: I'll be able to afford a modest rent."

Milly glanced shrewdly between her father and Rose. "Did you not say, Father, just the other day, that you could do with a housekeeper to help keep your fencing school in order and stop you walking half the way across town to have a hot meal?"

Silas smiled broadly at his daughter. "Aye, that I did."

Milly turned to Rose. "He may look a bit rough round the edges, but I can assure you, Mistress Isham, that my father is a gentleman and would treat you well if you went to work for him. And if he doesn't he'll answer to me." She waved the wooden spoon in his direction.

Rose realized she had been backed into a trap by the wily old soldier, getting his daughter to put his proposition for him.

"I have a room on a separate floor from my chamber, and a maid who sleeps in the closet off the kitchen, no one will raise a question about it, I assure you." Silas held out a hand. "What say you? Free board and lodging, a modest salary, and I will give you one day off every fortnight."

Could she trust him? The terms were generous and it would mean she would be free of the humiliating dependency on John.

"Diego is there every day—he'll report back to me if my father has stepped out of line," added Milly.

"Which I won't," vowed Silas with a laughing glance at his daughter. "I wouldn't dare."

"In that case . . ." Rose took the leap. "You have yourself a housekeeper, Master Porter."

"Milly-o!" A voice sung out in the street. "Anyone home?"

Diego rolled his eyes as he sharpened the carving knife. "Wonderful: another hungry mouth to feed."

"Be warned"—Milly got to her feet to answer the knock as her husband sliced the meat onto the plates—"it may be two if Tobias is still dangling at his heels."

Diego and Silas quickly helped themselves to a second serving of mutton.

"Mistress Isham, are you still hungry?" asked Silas solicitously. "Pray try this tart." He heaped food on her plate as if Lent started in an hour's time, rather than the week they still had left before the great fast.

"Stop, sir, stop!" protested Rose. "Enough! You've given me sufficient to feed a family of five."

"Ah, but you are about to witness one of the miracles of London, our own plague of locusts."

Milly soon returned with the young men in tow, a little tug rowing two galleons into port. Both towered over her and shared a family resemblance of dark hair and eyes, but one was already well known to Rose.

"You!" exclaimed Rose, jumping up.

Kit stared at her in astonishment. "Mistress Isham! What brings you to my part of town? Is something the matter with Mercy?"

Silas got to his feet to draw Rose back down to her place on the bench beside him. "I can see you know this rogue, so have no need of introduction. What's he done to upset you? Do I need to run him through?"

"Most assuredly, sir." Rose gestured to the young player. "He is the cause of my being put out of my brother-in-law's house."

"Oh, Kit," sighed Milly. "What have you done now?"

Tobias, unflustered by the scene before him, found a place on the bench and began helping himself to food. Diego gave him a pointed look.

"What?" he cried innocently. "Doesn't seem much I can do about it—Kit's got the lady in trouble, you're all upset with him as usual, end of story. I can't see why that should stop me eating."

Kit clipped his brother over the top of his head. "I didn't mean to get the lady in trouble. I merely called on her family to ask to court Mercy, her niece—that's the girl I told you about the other night, Milly. How that became cause for turning this good lady out of doors remains a mystery to which I would welcome an explanation." He turned to Rose and raised a questioning brow.

Rose had recovered from her initial surprise at meeting him so unexpectedly. "My brother took your pretensions ill, sir. He believes I have corrupted Mercy, making her easy prey to smooth-tongued fortune hunters."

"I'm not after her money!" spluttered Kit. "Why must everyone think that?"

Rose couldn't help smiling at the young man's genuine indignation at the suggestion. "I know that, sir, but you must admit that it looks a plausible reason for a player, such as yourself, to court a rich merchant's daughter."

Tobias swallowed a mouthful of meat. "Face it, Kit, you are doomed to be misunderstood. Have something to eat."

"Is there anything I can do to help, either Mercy or yourself?" Kit sank down on the bench beside Tobias.

"For me? Nay, sir, I have fallen on my feet." She smiled at Silas, who squeezed her hand under the table. "It is Mercy who should concern you. I fear the best you can do is leave her be."

He shook his head, not even protesting as Tobias finished off the last slice of tart. "I can't do that: I love her."

Tobias choked. "Gads, Kit, you've fallen! I'll never get a word of sense out of you again."

"Hold your peace and eat your food," said Milly to the lad, rather startling Rose because Tobias Lacey was clearly a young gentleman. However, he took correction from the seamstress in good part and returned to his meal.

"Tell me, Mistress Isham, what I need to do to win her?" Kit looked desperate.

"There is nothing you can do to change my brother's heart. You must know that he and his ilk are fiercely opposed to the theaters. As long as you continue a player, he will not let you darken his door."

"And if I stopped being an actor?"

"*What?*" squeaked Milly. "But, Kit, you love what you do!"

"And he can't do anything else," chipped in Tobias.

Kit ignored his brother's serving of truth. "Would that sway him?"

Rose gave the player a sorrowful look. "I'm afraid, Master Turner, that you can never make yourself good enough for John. He loves his Mercy, don't you mistake him, and only the most proper man, whose parents and grandparents had all been God-fearing folk, would do for her."

"You're shot, Kit, you'd better face it," Tobias commented helpfully.

Kit put his head in his hands. "I'm not giving up. I've promised Mercy."

Rose pitied the young man, secretly thinking this was a hopeless case and she wanted to let him down gently, let him work out the impossibility for himself. "Then you have to offer her enough for her to risk leaving her father's house. But, remember, she's very young, only sixteen, and very sheltered up to this point. To break with her family would be a terrible step for her to take and she would have to be certain of a soft landing."

Kit rubbed his chin thoughtfully. "I can do that. I can be what she needs."

Rose smiled wistfully at the young lover. "Then I wish you well. Mayhap, when his first anger has ebbed and if my brother allows Mercy to visit me in my new lodgings, you will be able to see her again. I would not press your suit just yet; the time is not ripe."

"Thank you, mistress. You are most kind. Where will you be living?"

"She's to be my housekeeper," announced Silas proudly.

"Excellent. Then I need not feel so guilty about causing you to be pushed from your pretty nest on London Bridge."

With that brighter prospect, Kit pulled his plate towards him and turned to the dishes still on the table. "'Swounds! Who's eaten all the food?"

chapter 9

OVER THE NEXT FEW WEEKS, Tobias found his brother very poor company. Kit was determined to save every penny he earned in the theater and had begun making noises about "investments" and "returns" that all sounded too dull to contemplate. Kit had even gone back to the Belknap home to ask the goldsmith for financial advice and was considering taking a loan to purchase some land near the Lacey holdings in Berkshire—a good prospect that Will had brought to his attention in his latest letter of family news from his estate. Being the illegitimate brother of an earl made Kit's credit good with the City merchants, particularly if he was buying on his brother's doorstep.

"Gads, Kit, you're turning respectable," Tobias complained. "I've got two other brothers for that. I look to you to set me an example in dissolute behavior."

Kit only shrugged and went back to the sums he was working out on a piece of paper.

If it hadn't been for Tom Saxon and his friends, Tobias would have counted his stay with his half-brother a disappointing affair. He became a fixture in their drinking circle, enjoying the riotous behavior of Babington, Pilney and Gage. They had managed to get themselves barred from most respectable taverns and had taken to supping in more dubious establishments near Love Lane. At times, Tobias got a little alarmed by their talk—Babington was a great admirer of the imprisoned Mary Queen of Scots, whom he had met in his youth when he served the Earl of Shrewsbury—but on the whole they were good sorts, always happy to stand the out-of-pocket Tobias a round or two.

Tobias accompanied his brother home from the theater one evening in March, spirits high from the successful performance, which he'd watched from the side of the stage, so close he had felt part of the action. They turned into Muggle Street and Kit gave every sign of intending to have another quiet night in. Tobias was having none of it.

"Oh, come along, Kit, don't be such a sobersides! You are acting as if you are ninety, not nineteen! Mistress Mercy wouldn't begrudge you a pleasant evening with a set of brave companions."

"I have some papers to read and a part to learn for the morrow."

Tobias danced ahead to prevent him slipping into his lodgings. "What about your poor brother? Think of me, deprived of the good influence of my elder. You've hardly taken me anywhere since I came to stay."

Kit put his hands on his hips and glared at Tobias. "Since you foisted yourself on me, you mean?"

Tobias feigned hurt. "Oh, cruel! You mean you don't like having me to stay?"

"I'm just wondering when Will is going to come and drag you back home. Isn't there something you should be doing? Latin to study or law to learn?"

Tobias flinched at the unwelcome reminder. "How did you know he wanted me to join one of the Inns of Court?"

"Simple. You do not seem suited to the church"—they both smirked at that idea—"and I can't imagine he'd want another brother to enter the military, not after what it did to Jamie; so that leaves the law. You could make yourself useful to him, you know—use that head of yours as more than a hat peg. It is an advantage to have a lawyer in the family."

Tobias shuddered. "I know. But not yet. Today we live! Come down to the Creeping Fiddler with me, Kit. Babington's promised a memorable night of entertainment."

"Wine, women and song, hey?" Kit scratched the back of his head. "You've been going to the Creeping Fiddler? I thought you were drinking at the Two Necks?"

"We were—until Pilney punched the innkeeper." Tobias mimed the stunned fall of the hapless host into a tray of drinks.

Kit shook his head. "Maybe I'd better come along and see what mischief you've been getting up to."

"Excellent. Leave your papers for tomorrow." Tobias hurried him past his door before he could think better of it.

Kit followed his little brother with a feeling of guilt settling on his shoulders. In his preoccupation to set himself up on a firmer financial foundation for Mercy's sake, he had neglected Tobias. If he was now drinking in the Creeping Fiddler, there were two chief perils: firstly, brawls there often turned murderous and, secondly, a visit to the wenches left many a man with lingering effects that only a bath of mercury could cure.

"Lacey!" cried Babington when he saw the two brothers in the door. "Turner! Well met indeed."

It was hard to see them through the fume-filled atmosphere. The chimney didn't draw properly, leaving the drinkers to be smoked like herring. Kit's eyes were already beginning to sting. Were people really supposed to enjoy themselves in this fug?

"And you like it here?" Kit murmured to Tobias. A few weeks ago he might have been impressed by the dangerous appeal of the place; now he found it dirty and loud. Kit laughed at himself, thinking how his little Puritan had begun to reform him whether she meant to or no.

He slid onto the bench next to Babington, keeping Tobias at his side.

"Can you stand them a drink for me?" Tobias whispered. "I owe them a few jugs."

With a sigh, Kit took out coin and passed it to Tobias under the table.

"You are my favorite brother," Tobias muttered fervently. "Jilly, bring us a jug of your best!" he called proudly to the serving maid.

Babington snorted into his ale. "What's this? Lacey-lack-coin is treating us? Oh rare!" His companions cheered but Kit thought their good spirits were rather at Tobias's expense than shared with him. He felt increasingly uncomfortable about the company into whose hands he had let his brother fall.

"So, Turner, we've not seen you about much, apart from on-stage, that is," continued Babington.

"I've been busy." Kit poured the ale, helping Tobias to only half a flagon, with a look daring him to say anything.

"So Lacey here claimed. Tell me, do you see much of your other brothers?"

"Nay, sir, we hardly move in the same circles." Having missed dinner as an economy measure, Kit was ravenous, so he tried a piece of the bread and meat on the table but quickly discarded it as inedible. Gads, there were weevils in the crust.

"Your brother told me that Master James Lacey is an intimate of the Queen thanks to his goodwife, the Lady Jane."

The Queen's name was not one to be bandied about lightly— and certainly not in a low dive like this. Kit was wondering if Babington was really a fool for all his hard slashing edge.

"Aye, it is no secret that she is one of the Queen's ladies." Kit didn't like the direction of this conversation. One of his least favorite topics was his much lower social status than his legitimate brothers'.

"But the earl is not particularly popular at court, I hear, at odds with the favorite, Raleigh."

Kit took a gulp of ale. If this were the Creeping Fiddler's best, then he would hate to taste its worst. Horse piss might be more palatable. Swilling the flagon, he did not give Babington a response. The man was clearly well informed about the various branches of his family without him adding to the stock of knowledge.

"Would you say he was content with the way Lord Burghley handled his estate during his minority? Most lords graze away the profits and leave but a barren pasturage behind."

Kit took up the knife by his plate and began carving the crust from the bread to keep from having to engage in the conversation. How soon would they decently be able to make their excuses? Tobias had managed to attract a wench to his knee and was paying no heed to Babington's interrogation. Kit sincerely hoped Tobias had better sense than to take the encounter further; the girl did not look a very fragrant specimen.

"Do you think he would be a supporter of change?" Babington leant back, determined this time to wait for an answer.

Kit put the knife down, crumbling the bread from his fingers. "My brother is a loyal subject, sir."

"To the Crown, as we all are. The legitimate holder of the Crown, whomsoever that be in future?" Babington bent closer, his breath soured with ale. "We have the Scottish queen wrongly imprisoned—what thinks he of her?"

It was time to leave. This talk was verging on treasonous. "Tobias, we have to go." He hauled his brother up, dislodging the maid from his knee. "Give her a penny for her pains, then we must depart."

Furious to have his dalliance halted in its tracks, Tobias rounded on his brother. "Why, Kit? Has your lady got such a grip on your bollocks that you can't be seen with us sinners?"

"Don't be such a bloody idiot!" hissed Kit.

"They'll think we're killjoys!"

"I don't give a damn for their opinion. If you had half a wit, you'd realize what they're about." He turned to the rest of the table. "My brother's taken ill, sirs; I bid you good even."

"He looks fine to me," muttered Saxon.

"Enjoy the ale." Kit firmed his grip on Tobias and dragged him from the room.

Tobias tried to squirm free, but Kit was determined and had the stronger fist. They stumbled out into the alley, Kit stepping ankle-deep in some unspeakable mire that did nothing to improve his mood.

"You're about as much fun as a frost in spring," Tobias grumbled. "I don't know what's come over you."

Kit only let go when they reached Wood Street. "I'm suffering from an excess of good sense. I pray you be struck down by the same infirmity. If you hadn't noticed, Babington was flirting with treason in there. What have you told them about Will?"

Tobias shrugged, but he looked a little sheepish. "Nothing that anyone about court wouldn't say—that he and Raleigh hate each other most heartily. Babington is no friend to Raleigh either."

"Babington is no friend to the Queen—have you thought what that might mean?" Kit wanted to shake some sense into his brother. Innocent of any experience of court intrigue, Tobias was dangerously unaware of the peril with which he flirted. "You're behaving like a green boy. They aren't your true friends in there and I wager you know it. Think for once! You've heard the stories, seen others fall. Surely you realize that you only have to be in the wrong place at the wrong time, laugh at a risky joke, or write a letter that can be misconstrued, and then you'll find yourself over your head in trouble—and your family with you."

Only having just emerged from the schoolroom, Tobias resented the implication that he was not old enough to judge his own pursuits. "I've done nothing wrong."

"But you have to be better even than that—your record must be lily white when it comes to loyalty to Her Majesty. If anything is written on the page about you, the words must be ones of respect and service, not crude jokes down the tavern."

"You're making too much of it, Kit. None of that talk means anything."

Kit felt truly frightened for the boy; he was sailing close to the reef without realizing it, and a player was no protection come shipwreck. "I think, little brother, it is time you went back to Will, or James—take your pick."

"You're throwing me out?" Tobias looked aghast to find his easygoing brother come down on him so hard.

"No, I'm throwing you to safety. Babington's ship is likely to sink if he's as unguarded in speech as he was this night. You need to get to shore before it goes down with all hands."

Tobias swore at him. The last thing he wanted was to have his freebooting life in London cut short.

"Oh, grow wise, Tobias, this isn't about you and your small debts! Will doesn't care about them. He's hoping you'll learn what the world is like outside the comfort of Lacey Hall, and this is your lesson: life is dangerous!" Kit pulled Tobias out of the path of a crew of drunks reeling across Wood Street to search for the ladies of Love Lane. "Look, I don't want to preach at you, but being about the Theatre since a lad has taught me a hard lesson or two. Men like Babington blaze bright, but then get snuffed out. None of us wants to see you follow that same path."

Tobias grimaced.

Time for the second lesson. "And that maid you were fondling?"

Tobias's smile brightened at the reminder. "What about her?"

"She had the French disease—you can tell by the condition of the skin. 'Sblood, Tobias, if you're going to go wenching, at least find a good sort of girl to tumble, a proper sweetheart."

Tobias looked sick and brushed his hose vigorously.

Kit dug his teeth into his lip to hide his smile. He knew his little brother was keen to lose his virgin status, but hadn't yet managed it for all his swaggering. It was a ticklish business for a fellow and he could sympathize, though his own experience had been forced on him somewhat younger when he'd had no older brother to counsel him.

He clapped Tobias on the back. "Save yourself for the right maiden, Tobias. You won't regret it."

Tobias cheered up at this thought. "You mean like you are with Mercy?"

"Yes, like me." Though it seemed likely that Kit's celibate state would last some time with all the progress he was making in his campaign to win his lady. He was the last man alive to volunteer to live as a monk, but somehow it had fallen to his lot to learn patience and restraint. "For the sake of our ladies, we both should keep our points tied."

Tobias nodded sagely. "Aye, maybe you are right. But at least you know who will have the unfastening of yours. I'm still looking."

Kit was growing distinctly uncomfortable. "Let's change the subject, shall we?" He searched for a suitably subduing theme. "Tell me about studying the law."

chapter 10

"WHAT'S HAPPENED TO ROSIE?" GRANDMOTHER Isham asked Mercy for the twentieth time that day.

Mercy tucked a blanket around the old woman. The milky surface of one of Gran's eyes had grown worse over the last two months since Rose had left, and Mercy suspected that she was now almost blind, which added to the confusion not to have her favorite child with her.

"She's housekeeping for Master Porter. You remember him, Gran, don't you? He called by last evening to bring you word. When the weather gets better, he'll take you to see Aunt Rose."

Grandmother pawed at the blankets. "But why can't she come here? I want her."

Mercy sighed, trying not to shoulder the blame for her aunt's absence. Rose had been right: the matter had been between her father and her aunt and Mercy's part in it was incidental. The only person who appeared happy with the change was Faith, who appreciated having her kingdom of the kitchen to herself. Still, it didn't stop Mercy feeling bad about the situation. "Aunt Rose can't come just at the moment, but she made this broth and sent it this morning. Would you like some?"

Grandmother shook her head, her eyes watering. "No, I want my Rosie."

Mercy's father came in from the street in time to hear Grandmother's last words. He glanced at Mercy then looked uneasily about the room. The balance in their relationship had shifted of late; Mercy no longer folded so quickly under a disapproving look, and he had begun to avoid her gaze when it came to matters concerning her aunt and grandmother.

"Where's your sister?" he asked, hanging his hat by the door.

"Visiting Mistress Kingsley. She was delivered of a stillborn child yesterday." Mercy put the cup of broth back on the warming ledge by the fire until Grandmother was ready for it.

"Sad news. I must call by later and offer my condolences to Kingsley. A house without children is like a grate without a fire— a cold place."

"I think that's what Gran believes too." Mercy patted the old lady on her hunched back. "Will you not let her see Aunt Rose?"

John Hart pulled a stool up to the table.

Ah well, so he still refused to answer.

"What's for dinner? It's been hungry work this morning—a convoy of ships finally come in from the Indies. They had to sail far into the Atlantic to avoid the Spanish pirates and we had begun to fear they were lost. There's many a relieved investor on the 'Change today."

"Will they have new cloth for you to trade?" Mercy set the chicken pie she had made on the table.

"Indeed. Fine silks, brocades—a treasure trove from the glimpse I had of the samples. I've Edwin down at the dockside with my men to take an inventory."

Mercy cut a slice for him and put it on a plate with a side serving of mashed turnips flavored with thyme. "May I have a look before you send it out to the warehouses?"

"You?" Her father picked up his knife. "You've never shown an interest before."

"I have a desire for a new gown, and mayhap a forepart and stomacher. Ann knows a good tailor who can make it at a reasonable price."

John Hart studied her warily. "This is not like you, Mercy. I know the folk at church have been unkind, but you've borne their foolish scorn like a Christian should. Don't do anything rash."

Mercy gave him a snip of a smile. "I do not think a new dress is rash. And I've outgrown most of my clothes."

Her father studiously avoided inspecting her blooming figure. It was true that she had continued to fill out her bodices and had shot up an inch over spring. "I don't begrudge you new clothes, Mercy, far from it. Order ten if that will make you happy."

Seeing Kit would make her happy, but her father didn't want to hear that.

John Hart spoke the grace and Mercy then sat down opposite him, her own plate only half full as she had little appetite. Mercy hadn't been able to speak to Kit since February and only heard word through Ann when Kit had had business with Alderman Belknap. Their sole contact came each Sunday when Kit would come to the same spot on the south bank. If the tide was right, he would write a message to her in the mud, some line of poetry or snatch of song. Thus far none of her family had asked why she was so assiduous at retiring to her chamber for private study as soon as they returned from the morning service, and she was grateful for their lack of curiosity. She lived for that day each week, amazed that he was still returning for so little reward—a wave, a blown kiss, that was all she could send him by way of thanks.

"What think you of Master Porter?" her father asked her abruptly.

"Why, I think him a very good sort of man." Mercy smiled at the memory of the old soldier charming Gran with his bluff manners and hearty laugh.

"Murky past." John Hart poured them both some ale.

"He seems in favor at the moment. Edwin told me that half the young men at court come to him for tuition—and where the court leads, the City has followed. He has met all sorts in the fencing hall."

"Aye, it's a fine place for your brother to mingle with men of influence and potential."

Edwin had also told her that he'd met Kit's half-brother James there. James Lacey had come to give a masterclass with Porter's blackamoor son-in-law, Diego, on the use of rapier and dagger. She wondered if Edwin had told their father about it. Edwin had been in awe of the two men's speed and skill, going on to confide his fears to her that he would never attain the same accomplishments and thus disappoint their father—another Hart child who put the fear of failing their parent before any other consideration.

John Hart cut another slice of pie. "Do you think your aunt is happy keeping house for him?"

Ah, here was the point to which he had been working, the thorn that had worried his paw until it had become sore.

"I have no way of knowing, Father. I haven't seen her."

"But did Master Porter say she was content?"

"He only said how happy he was with her services. She makes an excellent housekeeper."

"I thought perhaps that you might like to call there later, see how she fares."

Finally! All the family had known that John Hart could not long keep to his anger against any man or woman, his character tending to forgiveness more easily than condemnation. Mercy was relieved he had finally softened towards Rose, but she knew better than to sound too eager to repair the breach in case that made him suspicious.

"I can do that if you wish. And may I bring her back to see Gran?"

John Hart looked down at his plate. "Aye. There's no harm in her spending an hour here this afternoon. Just an hour, mind."

Mercy was intrigued to see her aunt's new home. She had heard much about the fencing and riding school from Edwin and knew where to find it as it was only a short distance from their London Bridge house. Silas Porter had taken a lease on an old tavern in a side street just beyond the bridge—a prime place belonging to the Bishop of Winchester, providing stabling for horses and a room large enough for the swordsmen to work when they could not use the yard outside. Fortunately, today was fine and she paused to watch the entertaining sight of six young men lined up in pairs practicing their strokes to Porter's stern orders.

"Dudley, your blade is not a willow-wand. Don't let me see it droop again like that! Good, Smith, good. And again—keep up the tip, keep it up, keep it up!"

Mercy decided it best not to interrupt him to ask for her aunt. He looked quite fearsome on the field of combat and she didn't want to be responsible for a gentleman putting out an eye of some hapless opponent by an ill-timed enquiry. Surveying the building, she saw the ground floor was given over to stabling, which led her to conclude that the family quarters must be above. A flight of stairs went from the yard to the first-floor balcony—the most promising way in.

Her entry into Porter's school did not go unchallenged. The next class of young bucks was hanging over the rail, watching the skirmish in the yard with keen interest—but not so keen that they didn't notice her climb the steps. One whistled appreciatively.

"Ho, lads, our luck is in. Sergeant Porter's employed a new tutor."

"You can teach me what you like, love, any how, any way," said another with a leer.

A mop appeared out of an open window and dowsed the amorous swain with grubby water. "Cool your fires, young sirs, and keep a civil tongue in your heads. This is my niece."

The gentlemen immediately looked abashed.

"Apologies, fair mistress." The sopping-wet one scraped a bow. "You know we meant no disrespect, but your charms robbed us of our senses."

Mercy didn't know any such thing, but whereas a few weeks ago she might have been shocked by their words, now she just whisked them away like bothersome flies. She ignored the gallants.

"Aunt Rose, are you receiving visitors?"

Rose opened the door and embraced Mercy. "You're not a

visitor. Family is never a visitor. Come in, come in. Your father's let you come at last?"

Mercy nodded.

Rose pushed Mercy to arm's length. "My, I do believe you've grown."

Mercy shrugged. "A little upwards and more outwards. When am I going to stop? It's getting quite tiresome to keep letting out my clothes."

"I doubt your Kit will be disappointed." Rose steered her into the kitchen.

"You've seen him?" Mercy untied the strings of her cloak and hung it on a peg.

"Several times. He's a good friend of Silas's daughter."

Mercy felt a twinge of jealousy. "How good a friend?"

Rose chuckled. "Milly Porter is very happily married and to a man who can more than fend off any rivals to her affections. Never you fear, I'm yet to see a more devoted lover than Kit Turner. He's still determined to have you, you know."

Mercy hugged her arms round herself and grinned. "I know."

"He's working hard to provide a home for you, saving his money to establish a little nest for you both."

"He is?" Mercy couldn't help laughing. Her flamboyant player turning wise investor: it had to be love!

"When he has enough, I think he'll ask for your hand in marriage again."

Mercy scowled at the reminder. "And my father will refuse."

"And your father will refuse," Rose echoed. "So what will you do then?"

"I don't know. I'm not of age and won't be for many years."

Rose put a plate of fresh-baked buns on the table. "If you find a priest to say the words, I suspect your father will not refuse to recognize the marriage if he thinks he's too late to do anything about it."

Mercy had thought of this herself. "Aye, but it would hurt him—and he'd never forgive me, not really."

Rose stroked Mercy's cheek. "Aye, well then, it will come down to whom you love more: your family or Kit. I'll stand with you whatever you decide."

"Why can't everyone just love each other and have done!"

Rose gave a bittersweet smile. "There's the rub. But the world doesn't work that way, as you well know. But somehow I think my Mercy is now old enough to make the right choice. A few months back and I wouldn't have been so sure."

"You think I should marry Kit?"

"No, no, I'm not telling you what you must think through for yourself."

Mercy knew she really had already made her choice. "Oh, Aunt."

Rose gathered her to her shoulder. "Oh, Mercy."

"Sometimes life is so bitter."

"It is indeed."

Tobias had to admit life wasn't too bad back at Lacey Hall: he had his pack of hounds to amuse him, a younger sister to tease, a nephew to spoil, his mother and his brother's wife, Ellie, to spoil him, and Will to argue with. If only these long spring and summer days didn't have to end. He'd promised on his honor to join Staple's

Inn in September as a stepping stone to joining Gray's Inn for his training as a lawyer. The prospect sat like a cloud hovering on the horizon of his sunny days. The thought of actually reading all that dry stuff—statutes, muniments, leases, testimonies—made his toes curl.

To divert his thoughts in a more pleasing direction, he challenged his brother to a game of tennis in the court their father had built in one of his richer periods near the stables of Lacey Hall. Only in his early twenties, Will was in danger, in Tobias's opinion, of forgetting to leaven each day with a pinch of fun. Fortunately, the earl's mood had improved since news had reached him that his ship had come in from the Indies. What had for a few sticky months seemed a rash investment now appeared a triumph, and Will was talking of going up to London to oversee the breaking up of the cargo, fearing otherwise his agents would cheat him of half his profit.

Imagining the ball a scrunched-up page from his law books, Tobias smashed it past his brother, winning a point.

"Hey ho, brother, where's the fire?" Will asked, scooping the ball up with his racquet. "I thought we were only warming up?" He tossed the ball high and served it with force off the wall. It bounced on the Hazard Chase one-yard line, requiring Tobias to stretch to reach it. His return went into the net.

"Got to keep you sharp, Will. We can't have you turning into a fat old nobleman who can't move without six footmen to lift him." Tobias threw the ball back to his brother on the service side of the net. To be fair to his brother, there was little chance of that, as Will led an active life, much of it in the saddle keeping an eye on his lands, but it was the task of the younger brother to goad the elder. "Do you know that the service was invented by old King Henry when he got too fat to pick up the balls? He had servants throw them up in the air for him."

Will lined up his shot. "Are you saying, sprout, that I'm going that way?" He struck the ball right at Tobias who only just moved in time to hit it into the side penthouse. It rolled back to fall on the Chase Yard. Will fluffed the return.

Tobias spun his racquet. "What's the score? Thirty–fifteen to me, I think."

"You crow too soon, cockerel. I'm only now getting serious."

The first set in the match stood at five games all when their sister Sarah and Will's wife, Ellie, came into the court to watch, taking refuge in the dedans behind the server. Ellie had the two-and-a-half-year-old Wilkins in her arms, having left the youngest of the brood, a little girl born in March, with her nurse. Will had the good fortune of being the one with the serve for this deciding game of the set.

"Go on, Will, smash him out of court!" yelled Sarah. The two youngest Laceys always took sides against each other as a matter of honor.

"Lord, what did I do to deserve this?" complained Tobias with a theatrical flourish to the heavens. "I face a hostile mob of marauding citizens—and Lady Ellie"—he excused his sweet-natured sister-in-law from the general condemnation—"with only my racquet to protect me."

Wilkins jammed his fist in his mouth and sucked very fiercely, wondering why his father and uncle were firing missiles at each other.

Will won the game, but barely, sneaking a crafty spin down

the service line. He ran to his wife and child, kissed Wilkins on the nose before passing him off to Sarah, then lifted Ellie and spun her on the spot.

"All hail the conqueror!" laughed Ellie.

"It's only the first set," grumbled Tobias. "And he had the serve in the last game."

"But the proof is in the score, Tobias: Will is clearly the better player." Sarah smirked at him, enjoying his temporary defeat. And it would be temporary, Tobias vowed.

Will clapped him on the shoulder. "I believe that time in London has made you a little soft, brother." He backhanded him in the stomach. "Too much beer and lazing about at the Theatre."

That was too close to the truth for comfort.

"I learnt a lot with Kit," Tobias said defensively, not that he could share those particular lessons with ladies present. "I think I might know an honest merchant who could handle your cargo for you—a mercer, John Hart."

"You can vouch for the man?" Will downed a tankard of small ale and wiped his brow and hands on a linen towel.

Tobias nodded. "I can swear that he's a man of the strictest principles." So strict he disapproved of players. If Will struck up a business relationship with Hart, Tobias reasoned, that might sweeten the man to accepting the earl's half-brother as a son-in-law. At the very least, he might think twice about upsetting Will by snubbing the Laceys and losing the prestige of having the Earl of Dorset for a client.

See, Kit, thought Tobias, *I'm not so green. I can plot with the best of them.*

Will threw the towel aside. "I'll pursue the matter when I go to London. Perhaps you'll come with me to make the introduction?"

Tobias grinned, delighted to be taken seriously for once. "My pleasure."

"Still, I'm pleased you came home when you did. It's a testing time for all of us and London is not a safe place to be. I wouldn't want you rattling about there on your own. The wars in the Low Countries aren't going well. Lord Leicester is having a hell of a battle with his so-called allies among the Dutch. The Queen is particularly"—Will searched for a phrase that did not smack of treason—"changeable at this moment, people falling in and out of favor with little warning." He kissed his wife and moved away from the spectators' gallery. "There's talk—most private talk—of a plot discovered against Her Majesty, one involving a certain queen in our keeping."

Tobias paled. "Is that so?"

"According to Lord Burghley. I think this year will settle that lady's fate, one way or another. We must all take care that no hint of disloyalty touches us. Jamie is in a very vulnerable position, what with his wife being so close to the Queen's person. Your serve."

chapter 11

KIT COULD NOT REMEMBER THE last time he felt this excited. He had received an invitation to accompany the Belknap family on a river excursion to Greenwich to celebrate the arrival of May, and Ann had whispered to him that Mercy was to be one of the party. Obtaining leave for the day from Burbage had proved easier than he anticipated as his manager was all in favor of him furthering his relationship with the wealthy goldsmith for the sake of the Theatre.

"If you can manage to slip into the conversation that the stage canopy needs new paint, I'd be most obliged," Burbage said as he dismissed his leading man to walk a very different kind of public stage. "A loan—or gift—right now would be very welcome."

Kit met the Belknaps down at the river steps. At first he could not see Mercy among them and feared that Ann had got her information wrong. Mistress Belknap, however, put his mind at rest when she brandished the lute before stowing it in the bottom of the boat.

"I do so hope, Master Turner, we can prevail upon you to entertain us again. I have secured the presence of your sweet accompanist, under the strictest terms of chaperonage, of course." Her eyes sparkled, suggesting she would be as effective a guard as her daughter. "She should be here any moment."

When Mercy finally arrived under the escort of her brother, Kit made himself inconspicuous, turning to talk to the boatmen at their oars. He waited until he heard the farewells to Edwin before coming out of hiding to face Mercy.

"Mistress Hart." He kissed her fingers and bowed.

Being forced apart for so long made the moment fraught with more emotion than it otherwise would have had. He could feel a slight tremble run through her, see her green eyes swim with tears. Of joy, he hoped.

"Master Turner."

He squeezed her hand before releasing it to involve himself in the bustle of departure. Yet with every laughing comment made to Belknap, every compliment paid to one of the Belknap ladies, he was aware of exactly where Mercy stood, like the sun beating down on dark raiment, heating the spot where it touched the skin.

The weather favored them with a sunny passage across the Thames. Kit found himself at the opposite end of the boat from Mercy, thanks to the alderman taking him aside for a conversation about the latest investment news. The goldsmith appeared to think such matters perfectly suited to a holiday, and perhaps for him, who lived and breathed news on the 'Change, it was the most fascinating matter. Kit might be a reformed man when it came to planning for his future, but his heart was more in the poetry of the stage than the prose of daily life. He finally escaped death-by-percentages when he offered to accompany their little voyage with a few tunes on the lute. It was duly passed to him by the eager

Mistress Belknap, and he spent the remainder of the journey working his way through the songs he had etched in the strand for Mercy over the last months. Their gazes often met across the length of the boat, and he loved how she mouthed the words along with him, too shy to join in, but too moved to resist this much.

The two oarsmen headed southeast to where the green pastures of Greenwich spread to the margins of the water. The Queen was not in residence in her palace, so the parks were open to citizens of good standing. Not one to stint on comforts, Alderman Belknap had sent servants on ahead to prepare a feast for them to enjoy under the canopy of the newly leafed trees. They were greeted by the welcome sight of trestle tables already spread with a generous dinner of many sorts of cold meat and other delicacies. Thanks to some maneuvering on Ann's part, Kit was seated next to Mercy at the end of the board, giving them as private a space as possible in open company.

"My love, how have you fared?" he asked in a low voice. "I feared that your father would punish you for my audacity in approaching you as I did."

Her lashes veiled her green eyes from his gaze. He could count the light sprinkling of freckles across her nose—a delightful feature that he would enjoy tracing with his lips, making sure he paid homage to each one. Did she have them elsewhere, he wondered?

"My father is not a harsh man, Kit, whatever else you may think. He hates to correct us and only uses words and reason."

"But he cast out your aunt."

"Only because he thought it his Christian duty." She sighed. "I fear he takes a very firm line on those he believes to be within the fold of believers and those who stand outside. But, fortunately, she is happily situated in service to a friend of yours."

Kit grinned. "Aye, I know. I think there may be an autumnal romance brewing there—Milly believes so. She is a great admirer of your aunt—but not so great a one as her father."

Mercy gave a little bounce of excitement. "Is that so? That would be very good for them both if it proves true."

After the board had been removed, the party broke up into smaller groups, walking beneath the trees in twos and threes. No one objected to Kit taking Mercy's arm.

"Stay within call!" cautioned Mistress Belknap as she oversaw the stowing of the plate.

"We will, mistress," promised Kit, hurrying Mercy along an unfrequented path. "Please take note she did not say 'stay within sight,' he added in a low voice.

Looking around him for a suitable retreat, he spotted a fallen tree, splayed roots making a barrier between them and the path. He guided Mercy to sit on the trunk, first brushing it off with a handkerchief so his lady would be perfectly at ease. A song thrush broke into its call somewhere in the beech canopy; leaves rustled in the impatient wind.

"Well," he said, eyes twinkling.

"Well," she echoed, close to laughing.

"Have you been thinking, as I have, that we must be the most fortunate lovers in all history to have such friends to bring us together?"

Mercy looked back to where the Belknap girls were playing with a tennis ball in the sunlight. They were teasing each other and cheating with the raucous familiarity of long acquaintance. "Yes, we are blessed."

Kit had so much he wanted to say, so much he wanted to do, he didn't know where to start. Mercy beat him to it.

"I hear you've been making some interesting decisions of late. Ann and my aunt have done nothing but praise you for the sober turn to your character. You are quite a stranger to the alehouses, they say."

Kit grimaced. "Believe me, the alehouses are no loss. Nothing contents me, but either to be with you or to make plans to bring us together."

Mercy reached out a hand to trace his jaw. "Oh, Kit, you make me feel very humble. I've done nothing to deserve you."

He smiled and turned his face to kiss her palm. "You are you: that is enough." Bending down, he plucked three strands of grass and wove them into a ring. "Here. I cannot afford gold—yet"—he winked—"but wear this for me." He bit off the ragged ends and pushed the grass ring onto her finger. "Mercy, I do not know any words for this. Perhaps I should have consulted the poets and learnt my part, but too late. You are left with the plain man speaking plain words, a worthless rogue daring to address a merchant princess. Will you marry me? Will you be mine?"

She covered her left hand with her right, caressing the ring he had made for her. "It is better than gold to me."

Kit smiled, though his heart was pounding as he waited for her response. He was not so sure of his own charms to think her refusal not a possibility. "I fear that is not good enough, my lady. I need a reply. See, you have me here on my knees; I'm not rising until you answer."

Mercy kissed the ring. "Is that so? You are planted there like a doorstop?"

His little Puritan was teasing him—and it was wonderful! "Aye, like an iron post. I cry you mercy, Mercy."

She leant forward and placed her hands on his shoulders. "When you call my name like that, Master Turner, how can I refuse? My answer is yes."

With a hoot, he jumped to his feet, seized her round the waist and lifted her into a kiss, her toes only brushing the ground. When their lips parted, he tucked her head next to his heart.

"Oh, sweet, I do so need you," he said fervently, squeezing her to him as if he would never let go. "I need you to keep me on the straight and narrow path. You must scold me if I slip back into my old ways, get mixed up in bad company."

She pulled back so she could see his expression. "What kind of company is that?"

He chuckled. "Oh no, no confessions of past misdeeds. We start anew, you and I. May I assume your father is unlikely to give his approval?"

Mercy brushed his hair off his face. "How did you come to that conclusion? Was it when he had insulted you and your ancestors or when he had you thrown out at sword point?"

"Oh, so you think he doesn't like me?" Kit said with mock surprise.

She gave his chest a consoling pat. "No, not yet. But my aunt thinks he will warm to the match if we proceed and come to him already having said our vows."

"And you—what do you think?"

She traced the pattern on his green doublet, absentmindedly

tucking her finger into the cuts on the chest where the fine cambric of his shirt peeped through. He thought she probably didn't realize what she was doing, but each touch was setting him on fire. "I think he will not reconcile to the match even so. He may agree for decency's sake—either that or see me disgraced before the congregation of believers—but he will never really forgive me."

"Ah, my love."

"But that is the price and I have no choice but pay it, for I love you, Kit, and will come to you barefoot as he threatened and make the best of it. I will renounce the name of Hart only to take on that of Turner."

He could do nothing to comfort her but kiss her. He lifted her again so their lips could meet.

"Ah, Mercy, kissing you is very heaven. There will be happiness, so much joy in our marriage, that your father's displeasure will not weigh too heavy on us. He is a good man—he will change his mind when he sees you are content."

"I pray so." Mercy initiated the next kiss, opening her mouth to let him deepen the caress, one step further on this path they had set themselves on.

He enjoyed the taste of her kiss for a good long while, but he wanted more. She was to be his wife; he wanted to learn her shape and feel, transform his imaginings into experience. His hands swept down her back then returned up her sides. Reverently, he brushed her bosom through her clothing.

At this, Mercy stiffened and pushed him away, reacting as if his touch had been a burning brand.

"What are you doing?" she asked in scandalized tones, clutching her hands to her breast.

Kit really didn't think it needed a diagram to explain. "Kissing you, sweet. Here, come back to my arms."

"*That* wasn't kissing!"

He had gone too far for his little Puritan. Through his frustration, he struggled to see the funny side, which he knew was there. His friends would laugh to see him spurned for so slight a matter. "What was it, then?"

"You were . . . you were touching my . . . my endowments."

Gads, she talked like a lawyer. Endowments, were they? "Mercy, you are to be my wife. There is much more to being man and wife than kissing, you realize."

From the confused look on her face, she clearly didn't know.

"I touched you most respectfully through I don't know how many layers of clothing—three at least. I wanted you to feel at ease with me before we wed." And, it had to be admitted, get a closer acquaintance with her most striking bounty. He thought he had been the model of forbearance till this point and had earned the right to this much.

Mercy was too shocked to consider that she might have overreacted. "I'm sure that isn't right. Christian husbands and wives don't do such things."

Annoyed as well as grimly amused, Kit threw himself on the ground and propped his head up on one hand while his lady paced off her own frustration. She was too innocent to realize that part of the agitation she felt was exactly because she hadn't let him continue.

"And tell me, Mistress Hart, what do Christian wives and husbands do? I'd be mighty interested to find out, because I've clearly been doing it all wrong thus far."

She clapped her hands to her cheeks to hide her blush—a futile task because it flushed her neck and what little of her chest he could see. "They . . . they meet in the privacy of the chamber to . . . to know each other. That's what the Bible says."

"*Know* each other?" He chewed the end of a stalk. "How do they do that, pray?"

"I don't know. But I know it doesn't happen in the open air with people touching other people's . . ." The poor lass ran out of words.

"Endowments. Yes, I understand you. But I've got news for you, my sweet, that is exactly how it often happens."

"Maybe for people of loose morals, but not for God-fearing folk," she declared mutinously. "And you said that you wanted me to help you be good, not mix in the wrong company. Clearly this is one of those points on which I need to correct you."

Anger was winning out over amusement. The last thing Kit wanted after months of the most irreproachable of living was to be preached at by Mercy.

"You want to correct me?" He sat up, letting his hands hang loose over his knees. "I suppose you have a list to bring to my attention?"

She paced, knotting her hands in the fabric of her dove-gray skirt. "Well, perhaps aside from that touching thing"—she waved vaguely in the air, not daring come anywhere close to her bosom—"you could stop wearing the earring. And your clothes"—she flicked her eyes over his costume—"well, obviously, they could be somewhat more restrained."

Kit thought the dark green doublet he had on this day was really the dullest he had ever ordered made—a recent purchase with Mercy in mind. "You don't like my clothes?"

She squeezed her hands together. "It's not that I don't like them, I just think that you will find you are more acceptable to other people if you don't stand apart so much in your choice of apparel."

Kit got up smoothly, his six feet making her five and a bit seem suddenly very small. He had not used his height to intimidate her before, but now he was angry enough to do so.

"I thought you said you loved me, mistress."

Mercy stopped pacing and wrapped her arms round herself, her stance rejecting his all too eager readiness to embrace her. "Aye, I do."

"But it seems to me that you've been expecting me to do all the changing. Willingly I have altered my way of life, even these clothes are not the kind I usually favor, but you still keep to every sign of your God-fearing upbringing." He flicked the dull skirt contemptuously. "I've not tried to change you."

"But, Kit . . ."

Kit wagered she was going to say that she didn't need changing as she was accepted as she was and he wasn't. He didn't want to hear this. It all depended on which crowd you moved in and Kit suddenly wasn't sure he wanted to belong in hers. He knew more than enough about judgmental Puritans.

"Save your words, Mistress Hart. I think we should return to the others."

Mercy bit her lip, tears brimming in her eyes. "Aye, we should."

They walked back in silence, the grass ring still on her finger, but wilting with every second that passed.

chapter 12

MERCY SPENT A LONG TIME ON HER KNEES in prayer after the service ended that Sunday. The previous day's outing had turned from a beautiful dream into a nightmare, and all because of a thoughtless word on her part. She had reacted from instinct and that had sent her off on the wrong tack. She should have seen that Kit, more used to sinners than God-fearing folk, would not think anything wrong with touches that she found shocking. Her fault had been to go about telling him so gracelessly, prompting him to think she was finding him unworthy of her when she had intended it in the spirit of one Christian correcting another.

Looking about her at the sober faces of her neighbors as they exchanged Sabbath greetings, she was sure she was right to try to curb him. She couldn't imagine Master and Mistress Hudson caressing each other in that fashion, nor Reverend and Mistress Field, God forgive the thought. No, she was certain that whatever "knowing" one's wife entailed, it did not mean that.

Her father caught her arm. "Mercy, there's someone I want you to meet." He steered her to face a young man dressed in gray, much like the hue of her own skirt. "You may not remember him, but this, Mercy, is Righteous Field, our priest's eldest son. He's been in Antwerp the last few years, studying with the brothers there."

Mercy bobbed a curtsy. "Pleased to meet you, sir." Though she could not remember meeting him, she had heard much about him from his mother. They were hoping Righteous was going to follow in his father's footsteps and become a minister.

Field bowed. "Mistress Mercy, it is a pleasure to meet you. I had the honor of being introduced to your sister earlier." He turned his round moon of a face on her father. His gray eyes never seemed to blink. "God has blessed you with a fine crop of daughters."

"Aye, they are a credit to my house, no matter what loose tongues might say," her father said testily.

Kit's incursion into the church had given many of the gossips fuel for months, but thankfully it was now beginning to die down with no further evidence that Mercy was about to disgrace herself with a player. *And mayhap I'll never now get the chance*, she thought glumly.

After a further exchange of words with the young scholar, ones that Mercy scarce paid attention to as they dealt with dry matters of theology, her father bade Master Field farewell and escorted his family home. On return from church, Mercy rushed to her bedroom—she couldn't get to the window quick enough. Would Kit come? She had already decided that failure to appear would signal that he withdrew his suit, but she hoped he would find it in his heart to forgive her for her incautious words. She'd kept his ring, tying it by a silk thread round her neck where none would note it.

The river beach was deserted.

He had to come; he had to! Mercy couldn't bear to think she had offended him so greatly that he would give her up. Surely her ill-judged words had not destroyed any hope they had of being together?

But he fell in love so swiftly; would it not be like him to fall out the same? a traitorous voice whispered, feeding the doubting part of Mercy's mind that could not understand why such a bold fellow should be attracted to a dull duck like her.

She got on her knees again and bent her head.

"Dear God, if it pleases You, make Kit forgive me," she prayed.

Faith hurried into the room. "I beg your pardon, sister, for interrupting your devotions, but there's an earl below and Father needs us all in attendance."

"A what?" Mercy reeled. Faith could have said "elephant" and she would not have been more surprised.

"A real earl." Faith, who was impressed by few worldly things, couldn't help but be astounded by the honor visited on their family: a merchant household favored by the personal attention of a noble—it just was not done under any but extraordinary circumstances! "You must come."

Mercy rose, sneaking a last look out of the window, but she couldn't see Kit's beach, as she called it, without making a more betraying movement in that direction. Following her sister, she hurried down to the parlor.

Her father was standing in humble stance before a handsome young man dressed in noble scarlet and gold. Three men attended him: two servants in brown and Tobias Lacey, the very same brother she had met with Kit outside the theater that fateful day. Her heart squeezed painfully as he looked so like his player-brother with his shaggy black hair and amused expression. But why were they here? It could not be coincidence. Could Kit have sent them to tell her he had irrevocably withdrawn his suit? Surely an earl would not run such an errand for his brother unless they wanted to grind in the point that she was missing out on a noble connection that any other family in the land would sell their first-born to gain.

"Faith, Mercy, fetch the earl some refreshment," ordered her father, not thinking such an exalted nobleman would desire an introduction to such unimportant people as his own daughters.

The two girls hurried into the kitchen. It was the maid's day of rest, so they had to prepare the offerings of cold meats and wine themselves. Faith carried the platter while Mercy followed with the jug and glasses, which they only used on very special occasions. They had both agreed in whispers that this visit surely qualified.

The earl was now seated in her father's chair while John remained standing in his presence. "I pray your pardon that I have called on the Sabbath." The earl's manner was kind but clearly used to command. "This is not the day to discuss business, but I wanted to meet you after hearing about you from my brother."

Mercy rattled the tray of glasses in terror.

"Yes, Tobias heard you were a man of unimpeachable probity. I need such a one to help me put my new shipment of cloth to the market."

The earl might be ignoring her, but Mercy saw that Tobias was watching her every move. Hands shaking, she almost overset the jug as she tried to pour the wine. He came to her side and relieved her of the burden.

"A pleasure to meet you again, Mistress Hart," he murmured.

Mercy swallowed. It didn't sound as if he'd spoken to Kit recently if he was still talking about pleasure. "And you, Master Lacey."

He took two glasses from the tray. "Here, my lord, do you wish for some wine?"

The earl waved the drink away, too intent on his talk with Mercy's father.

"But I won't say no." He put the rejected glass back on the tray and took a sip of his drink. "So, Mistress Hart, what have you done to our Kit?"

Mercy almost knocked the jug flying again as she started, but Tobias caught it and carefully set it on a side table.

"I think I'd better put this out of harm's way," he said, obviously amused by her discomposure.

"I haven't done anything to Kit," Mercy replied when he turned back to her.

"Oh, but you have. He's a different brother—much more like the earl here, and my brother James if you knew him. He's suddenly got a passion for making a future for himself; until you entered the scene, he was all about living for the day." He leant closer. "I won't tell him this, but I think you've been a good influence."

It came then to Mercy that Kit had been right yesterday, but she hadn't listened properly to him as she ought. He had changed for her and she had not given him the recognition he deserved. She would never have been happy married to a dissolute player living on credit, and he had made sure she would not have to. But had she said a word in praise of his efforts? No—she had reacted like a fool at the first hint of a difference of opinion between them.

"I think I have made a mess of things," she whispered, half to herself. "We've argued, you see."

Tobias raised his glass to her. "Never fear, Mistress Mercy. Kit is without defenses where you are concerned. If you have offended him—which I doubt very much—he will soften at the very merest hint of a gentle word from you."

She hoped he knew his brother better than she did. The last she'd seen of Kit had been a very cold farewell on the steps where they had got out of the boat. Eagle-eyed Ann had noticed the chill between them, but Mercy had been too despondent to admit what was the cause.

"I pray you are right, Master Lacey." She didn't have long: the earl was rising, agreeing to meet her father again on the morrow when business resumed. "If you see him, tell him I . . . I . . ."

Tobias touched the back of her hand comfortingly. "Don't worry, mistress. I know what to say."

"Awake, my lord, and face this happy day," Tobias chirped, when he found his brother still abed despite the fact it was Sunday afternoon. "Will is below being waited on by your landlady. He wants to take us out to dine. We can't leave him alone with the lady too long—Dame Prewet is in danger of expiring from the honor of having an earl in her kitchen."

"I've been up already," Kit growled, "but decided I didn't like the poxy day so I've gone back to bed." In two minds if he should go after yesterday's argument, he had arrived a little later than usual at his spot on the bank, but Mercy hadn't even had the

161

patience to wait for him. He'd faced an empty window and the chuckles of the boatmen who had been charting the course of the young lovers' amour each week with hearty interest. The souring of the affair had made one man the richer from the evidence of the coins that changed hands as Kit stormed away and taken his bad mood back to bed with him. His humiliation had been complete.

Tobias ignored his ill-tempered brother as he cast back the shutters.

"I saw Mercy but an hour since."

Kit rolled onto his back and put his hands beneath his head. "Let me guess, she was out with her God-fearing folk singing Sabbath psalms."

"No, she was serving Will and me wine in her father's house."

"What!" Kit jumped up.

Tobias pretended to cover his eyes. "Gads, Kit, when are you going to start wearing a nightgown like a Christian?"

Kit grabbed his shirt and pulled it over his head. "It's too hot. Tell me, sprout, what were you doing at Hart's?"

Tobias grinned and folded his arms, playing his hand to the full advantage. "Tell me, *my lord.*"

"Tell me, *my lord sprout,* what were you doing at my lady's house. Will's not heard about her, has he?"

Tobias shook his head. "Not from me—though I think you should let him in on the matter. He and Hart are going to do business together. He might be seeing more of the Harts than you."

Kit ran his hands through his rumpled hair. "What's going on?"

Tobias rubbed his palms together. "I've been plotting on your behalf. Think about it: if Hart meets the decent side of the family, he might soften towards you. It's no small matter to offend an earl."

Kit wasn't sure if he wanted to thank or beat his brother for his interference. "'Sblood, Tobias, it might be too late. Mercy and I had an argument yesterday."

Tobias acted as if this was news to him. "What about?"

It was a delicate matter to describe to his brother. "She objected when I touched, well, you know, her . . ." He made a gesture to his chest.

Tobias fell about laughing. "You rogue, you!"

"It was all very decent," Kit growled, "no bare flesh. She's so beautiful—and we are getting married—I just couldn't help myself taking the liberty."

This made Tobias laugh even harder. "I don't blame you, you lucky dog."

Kit decided he really didn't want to discuss his relationship difficulties with Tobias: he'd managed to rub off all the romance with his amusement at Kit's expense. He began fastening the points of his doublet to his hose. "How did Mercy seem to you today? Did she seem at all regretful about our argument?"

Tobias beamed. "Nay, brother, she was as bright as a lark. Seems to me you've got your tail tied in a knot for nothing. You'll have to go crawling to your little Puritan if you want to win her back."

Kit frowned.

"Of course, if you don't think her worth it, then mayhap I could call on her and tell her the match is off . . . ?"

Kit cut him short. "No, it is not." He kicked a stool across the room. "'Snails, I hate crawling to a girl, especially when she's the one in the wrong."

"But she's not just any girl, is she?" prompted Tobias, watching his brother with keen interest.

Kit paused in his angry progress around his chamber, threw his head back and closed his eyes. "Nay, she's not. She's my Mercy. I'd crawl through the Fleet ditch for her."

Tobias ushered him to the door. "Somehow, Kit, I don't think that will be necessary."

The following day, John Hart asked Mercy to stay behind after breakfast for a private word. Mercy's brain spent the rest of the meal in a spin. Had he heard something about Kit from the earl? She had been wondering how long it would take her father to realize that the earl was the half-brother of her scandalous suitor—Kit had blurted out his origins for all to hear at church, of course. What would this mean for her father's attitude towards a match with her? If anyone had asked her before yesterday how John Hart rated worldly considerations of rank, she would have laughed at the notion that it could sway his opinion of a man. But after seeing how impressed he had been by the patronage of the young earl, she was reevaluating that opinion and had begun to dare to hope.

Faith and Edwin left her alone with her father in the parlor, not without some last-minute shuffling and tidying in the hopes that they might overhear what would doubtless be a very interesting interview. But John Hart waited until the kitchen door was firmly shut before speaking.

"Mercy, a most promising offer has been made to me. It seems you have attracted the attention of a worthy young man."

This was better than she had hoped. Had an earl so easily made him change his tune about Kit?

"Indeed, sir?" She tried for maiden-like interest—not too eager, but ready to please.

"You know the fellow, and I'm sure you'll agree that he is a very suitable match for you, connecting us to a leading family and forever silencing any doubts about your character that arose so unfairly in the winter."

Mercy could feel a bubble of happiness forming inside her. She felt she was floating an inch above the ground. "I am a very fortunate girl, sir."

"Aye, I think so. I have given permission for him to call on you this morning and make his own proposal."

"You have?" Mercy wished she'd put on the new kirtle she'd had made from a pretty blue camlet. Did she have time to change? "When will he be here?"

John Hart got up from his chair and put his hand on his daughter's shoulder. "I'm pleased that you are taking this so well. I had thought that Faith would be the first to leave my house to go to a husband and I was content to have you by my side for many years longer, but it appears that God has other plans for you."

Something about this speech made Mercy halt her rush of plans for her meeting with her betrothed. Why would she not take it well when her father knew she loved Kit?

"Who is coming to call, Father?"

"Ah, you've not guessed?"

Biting her lip, she shook her head, willing him to give the answer she wanted to hear.

"Why, Righteous Field." He chuckled. "He says he has heard much about you from his family and thought you very comely and well behaved when he met you at church. He returned to London with the intention of settling on an English wife drawn from his father's congregation. You would go back with him to Antwerp for a few years until he is ready to enter the church here."

Mercy felt as if the floor had just disappeared beneath her feet and she had plummeted into the river. "Master Field?" That could not be: Mistress Field, his mother, had been one of those most harsh in their opinion of her after Kit's appearance in church. "He barely knows me."

"Ah, my sweet Mercy, few marriages start with love. It grows as each earns the respect and care of their partner in the union. Only poets can afford to indulge in such dreams of romance; real life is rather more prosaic." John Hart took note of his daughter's horror-struck expression. "Have you any reason to dislike the man?"

Mercy shook her head.

"Then you'll give him a hearing?"

She had to tell the truth. "Father, I love another."

He tightened his grip on her shoulder. "Aye, perhaps you think you do, but listen to Righteous and we'll talk more about it when he has gone. I think between us we can help you make the right decision."

chapter 13

RIGHTEOUS FIELD CAME CALLING AS the bell of St. Mary Overie struck eleven. He stood in the parlor, hat in hand, the epitome of humble youth.

"Master Hart, I wondered if I might beg the pleasure of escorting your daughter Mercy for a walk in the fields? It's a lovely day, and it does the heart good to appreciate God's creation in the midst of His wonders." He turned to smile at Mercy. "And I have some things to say to her that I would prefer to air in private."

Mercy hoped her father would refuse. She had expected a brief interview in the family parlor with her suitor; an excursion would drag the torture out to an hour at least.

John Hart rubbed his hands together eagerly, not seeing the silent pleading looks of his daughter. "I'm sure Mercy will have no objection. I know she loves to be out of doors."

Righteous creased his brow in a serious expression better suited to an older face. "And I promise to return her safely in time for dinner. You dine at twelve?"

"Let us make it one today," said her father, bending over backwards to accommodate the suitor's wishes. "And you will make a fifth at the table, I hope?"

"Aye, if it please you." He held his arm for Mercy to take. "Are you ready, fair maid?"

Better to get this over with. Mercy had already decided that her father did not expect her to give the man an answer today, so she could listen and remain silent: no one could complain about that. That was what God-fearing girls were taught to do. She took his arm.

"Do you have a preference where we should direct our steps?" Righteous asked.

"Nay, sir, but you have to walk a long way before you meet any fields inspiring of God's creation."

"I thought we would wend our way past the bishop's palace and the bear-baiting pits of Bankside. There are pretty enough fields beyond, if I remember rightly." He turned to the southern end of the bridge.

Mercy wondered if he had been away too long and forgotten that the area he thought to walk through was not known for its decent citizenry. She had left her money pouch at home, but the nippers were like to relieve him of his if he did not watch his belt closely. She avoided going that way if she had a choice in the matter. Still, it was the broad light of day, not too grave a risk if they kept alert.

They talked of inconsequential subjects until they turned to walk along the southern bank of the Thames.

"Have you been to a bear baiting?" Righteous asked as they approached the pens where the mastiffs were kept. The scarred dogs lolled in the sunshine, barely twitching as they passed, all their energy saved for their deadly afternoon's sport.

"Nay, sir. It is not a godly amusement." She wished he wouldn't keep asking her questions; it was playing havoc with her desire to remain silent.

He paused to admire one particularly vicious mastiff as it gnawed a bone with obsessive focus. Saliva coated the ham knuckle, giving it a dull sheen; tongue licked at the marrow. "You think so? I've been to them in Antwerp and think them a most intriguing spectacle: Nature at her most raw. It reminds a man that we are all creatures of flesh and blood as well as spirit and soul."

"Marry, sir, I never saw the attraction in watching animals fight to the death. I struggle to imagine Our Lord would approve."

"But would He approve of a play?" Righteous opened a wicket gate leading out into the first of the fields around Southwark. This one was given over to pasturage for horses, but they stayed down the far end, watched over by a boy from one of the local stables. He wasn't doing a very good job, lying on his back, hat over his eyes, in a patch of sunshine. The hedgerows brimmed with flowers, primroses and meadowsweet, a hint of country spring creeping into the city. Mercy wished she were free to enjoy the sight on her own.

"I . . . I don't know. I do not remember plays being either praised or condemned in the scriptures." Mercy edged round a puddle of muddy water at the entrance to the pasture.

"And yet you went to one, I understand."

"Aye. Once." Where was he leading her in this conversation? If he disapproved of her activities, why ask to court her?

He took her arm, making great show of helping her avoid the mud when really he did nothing but upset her balance. "Do not think I consider this wrong. On the contrary, it proves that you possess a questing mind, an attribute I value in my future wife. I need a . . ." He paused. "A broad-minded woman by my side in Antwerp."

"Broad-minded?" What did he mean by that?

"Aye." He stopped under an oak tree that grew in the middle of the hedge, a screen to the farm buildings beyond. In stature, he made a thin gray post against the riot of greenery behind him. "The brothers here in London are apt to be too narrow. My friends on the continent have the right of it: our salvation or damnation is in God's hands; no works we can do will earn it. Therefore, we need not trouble ourselves overly about the smaller matters of the world, how many sins we incur and the like."

Mercy knew from her father that some believers argued thus, inspired by the teaching of the Calvinists, but never had she heard that they concluded that sins did not matter. She wasn't sure what Righteous meant, in truth.

"I don't understand. Surely sins always count?"

He dropped his hat on the ground and took her hands. He smiled at her. "I think you do comprehend in your heart of hearts. You have already garnered some experience in your few years of the world. I want such a woman who will understand the weaknesses of the flesh, not a porcelain saint like your sister." He edged her back until she was against the tree trunk, looking at her with an unsettling expression—intent, like a mastiff spying weaker prey. She stumbled, foot slipping on the uneven ground at the roots. "And if you still do not understand, perhaps I can show you, for there is no need to wait with you, is there?" His mouth descended on hers, pressing her lips in a grinding, slobbery kiss.

Mercy was too shocked to react. When she did not soften for

him, he moved his hand to her throat, pressing the corners of her jaw. "Open your mouth for me. You know you want this."

She absolutely did not want his kiss. Mercy struggled, but his fingers dug into her cheeks, forcing her jaws apart. He then filled her mouth with his thrusting tongue, stopping her protests.

Stars, now she knew what Grandmother had meant about unpleasant kisses. She felt as though she were going to suffocate.

While she battled to push Righteous away from her mouth, his other hand was busy raising her skirts to touch her thigh. When she realized, she squawked in fury, trying to stamp on his foot or knee him as Rose had done that man at the Theatre, but he was pressed too firmly against her to allow her enough movement to succeed.

"No, sir. Let go of me!" Mercy protested when he raised his head from the assault on her mouth. "I'll tell your father!"

"Peace, sweet. Our families approve the match. There's nothing to stop me tasting the fruit before our vows."

He seemed determined to press this encounter further—far further than she knew possible. His hand was now thrusting down the neck of her bodice, reaching for the bare skin of her breast. She had to take desperate measures. Giving up on the unequal struggle of pushing him away, she freed her arms and clapped her hands to both his ears with force, then scratched at his eyes.

"God's sake, girl, what's got into you?" Righteous cried, stumbling back from her.

"Nothing, but the Devil must have got into you, sir!" She picked up a fallen branch to swing at him, but he was shaking his head, ears ringing, and no longer appeared likely to press his suit. "I fear, Master Field, I am not the broad-minded woman you seek if that is what you think the word means. Touch me not again." She turned to leave. "And take not the Lord's name in vain. Did not your father teach you anything?"

Field snatched up his hat and brandished it at her. "Mercy Hart, you should go down on your knees to thank God that I am willing to marry you. No one else in our congregation would consider connecting themselves with you after your dalliance with the player!"

"Nay, sir." Mercy swung the branch threateningly at him. "I go down on my knees to thank God I do not have to wed a hypocrite like you. Give me a sinful player any day over a painted sepulchre like you."

She stormed away, her fury carrying her back through the dangerous alleys of Southwark. Even a cutpurse would think twice about approaching an enraged maiden bearing a stout oak staff.

Not being able to stomach going home, Mercy ran to take refuge with her aunt. Pushing her way past the astonished gallants waiting in the fencing yard, she burst into her aunt's home without even knocking. She interrupted Rose and Silas at their dinner.

"Mercy!" her aunt cried. "Whatever is the matter?"

Mercy took one look at the branch in her hand then threw it down. "Oh, Aunt, I'm in a fearful tangle." And she burst into tears.

It took Rose a good half-hour to calm her niece. Silas had surmised something out of the ordinary had happened to the lass from the disturbed state of her clothes and hair.

"Leave me with her." Rose motioned him to the door.

"When you find out who it is," Silas growled, "I'll go . . ."

172

"Yes, you'll go skewer him for her." Rose's eyes shone with exasperated love for her rough soldier. "Let us have a quiet word first. Skewering may not be the best course of action."

Mercy poured out her story between fits of sobbing—the argument with Kit, the fact that he hadn't come as usual to his Sunday trysting spot, the suitor her father had lined up for her and the disastrous walk in the fields.

"What did he do, Mercy?" her aunt asked with genuine concern. "He didn't . . ." She feared to put the thought into words.

"He kissed me," wailed Mercy, "and it was horrid. Not like Kit. He tried to touch me under my skirts and my . . . my breast, but then I pounded his ears like you used to do to us when Edwin and I argued—but harder—and then I scratched him."

"I see." Rose began to realize her worst fears had not come to pass.

"When he let me go, I threatened him with that." She gestured to the oak branch. "He backed off. I just wish now I'd got in a couple of good blows before I left him."

Rose was only grateful that the scoundrel had not been a bigger, more violent man. She wouldn't fancy her little niece's chances against one such as that. "Oh, love, we need to get you safely married to our Kit, don't we? We can't have every Puritan boy who thinks you're a woman of easy virtue trying his luck with you."

"But Kit doesn't want me anymore." Mercy mangled the handkerchief in her lap.

"I don't think that is true for one moment. Lovers quarrel all the time. It is part of the growing together each pair must go through." She thought how she and Silas had had several loud disagreements since she had come to live with him, neither swift

173

to back down and beg the other's pardon. It all added spice to the mix. Her sweet niece was still at the stage when she believed every up and down was life or death to a relationship.

Mercy was not ready to hear such comforting words, her mind still predicting dire consequences from their tiff. "But a quarrel might also drive them apart, might it not?"

That was undeniably true. Rose did not know Kit well enough to guess if he had the constancy to stay when the going got difficult. Still, she had liked what she had seen of the young man thus far.

"You mustn't give up so quickly, Mercy. Wait until you see Kit again. It sounds to me as if you owe him an apology."

Mercy smudged her tears across her cheeks with her wrist. "But I really thought it wasn't like that, you know, between men and women. But I was wrong: even God-fearing folk grope each other—in broad daylight. And he's the minister's son!"

Rose wisely hid her smile. Ignorance through innocence was not to be mocked. All have to come to the realization one day that marital relations involved more than the chaste kisses of the poets. This was Mercy's moment.

"It sounds to me that you are in very good hands with your Kit. He will show you what you need to know at the right moment and it won't disgust you as today's experience has done. But I think it is past time I had a word with your father. We must keep you out of the clutches of that Field boy or I really will have to send Master Porter to skewer him."

Mercy shrank back, skin flushed red with embarrassment. "Must you, Aunt?"

"Aye, I must. Your father is blinkered as to the true qualities of the boy, and it is only fair to you that he is put right on a matter or two."

Mercy shook her head. "I'm not sure I want to be there. He's convinced that Righteous can do no wrong."

"Then we'll have to tell him, won't we?"

"What?"

Rose grinned and shaped her niece's face gently in her hands so she would pay attention to every word. "That righteous is as righteous doth, not as named."

Mercy realized that she had made a tactical error going to her aunt's first when she discovered Righteous Field already in possession of her father's parlor. Pushing open the door quietly, her aunt at her shoulder, she was just in time to hear the tail end of his version of events.

"And then she marched off, leaving me kneeling in the mud, most respectfully I might add, shouting at me that she would wed a player, not a minister's son." Righteous clutched his hat to his breast. "I fear, sir, your child is possessed by a demon. You must ask my father to drive it out before it brings greater grief upon you."

Aunt Rose shut the door with a bang, startling Field into tripping backwards. Mercy's father, Edwin and Faith stared at her as if she had just fallen from the moon among them.

"Demon, my stars! It was no demon that possessed my darling girl but a presumptuous boy who would've forced himself on her if she had not fought back!" Rose snatched a twig broom from its usual place by the door and took a swipe at Field.

"Aunt, please!" Mercy was not sorry to see Righteous punished, but it was not helping her case if her family thought them both possessed.

"What is this!" spluttered Field, holding his hands in front of him to fend off the birch twigs aimed at his groin. "Stop her, someone!"

"Keep back!" warned Rose, showing she had thorns for all her pretty name. She got in another good blow below the belt. "This snake-in-the-grass needs to be taught a lesson!"

The paralysis that had struck the Harts at this unexpected development lifted. Faith rushed to Mercy's side.

"My dear, is this true? Did he attack you?"

Mercy suddenly realized that whatever Righteous believed he could achieve by poisoning the ground before her seed of truth could be scattered would not work. Her family knew and loved her; they would stand by her.

"Aye, he tried to . . . to anticipate the marriage bed." Mercy couldn't bring herself to be more specific before her father and brother.

"*What?*" roared John Hart. The kindly merchant seemed to swell as he rounded on the much-harassed Field. "You dare touch my daughter in that lascivious fashion?" His anger was such that even Rose eased her onslaught to look at him in surprise.

Field gave Mercy a look of contempt. "I only went where others have doubtless gone before."

At that insult, Faith pushed past Rose and delivered a sound slap to the man's face. "You fiend! How dare you insult my innocent sister without cause!"

"Villain, take that back!" Edwin stepped forward to add his

own ha'penny worth to the dispute, but John Hart swept him aside.

"Leave this to me, Edwin. It is for me to punish your sister's attacker." Mercy's father stood in front of the smirking suitor— Righteous was foolishly convinced that his connection to his father would protect him from an irate member of the congregation. "Master Field, I trusted you with my daughter, thinking you meant only to honor her, but you have proved yourself a rotten sinner, not worthy to touch the hem of her cloak, let alone her person. We are going to your father, but first you will feel what it is like to be at the mercy of someone who is bigger and stronger than you."

And then her peace-loving father drew back his fist and laid Field out on the rush mat with a punch to the jaw.

Rose applauded and hopped on the spot with delight. "Oh, John, that's splendid! But what happened to turning the other cheek?"

"Humph!" He hauled the dazed Field up by the front of the jacket. "I'd be happy to hit the other one too if he begs me. Come along, master, I think it's time you and your father had a little talk about your future."

Waiting for the performance to begin in the tiring-room, Kit pondered what means he could find to deliver his crawling plea to be back in Mercy's favor. If it meant tying his hands behind his back whenever they were together, he would do it. He was almost dressed for his role in today's play, all ready bar his doublet, so could afford the time to sit on an empty trunk, surrounded by a curtain of cloaks, swords and armor, and ponder his situation. Unless the Belknaps arranged another amusement for them both, he had no common ground on which to meet her. He supposed he could linger outside her house in the hopes that she would come out, but he had his rehearsals to attend and performances to give. He valued his regular wage too much to risk his employment on what might prove a fruitless watch. The best he could hope was that her aunt would pass her a message, but that would not do justice to the words he wanted to say.

James Burbage patrolled the room, checking that all the actors had come in good time. He slapped his son, Richard, on the back, making him stagger as he tried to put on his hose, causing much hilarity at that end of the room. Kit let his gaze drift, noticing how the dust spun in the shaft of sunlight coming through a high window. Beams fell on a spot where one trunk sat neglected and unopened.

"Turner, have you seen Tom Saxon?" Burbage kicked the chest.

"Nay, not since yesterday."

Burbage whistled for the Theatre's messenger boy. "Here, lad, go knock on Master Saxon's door and see what's keeping him." He checked the prompt's copy of the day's play, *The Two Widows of Eastchepe*. "Hi, you, Shakespeare. Look, man, if Saxon doesn't show, you'll have to take the part of the merchant. Can you do it?"

The Stratford man shrugged. "Aye and stand on my head, if it please you." He was famous in the cast for having a prodigious memory, knowing everyone's parts as well as his own. Sadly, his acting skills were not as strong, and he had yet to be given a big role.

"Nay, doing the merchant on your own two feet will be

enough." Burbage moved on, grumbling about sottish lads not turning up to do their duty.

Worried for Tom, Kit finished donning his costume of the merchant's son, suitor in the play for one of the widows. He hoped it was merely a hangover that was keeping his drinking companion at home and nothing more serious. There was as yet no sign of plague this year, but strange disappearances were often the first hint. Tom had always managed to show up on time before, even if he was nursing a crushing headache.

Still, that was none of his understudy's fault. Kit decided to rally the new actor before nerves struck.

"Hillo, ho, Dad!" Kit called cheerily to Will Shakespeare. "How d'you like your new strapping son."

Will smiled and shook his head. "All I can say, lad, is that my goodwife must've danced the shaking of the sheets with my lord's fool."

He'd walked into that one. Will had the knack of turning the tables on a man.

Seeing the hour was almost upon them, Will began putting on Saxon's costume. Kit helped him find the various parts in the trunk—rich gown, false stomach, long gray beard.

"Saxon's going to catch it hot for this." Kit buckled on the wide gold belt to hold the cushion in place.

Will adjusted his paunch. "Aye, Burbage will be down upon him like a Fury crowned with snakes."

Kit snorted. "You speak poetical, Master Shakespeare. I didn't know you were a man of learning."

"Little learning and less wit, according to my goodwife," he replied modestly.

"I think the lady underestimates you." Kit twitched the back of the merchant's cloak into place. "Burbage is talking about giving you a trial as a writer."

Shakespeare's eyes woke with a glint of fire. "He is?" He grabbed Kit's wrist in a surprisingly forceful grip. "Put in a good word for me, will you? He holds you in high esteem. It's hard for a plain man like myself to make entry to the profession when there are so many plaintiffs and only one judge."

"Meaning aspiring playwrights and Burbage?"

"Aye. His ears ring each day with the poor scribblers from the shires who swear they can write the next triumph. A word from you would raise me above the common pleas and mayhap bring a favorable verdict."

"I'll do that—though I pray he does not cry 'guilty' when he reads your submission. Are you sure you have a play in you? 'Tis not everyone who understands stagecraft. I'm happy to give you any pointers along the way if that would help."

"Aye, Master Signpost, that might well be of use to me. I'll give it some thought."

Kit wondered if the thrum of affectionate teasing in that last speech had been only in his own imagination. The stubborn set to the man's jaw told him that Shakespeare did not really need his advice; the older man already had his course set and was just waiting for a fair wind to make sail.

The trumpets sounded from the Tower.

"Our cue, Dad." Kit took Will Shakespeare's arm to steer him to the right side of the stage for his first entrance.

"Aye, readiness is all," the actor said with a grin.

Returning for a brief while between scenes, Kit discovered that the messenger had come back and already spilled his cargo of news to the other actors.

"What! Saxon's been arrested? By whom? And for what?" spluttered Richard Burbage, half in his next costume. "I must tell my father."

"It has to be debt," said Appleyard, the elderly player now only taking very small roles as he could not be relied on to remember long speeches. "That boy always runs in bad company. They play for high stakes."

Kit shivered as the hairs prickled on the back of his neck. There was another possible explanation—one involving treason. He had anticipated such an outcome when he had dragged Tobias from the clutches of Babington and his crew. He hoped he had moved swiftly enough to mask that particular scent on Tobias's trail. But he feared Tom had not been so lucky. He would have to warn his brother, suggest he get well away from London. Such wildfires of suspicion had the habit of consuming all in their path.

"Know you something of the matter?" Will Shakespeare asked in a low voice as he changed next to Kit. His sharp gaze must have read the thoughts flitting across Kit's face.

"I'd prefer not to say."

"But you know in what company the lad has been running of late?"

"Aye. Not good."

"Vile politicians, the three of them, and your friend Saxon has not so much brain as earwax betwixt his lugs."

Kit offered no defense, for it was true.

"I pray that he squeaks clear of their traps or it won't go well for us." The actor nodded to the men of the troupe. "Soot lingers even when the fire is smothered."

The man's world-weary tone made Kit realize what he had already sensed: that Shakespeare had years of experience on him and a deep knowledge of humankind, very likely trouble with the authorities too by the sounds of it. "Your advice to a fellow player, Will?"

The sparkle came back to the actor's eyes as he approved the young man's willingness to learn. "If taken, play the fool and speak an infinite deal of nothing. If they try to capture a cloud, they'll come away with nothing for their pains." He tapped his head. "Earwax may yet save your friend. It's the clever fellows like the pair of us who really have to worry."

They did not knock when they came for Kit. The first he knew was that he was on the floor, a sword pressed to his neck.

"Get dressed, Master Player, there's someone who wants a word with you."

Seven men in dark cloaks filled his small chamber. If Kit had thought to make a run for it, he would not have got very far. Despite the warning of Saxon's arrest, he hadn't anticipated this when he went to sleep, thinking himself clear of the matter, but now it had come there was an awful inevitability about the summons.

"Oh, Master Turner, whatever do they want with you?" sobbed Dame Prewet, restrained at the door by one of the men. "He's a good boy, sir," she implored the leader. "Like a son to me, he is. He'll go quietly, just don't hurt him!"

Her plea worked, for the sword lifted and Kit rose to his feet. He pulled on yesterday's clothes lying where he had dropped them at the end of his bed. "I've no idea, dame, why they have come, but the sooner I go the sooner I'll be back." He tied his money pouch to his belt. Any Londoner knew a sojourn at Her Majesty's pleasure required bribes. He didn't have much coin so prayed this would be but a brief stay. "Pray send word to Master Burbage and my other friends if I do not return by morning. They will want to know where I am."

He didn't want to mention names before these men, but hoped she understood he wanted her to alert his brothers. If this trouble had reached out to encompass him, it might well swell to grab them next, and they had to make plans to get clear. A player was small beer; an earl and his noble brothers were like the finest wine to those tasting for plots.

The men marched him at the double through the quiet streets of sleeping London and, ironically for Kit, past Mercy's very door on the bridge. If anyone was stirring, they had more sense than to get in the path of such a determined party. They stopped only to gain admittance to one of the last places Kit had ever intended going: the Marshalsea prison in Southwark.

"Well, well, who do we have here?" asked the jailer, a square-jawed brute of a fellow, holding a lantern up to Kit's face. He did not look a tender guardian for his wards.

"Christopher Turner, vagabond player, to await Sir Francis Walsingham's pleasure," replied the chief of the guard.

"Do I put him in with the other one, or keep them separate? I'm right full at the moment, what with all these Catholics that keep creeping back into the realm. I swear this place has more of 'em than Rome."

"Apart. He is wanted for questioning. We've got to keep them from colluding."

Other one? Kit prayed most fervently that it wasn't Tobias. Bastard that he was, Kit did not think himself a person of enough importance to hold official attention long, but the legitimate brother of an earl was another matter entirely.

The jailer led Kit to a small cell half underground. Gads, it smelt like a sewer. Kit covered his nose with his hand.

"In you go, Sir Player." He shoved Kit down the single step onto the fetid floor. "Make yourself at home." The jailer chortled at his own wit before taking the light with him.

Kit saw enough of the cell from the lantern light to know there was a pallet in the right-hand corner. He groped his way to it and patted the covers, fearful of what his fingers might encounter. It was not occupied by anything other than bedbugs as far as he could tell. He chose to sit on the cover rather than risk lying down. Tomorrow he would see what he could do about paying for clean bedding and a better cell; this night he would have to make do.

Staring into the dark, he was struck with the absurd urge to laugh. But a few hours ago, his biggest problem had been how to woo a shy maid; now he was dodging a charge of high treason, the penalty for which really did not bear thinking about. Hanging, drawing and quartering—making death a blessed relief after inflicting every cruelty on the body; all this carried out in front of a

jeering audience who ate, drank and made merry while the condemned man was forced to watch his own innards . . .

Kit vomited in the corner, then collapsed back on his pallet.

God above, if his damsel was going to run shy of him, this
would be an excellent moment to choose to do so. Indeed, he
hoped all those he loved steered well clear of him. Ships on the
rocks offered danger only to those who sailed too close in the
hopes of pulling them off. He prayed Will would keep a firm hand
on Tobias, as his younger brother would be just the sort to try a
desperate rescue. His best hope lay in the whole matter fizzling
out like a fire with no fuel. Tobias rushing to his side would be oil
on the flame.

chapter 14

TOBIAS WAS STILL LAZING ABED in his comfortable chamber in James Lacey's splendid Broad Street town house when Will and James barged into the room with no ceremony.

"Kit's been arrested," Will said abruptly, throwing back the heavy velvet bed curtains.

"Jane heard word privately at court from Robert Cecil," confirmed James, running worried hands through his shock of chestnut hair. "She sent a message immediately."

Tobias wished he could be one of those who woke up alert. His brain felt more like it was wading through cold porridge. "When? Why, for God's sake?"

Will checked the room was clear of servants. "Walsingham has a scheme in the making and he is adamant that no one will upset it—something to do with the Queen Mary. He is ruthlessly pruning off any offshoots, as he puts it, from the main stock. Kit has become such a one."

Tobias began dressing. "But this makes no sense! Kit has nothing to do with plots or politics."

Will shook his head. "It seems we are wrong in that. A number of witnesses have come forward to say they saw a man of his description in the company of one Tom Saxon, player, and a set of the most dangerous men in England, Babington and his confederates. They are staunch Catholics and caught up in some drunken dream of rescuing Mary from her prison and putting her on the throne."

Tobias stopped halfway through pulling on a boot.

"Whatever is afoot at Chartley with the Scottish queen, Walsingham does not want the theaters involved stirring up trouble in favor of her cause, so he's moved secretly against the players. No one is to know they have been arrested. The word is being put out that they have been imprisoned for debt—a plausible enough story considering our brother's way of life. It is only thanks to Jane's position in the Queen's household that we've heard this much."

Tobias threw his boot at his oldest brother. "You don't know Kit at all if you say that. Kit's saving to be wed—not gambling his gains away in the stews."

James intercepted the boot and threw it back. "Have some respect, sprout. That's the twentieth most important man in the realm you are throwing your boot at. And what's this about Kit wanting to be wed? Why haven't we heard of this before?"

"Rather a moot point, I would say, if he's in the Marshalsea." Will pulled a stool up to the table under Tobias's window. "I think you have some explaining to do on behalf of our brother. If he's been living like a model citizen, how come people have seen him with an arrant traitor?"

Gads, there was no way to say this gently. "That was me." Oh, dear, that came out ill. "What I mean is that I fell into drinking with that crew earlier in the year. Kit discovered what was happening, opened my eyes to the dangers and sent me packing."

"God's bones, Tobias, how could you be so stupid?" spluttered James, looking for his own missile to throw at the youngest Lacey boy. "I can't believe you'd be so dim-witted! Are we safe, Will? Need I recall Jane from court and take a leave of absence on one of her estates? God knows the babe provides us with excuse enough."

"I didn't mean to get you in hot water!" protested Tobias. "They were just men I met down the tavern, not a conspiracy."

Will's anger was of the quieter, more dangerous sort. "Did you tell them anything about us?"

Tobias was determined to make a clean breast of this confession. "Nothing but that you do not like Raleigh."

Will shrugged this off: if not liking Raleigh were treason, then most of England would be guilty. "You did not say I would be sympathetic in any way to a plot to put Mary on the English throne?"

"No, I swear by my own salvation, Will, I did not. I will say that to whomever you wish, put my name to anything you want me to sign."

"I take it the person in the witnesses' accounts is you and not Kit?"

"Aye. You know we look much alike."

"And he is bearing the blame."

"Saxon is much deeper in with those fellows. If there's any plot, he'd be the one to know about it."

"And will be wanting to spread the blame to take the heat from himself. Who better than a player with the unusual link to court through his blood tie to us? We make much better suspects for those looking for a conspiracy than a couple of actors. By all that's holy, Tobias, you've made a fearful mess of things."

Wracked with guilt, Tobias still felt he should defend himself from the charge that it was entirely his fault. All he'd done was have a drink with the fellows, like scores of others. "I think you should remember, Will, that it was you who wouldn't help me out in February. If you'd settled my debt then, I would never have been at Kit's to meet these men." Ah, pox on it, that sounded petty. "I pray your pardon: I don't mean to blame you. I only drank with the Babington set; I never discussed anything beyond ale, women and dice—in roughly that order."

"That's going to sound a fine excuse if this reaches the Star Chamber." Will put his head in his hands.

"They'll take one look at the idiot and believe him," said James, cuffing his little brother.

This return to normal fraternal violence gave Tobias leave to hope that the worst of the confession was over. Will sat up and drummed his fingers on the table to gain their attention.

"Our course is clear. Unfortunately, we must make no move in public to help our brother. Kit has largely kept his distance, certainly from James and me, and that fact will now assist us. We must maintain that he has no connection with the family and that he is not admitted within doors. All must think he is of no account to us. If anyone questions your staying with him, Tobias, we will keep to a version of the truth: that you were living with the black sheep as a moment of youthful rebellion and now have come back within the family fold having seen the error of your ways."

Tobias opened his mouth to protest, but Will held up a finger.

"I say this not because I'm in any way ashamed of our brother. He's proved himself in this business a fine man and I'd be proud to own him, but we do him no favors if we draw more attention to him in the mind of Walsingham and his men by trying to use our influence to get him free. He has to do that himself by proving he is of no interest to the Crown, not when they've bigger fish to catch."

If that was the correct strategy, then it seemed a cruel one. What would Kit think of them all? He'd had a basin full of rejection from the Laceys when he was little; were they going to repeat it now that he needed their help?

"But we can't leave him in prison with none to comfort him," said James, giving voice to part of Tobias's objections. "The Crown often takes months to lose interest."

"No, we can't." Will sat back, hands spread open on the table. "Any suggestions? In sooth, I would welcome ideas on this."

"Burbage?" offered James. "He's cared for Kit like a father."

"But he's in a ticklish position if two of his company have fallen foul of the authorities. Besides, Walsingham wants the theaters kept far out of this as they have too much influence to sway the mob."

Tobias raised a hand. "I've an idea."

Will cocked an inquisitive eyebrow.

"His ladylove. No one will suspect his sweetheart of any ill intentions if she visits him."

Sitting back, Will was about to dismiss the notion. "But if she's connected with the company, she cannot help us—Walsingham won't like any word getting back that way."

Tobias smiled bitterly. "No fear of that. She has no connection with that crowd and is the least likely person to be suspected of supporting Catholic plots in the realm."

"You jest—she'd have to be a Puritan for that!"

"I conclude my case, my lord." Tobias gave a mock bow as if to the judge's chair. "It appears our brother was very farsighted when he picked Mercy Hart for his sweetheart."

Mercy was paying her daily visit to her aunt when Tobias found her. The two women had been making a cherry pie, taking advantage of the brief season when the fruit was abundant. She felt somewhat at a disadvantage in receiving a young noble, for her hands were stained red like a murderer thanks to the cherries she had just pitted.

"Why, Master Lacey, what brings you here?" called Rose cheerfully when she saw the gentleman hovering at the kitchen door. "If you seek Diego, he's gone out for a ride with Lord Bergavenny and should be back by midday, and if it's Master Porter you want, he's gone to Westminster to give a lesson."

"Nay, mistress, it's your niece I wish to speak to."

Tobias looked very somber, not his usual mischievous self at all. A shiver ran up Mercy's spine. Something was wrong.

"Well, if it's my niece you seek, then you've found her. Stay awhile and have some pie with us. I'm just carrying it to the oven now. It shouldn't take long." Rose lifted it onto the paddle to slide it in to bake in the hottest part of the oven.

As soon as Rose's back was turned, Mercy asked: "What has

happened, Master Lacey? Is it Kit?" She rinsed her hands in a basin, the red stain leaving a purple mark behind that she could not rub off.

"Aye. Please, sit down." Tobias gestured for her to take a seat on the bench. That could not be good.

"He's . . . he's sent you to say he doesn't forgive me?" she whispered.

"Nay. This is far more serious than a lovers' quarrel. He loves you still, don't you dare doubt him. Mistress Hart, Mercy, I . . ." Tobias gave a frustrated sigh. "I can't think how to tell you. He's been arrested. They're saying it's for debt, but that's a lie. He's got himself clear of anything he owed months ago, thanks to you."

"Arrested!" squeaked Mercy.

Rose heard her exclamation. She swung round, bearing the paddle like a pike. "Who's been arrested?"

Tobias held up his hands in surrender. "Ladies, please, keep your voices down! This is a matter of the utmost delicacy—and danger."

Placing the paddle by the hearth, Rose hurried to her niece's side so they could huddle close around the table. "Tell us, sir, what's going on?"

"My brother Kit has been arrested. The official story is that he's been put in the Marshalsea by his creditors, but the truth is he's there for treason."

"Kit! Impossible." Mercy dug her fingernails into her palms.

"Aye, it's a mistake—and it's my fault he's there." Tobias tugged at his ruff, not liking this part of the confession. "I got into the habit of drinking with the wrong set earlier in the year. The reports made it sound as if it was Kit, and he's been taken in for questioning. I cannot tell you more of the matter without endangering you, but suffice it to say that my part was foolish rather than evil."

"So why can't you tell the authorities this and get Kit out of jail?" asked Mercy.

"Because the men behind the arrest are playing for the highest of stakes. They look for disloyalty near to the Queen. If I, or my brothers, try to gain Kit's release, we would cast suspicion on ourselves and all associated with us, as well as give the questioners reason to think my brother is more than just a player going about his usual business of drinking in rough company. If he looks isolated from us, then their interest will die and he will probably be released quietly and without charge."

"I see that, sir," said Rose, placing her hand over Mercy's clenched fists to calm her, "but what if you are wrong and they take this to trial?"

"Then the Laceys will stand by Kit, of course, and do our utmost to exonerate him. But I trust my brother, the earl's, judgment in this: charges of treason prompt the least rational process in the law. Any activity can be taken ill, and we should only move from this position when all other courses have been tried."

Mercy resented the young noble's calm words when she wanted to run to the Marshalsea and kick down the door. "So why are you here, sir? To tell me to abandon Kit as you have done? For I won't, you know!"

He had the grace to look guilty at that. "I have no intention of abandoning my brother, mistress, and I rather hoped you would feel that way. We want to support him, make sure his time in prison passes as painlessly as possible, but we fear to approach him directly, as his defense rests in seeming to be cut off from the Laceys. We would like you to go between us and Kit, offering the comfort that we cannot." He placed a heavy money pouch on the table. "This is for him—and for you, for your pains."

Mercy pushed the pouch away. "I need no pay for helping the man I love."

"Nay, I know that, but unfortunately you might need it more than you think." He looked regretfully at Rose.

"How so, sir?" her aunt asked.

"What do you think your father will say, Mistress Hart, when you tell him that you are going to visit Kit in prison?"

Mercy hid her face in her hand.

"Aye. I guessed he might be very angry, even to the point of making you choose between staying under his roof and Kit."

Rose folded her arms. "Then she can come here."

Tobias shook his head. "Think, mistress. As soon as your niece announces herself to the prison guard as being Kit's lady, she will become a person of great interest to the Queen's ministers. She will be followed—her least conversation judged for signs of conspiracy."

"What's that to me? I'm her aunt."

"Yet you are keeping house for one who spent years in the Tower suspected of aiding Catholic plotters. You will draw Master Porter into this, and he will be exactly the sort of character the authorities would expect to trap."

"But he's innocent!"

"Aye, but this, as my brothers have so forcibly made the point to me, is not about true guilt and innocence, but about the appearance of either." He turned to Mercy. "You will have to cut yourself off from those who would be harmed by this—your aunt, your friends, the Belknaps—and stay only with those above suspicion. There must be some good Christian souls of humble status in your church who would offer you refuge even if they disapprove of your choice, people who are so lowly that no one would dream that they had been dragged into any plots."

Mercy drew a pattern in the flour still dusting the table. Would her father throw her out? And would anyone step forward to shelter her? She would not know until she put the matter to the test. Really, what was she waiting for?

"Tell me what I must do."

Tobias kissed her floury, purple-stained fingers. "You are a pearl without price, Mercy, and my family stands in debt to you."

"Hold, sir," interrupted Rose. "Is there danger for my niece in this?"

"Very little, we think." Tobias squeezed Mercy's fingers then let them go. "Kit is famous for his attraction for the fairer sex; the authorities will most like consider her a maiden enamored of his charms. When they look into her connections, they will discover a girl from an unimpeachable God-fearing background, well known to her church and to her neighbors. Her family's relationship with the Laceys, as far as any can tell, is business only; as Mercy's father handles half the cloth dealing for the City, that is unlikely to raise any eyebrows. To suggest that the Harts would support a Catholic-inspired plot would be absurd and rapidly dismissed."

"I know what I shouldn't do." Mercy wrote Kit's name in the flour. "But I do not know how to go about helping him."

Tobias pushed the pouch back towards her. "Take him half of this money. Try not to be parted from it before seeing him. You may need to bribe the guards to get in to visit him, but that shouldn't cost you more than a few shillings. If you are allowed to be private with him, tell him what we have discussed, but only if you are certain no one can overhear you."

"And if they do not allow me to see him?"

"Pay for better accommodation and food. Ask for the jailer to give you a receipt to that effect or they will just pocket a foolish young girl's money and forget the rest."

Mercy brushed her fingers off on her apron and rose. "I can do that and I'll go now. How long has he been in there?"

"Only since last night. We were fortunate to receive word at once."

She paused as she untied the strings of her apron. "What about the Theatre?"

"Aye, we can't have him ruined in his profession because of this. I'm going next to ask Master Burbage to hold his position in the company and explain to him that he had best keep clear of the trouble. Master Burbage is likely to feel as you do and want to rush to Kit's aid, but I'll counsel him against this course of action. It would be doing Kit no favors if he came out of jail to find the authorities had closed down the Theatre because Burbage had shown himself too loyal to a suspect character."

"This is not fair!"

"I know." Tobias sighed. "Fortunately, the players are about to go on summer progress; Kit's absence will not be so obvious."

Decision made, Mercy could not wait to go to Kit. "Do you have any message that you wish to send him?"

"Aye, that I'll take over his lodgings permanently if he doesn't talk himself out of this quickly." Tobias winked. "So if he wants his things where he left them, he'd better put his silver tongue to good use."

Mercy managed a wavering smile. Realizing nothing would stop her from going, Rose hugged her and kissed her farewell.

"You look after yourself, dearest one," her aunt said fiercely. "I'll be here if you need me. Come back as soon as it is safe to do so—and before if you get into trouble you can't handle alone."

Tobias handed her to the door like a princess. "Mercy, you can also tell the rogue that we all love him and will move heaven and earth to make sure he is safe."

She nodded bravely. "Aye, I can do that."

Tobias rejoined his brothers and their horses where they waited incognito by the porch of St. Mary Overie. He could see Mercy's gray-clad figure hurrying back to her house to prepare herself for a visit to prison. Rose had insisted she take the cherry pie with her and Mercy had gone home to gather some other necessities for the prisoner: clean linen, more food, paper, ink and quill, if he was allowed them.

James followed his gaze. "Is that her?"

"Aye."

"Did she agree to go?" asked Will.

"Wild horses wouldn't keep her away."

The earl shook his head. "She looks very young."

"And very innocent," added James. "Gads, perhaps we should come up with another plan? Jail is no place for girls like her. Jane'll have my ears for putting a maiden in this position."

"I think Ellie might go for something lower," sighed Will.

Tobias mounted his horse, eager to get on with the second part of his task: talking to Burbage. "Too late to stop her. We've started that stone rolling. Don't underestimate her: I have the feeling that Mercy Hart can produce a landslide to get her way."

James gave a weary chuckle. "Perhaps then, brothers, we should thank God for small Mercies."

chapter 15

"NAY, YOUNG MISTRESS, YOU CANNOT see him." The jailer folded his arms and stood barring the door to the Marshalsea, a square block of a building with grated windows not far from the southern end of the bridge. The man was built like the prison he maintained: low and squat with not an inch of yielding about him.

Mercy fumbled with the money pouch. Taking Tobias's advice, she'd stowed half of it at home, but it was still more than she'd ever carried in her life. She drew out two shillings. "Will you not reconsider, sir?"

"I've my orders, see," he said regretfully, though he took the coins from her. "He's not to talk to anyone."

"But I don't want to talk to him."

The jailer leered at her. "Aye, I don't suppose you do. Young lovers have better things to do than talk."

Mercy tried not to blush. She was here as Kit's sweetheart and the jailer had to believe her bold enough to demand entrance. "I've some things for him to make the time pass in more comfort." She lifted the cloth hiding the contents of her basket, releasing the delicious smell of pie.

The jailer's eyes glinted with interest. He glanced around him. "You'd best step into my office, mistress."

Mercy wasn't eager to be alone with the man, but at least this meant she got within the doors. She followed him into a dingy room, not much better than a cell itself, digging in her pouch to take out a few more coins while his back was turned.

"Put your basket here. I've to inspect anything sent in to my prisoners." He tapped the table.

Mercy put it down and took off the cloth.

He rejected the parchment, ink and quill immediately. "Strict rules, no communication with anyone outside the jail." His eyes went back to the pie.

Mercy knew what she had to do. She took it out and placed it on the table, laying two more shillings by its side. "You must get very hungry fulfilling your duties here, sir."

"Aye, that I do."

"Perhaps you might like this pie as a token of my thanks. It's fresh-baked with a cherry filling."

He licked his lips. "That'd go down well with a sip of wine."

With a sigh, she took out the bottle of Burgundy she had carefully transported this far.

The man took the wine, signaling she had given enough—for now. "He's in the pit. I'll bring him up to a cell aboveground so you can see him." The jailer jingled his keys. "No talking, mind. No carrying of messages to the outside."

Mercy nodded, taking his injunction literally. She only brought word in, and had no intention of taking any out with her. A few minutes later, he came back to fetch her, steering her only a short step down the corridor to the first cell. The place smelt damp and musty, the odor of human misery, she thought. He gave her a salacious wink as he ushered her in.

"I wager that with you to eat, your young man won't miss that pie," he chuckled. "Ten minutes—that's what I'll give you. Twenty if the pie is as good as it looks. Can't say fairer than that."

Kit couldn't understand why he was being moved. At first he thought he was being taken for questioning, but then the jailer showed him into an empty cell. A vast improvement on the dank hole he had been put in, and he hadn't even had to bribe the man for the privilege.

The door opened again and Mercy stumbled over the lintel, in a hurry to put some distance between herself and the slop bucket of a jailer.

"Mercy, what are you doing here?" This was terrible. She had to stay away. He couldn't bear it if his misfortune reached others. "Go away!"

"That's not very gentlemanly of you, sir," laughed the jailer. "Your little sweetheart's gone to all this trouble to see you and I've been so kind as to let her; I'd make the most of it." He shut the door on them, turning the key.

To his sorrow, Kit saw that his harsh words had bewildered his Mercy. Instead of running into his arms as she had plainly been intending, she hovered by the entrance, nervously squeezing the handle of a basket. "Master Turner, I've been told not to talk to you, but I've brought you some things to make your time here pass more easily."

He took the basket from her and put it down without even

looking at the contents. Wrapping his arms round her, he folded her to him. "Ah, sweet, you shouldn't be here." She smelt of home-baking and lavender, the complete opposite of everything in this place.

He could feel her swallow against his chest. "You . . . you don't want me?"

"Of course I want you. I meant that I don't want you caught up in this. It's going to take some time to sort out and it could get worse before it gets better."

Mercy nodded. "Aye, I know." She went up on tiptoe. He hoped for a kiss, but instead got a whisper in his ear, which was almost as good. "Your brothers sent me. I would have come anyway, of course, but they asked me to be their go-between. There's money in my pouch to pay for better accommodation. They said that they could only keep you safe by staying away."

"That's true." He kissed her neck. "I pray you, don't mention them again. We must be strangers, they and I."

"Just one more thing. They send their love. They thought it would be safe for me to come, as I have no connection to any political faction. If your situation worsens, they'll take steps to plead on your behalf, but for the moment they'll keep away."

"Let's not talk about my brothers," Kit whispered, making free with her ear for a nibbling caress. "In fact, let's not talk at all. There's little to say other than I love you, Mercy. Forgive me for upsetting you at Greenwich."

She sank back down, heels on the ground, which had the most unwelcome result of moving her lips out of range of his mouth. "No, it is for me to beg your pardon. I was wrong. You . . . you spoke true when you said people did such things. Can you forgive my ignorance? I was so arrogant to think I should correct you and I feel very foolish."

He held her serious face in his hands, tracing her cheekbones with his thumbs. How her skin could be so soft was a miracle in this place of stone and iron bars. "There is nothing to forgive."

"There is. You were treating me with care and respect; I was the one to go too far with my reaction. I've since learnt that not all men are so kind."

What was this? He brushed his thumb across her smooth cheek to touch the corner of her mouth, seeking the smile that usually put a dimple there. "Has something happened, Mercy? How do you know this?"

Her eyes slid to the wall behind him and she pressed her lower lip between her teeth.

"Come, sweet, nothing you can say will anger me."

Her fingers plucked the cording on his doublet. "My father arranged for a suitor from my church—a horrid man called Righteous Field."

Kit reminded himself he had promised not to get angry. "And what followed?"

"He took me for a walk." She glanced up at him, her green eyes earnest. "I didn't want to go, I promise."

"Aye, I know you didn't."

"He accosted me when we reached the field beyond the bear baiting."

"Accosted you? In what way?" His voice shook, but he continued to soothe her by stroking her face.

She gave an embarrassed shrug. "Well, you know, kissed me and tried to . . . um . . . touch my legs and . . ." Her gaze went to the center of his chest so he got the message.

"He's a dead man." Kit wished he weren't in jail so he could go douse the man's pretensions in the nearest horse trough—but only after rearranging his features into a more pleasing shape.

"There is no need, truly, Kit. I drove him off with a branch—"

Kit choked.

"—and then my father gave him a drubbing when my aunt told him about it."

"Your father!"

Mercy smiled, restoring the dimples in her cheeks that he loved to see in their rightful places. "Aye, he does not approve of any such meddling before marriage. He's quite changed his opinion of Master Field."

"Then there's hope for me yet." Kit kissed her forehead, promising himself that, if fate allowed, he too would have serious words with the would-be suitor. He glanced behind him to the door. "How long do you think you will be permitted to remain?"

Mercy gave him a proud look. "At least another quarter of an hour. Aunt Rose and I are masters of the cherry pie."

He chuckled. "Explain."

"Where avarice failed, gluttony prevailed. I now know how to gain entry to this place: keep the jailer supplied with pastries."

"In that case I have time for this." Striking swiftly, he pulled the coif from her head. "I've had many dreams about doing this. Let me see what you've been hiding from me." He unraveled her braid. "In sooth, mistress, you are full of surprises."

Mercy clapped a hand to her hair. "Oh, Kit, it's a terrible mess."

"Is that what you call it? I call it a beautiful mane." He picked up one lock, stretching the corkscrew curl straight so that it reached the small of her back. When he let go, it sprang to rejoin the others by her shoulder blades. "You have every color here from the lightest sack to the darkest Bordeaux. I can drink of you and never tire of the taste." Weaving his hands into the locks at her temples, he tilted her head to kiss her lips.

"Oh, Kit."

"It'll turn out right, I promise." And, in her presence, he could not doubt. If God had let this angel visit him, then He had Kit's interests at heart. It was time to mend the breach between him and his Creator. He knew Mercy would have it no other way.

"I'm so scared for you," she confessed.

"Don't be. I've friends on my side—and I've you to visit me. Many in this place are in far worse straits than I, for I know I am innocent. I count myself blessed." He kissed her again, shaping her to his full length, one arm angled across her hips, the other on her back.

Coming up for air with a sigh of contentment, she took his right hand and moved it to cradle her breast. Kit smiled into her hair. It had taken a spell in prison, but he and his little Puritan now understood each other perfectly.

On the jailer's return, Mercy reluctantly left Kit, promising to return as soon as she was able. The warden showed her to the door.

"I'm partial to a savory pie now and again," the jailer said to the air as he let her onto the street.

She bobbed a curtsy and hurried away with her empty basket.

The rest of her family was home when she entered, her brother and father at the table, her grandmother dozing by the fire and her sister bringing in a tray of food. Faith's eyes went to the basket on her arm.

"Ah, my dear, good: you're back just in time for dinner. I thought you'd gone to market."

"No, sister, I was visiting." She put the basket down on the table. "Do we need anything? I can go out again."

John Hart beckoned her to the table. "You've not eaten. Have your meal first."

Edwin pulled out a stool next to his and served a portion of meat on a plate for her. All were showing her particular marks of their concern since the Field affair—it had shaken them all profoundly that they could have been so mistaken in one of their congregation. But each caring gesture of her family was a twist of a knife in a wound, making the coming confrontation more difficult. Mercy couldn't help but delay the moment, taking a seat and cutting the ham up into small strips. Every mouthful tasted like sawdust and swallowing was almost impossible.

John Hart pushed his plate away with a satisfied sigh. "Excellent, Faith. That Seville orange sauce is very good."

Faith looked a little embarrassed. "Aunt Rose gave me the recipe."

"Aye, she's a fine cook. I'm glad you learnt so much from her." He turned his attention to Mercy. "You're very quiet, my dear. Is there bad news? Which neighbor did you say you were visiting?"

Oh, Lord. Here it came: the moment she'd been putting off.

"I was visiting Master Turner. He's in prison."

Edwin's spoon clattered onto his plate.

"*Master Turner?* In *prison?*" repeated her father.

"Aye."

He got up abruptly, his chair falling backwards to the floor with a dull thump. Grandmother jerked from sleep and blinked confusedly around the room. "You know what I said about that man?"

Mercy nodded, squeezing her hands together in her lap.

"Obviously you don't remember clearly, for you are sitting here at my table. Tell me what I said."

"You said . . ." Mercy cleared her throat. "You said that I had to leave the name of Hart and go to him barefoot if I wished to see him again as you'd have nothing to do with me if I chose him."

"And yet you went. To prison of all places, exactly the place I would've predicted a man of his nature would end up."

She ignored that unfair swipe as she could not enter into the reasons Kit was there without involving her family in the dangerous business. "But in the Gospel of Matthew, chapter twenty-five, we are told to feed the hungry, clothe the naked and visit the sick and those in prison."

John Hart swept his plate from the table so violently that it clanged against the wall. All three of his children flinched. "Do not quote the scriptures at me, Mercy, for it also says, in the ten commandments, 'Honor thy father and mother,' and you have just ignored a most solemn order from me. You will beg my pardon and go to your room. From this moment on, you must not venture out of doors without one of us to accompany you. And you most certainly shall never see that villain again."

Mercy stood up. "No, Father."

Her father gaped at her—the first time she had seen him so floored by a remark of hers. "What do you mean, no?"

"Kit is the husband of my heart and I will not abandon him. I stand here the sorriest girl in Christendom for the offense I cause you, but it seems that I cannot reconcile my duty to you with my love for him." She took up what was left of Tobias's money, which she had put aside before going to the prison and slipped it into her own pouch at her girdle. "Knowing this, do you still wish me gone?"

"Are you going too, Mercy?" quavered Grandmother. "Not like Rosie? No, you can't."

Mercy silently prayed that her father would change his mind. He had been her staunch defender against Field; would he now put his convictions before her wishes? When she plucked up the courage to raise her gaze to his face, she saw that he trembled with emotion—rage and distress at the breach opening between them. Tears flooded her eyes.

"Nay, do not try to soften me with crying." John Hart flung away from her, taking refuge at the far end of the chamber. "I cannot . . . I cannot let a willful sin go unchallenged in my house, no matter how I love the sinner."

Faith reached out a pleading hand to their father. "Please, let Mercy think awhile—give her space to pray and seek guidance on this matter."

Mercy brushed a sleeve across her eyes to blot her tears. "Nay, sister, I am afraid I cannot change my mind. Kit needs me."

Faith swallowed, then nodded. "Aye, I see that. I'll get your things for you."

Edwin stepped forward. "Come, sister, I'll take you to our aunt's. She'll take you in until this storm passes."

"No." John Hart brought his hand down on the table, making the crockery jump. "If she leaves, she leaves alone and with nothing, as I said she would. I will not let her actions make me a liar. If she leaves, she is no longer your sister. No longer a Hart."

"But, Father!" protested Edwin.

"John, I forbid it!" cried Grandmother.

John Hart turned on his son in a fury, discounting the old woman's words entirely. "Do you think I want to treat the child of my heart like this, Edwin? Can't you see what this man is doing to her? If he thinks we'll relent and pave his way with riches, he'll never let her go. We must cut off the sinner until she realizes her error and repents. It is the only way."

Mercy had known in one part of her mind that this moment would come, but she had still been hoping against hope that her father would yield. But, no, he was not bending. By his own reasoning, he could not.

"Very well, I will go alone and as you said." She knelt to take off her shoes.

"What are you doing?" gasped Faith. "Stop!"

"Father said barefoot, so I go without the shoes he provided for me. I pray you excuse me taking these clothes. I will send them back as soon as I have obtained others for myself."

Mercy's heart almost shattered when she straightened up and saw a tear run down her father's cheek.

"You mustn't worry." She addressed the room in general, knowing if she met anyone's eyes, she would crumble. She had to be strong—for Kit's sake. "I'll be able to provide for my needs. I'll send word when I know where I am staying."

"Oh, Mercy," wailed Grandmother.

"You're not going to our aunt?" whispered Faith, now also crying. "Please—you must! You don't know what it's like out there. Go to Aunt Rose—she'll take you in."

"I can't. Don't ask me to explain." Mercy took her cloak from the peg by the door and wrapped it around herself. "God be with you."

Opening the door, she stepped out into the street. Oh, God. It banged behind her with a terrible finality.

The stone of the alley was rough beneath her stocking-clad feet. Setting her shoulders back, she walked determinedly the ten yards to the shoemakers and entered.

"Excuse me, sir," she asked the shopkeeper. "Do you have any shoes ready to wear? I'm this size." She displayed her unshod foot to the astonished man.

He quickly regained his poise. "Aye, Mistress Hart, I've a pair that was never collected by the one who ordered them. You can have those." He took a fine pair of red leather shoes from the window.

Mercy thought they would be the sort Kit would favor, though too garish for her tastes. She slipped her toes into them. They were a good enough fit. "Thank you, I'll take them."

"Shall I put them on your father's account, Mistress Hart?"

Mercy felt a lump in her throat. "Nay, Master Hudson, I'll pay for them now. And I'm no longer Mistress Hart."

He clucked his tongue. "What business is this? You've not fallen out with your family, have you, young lady? You're not the first to do so—all over in an afternoon, usually."

She had no desire to parade her woes in front of their neighbors. "Thank you for the shoes, sir." She put a handful of coins on his worktable. "Is this enough?"

"Aye, enough." He patted her on the arm. "Never you fear, your family will have you back if you beg your father's pardon. He's a fair man."

She smiled at him through her tears. "Yes, he's a fair man," she agreed. But sometimes there were two kinds of fairness and they did not reconcile. "Good day, Master Hudson."

She left the shop, the heels of her new red shoes clicking on the pavement as she headed towards Southwark.

chapter 16

Two days after Mercy's visit, Kit's accusers finally appeared. He'd had nothing to do in the interim but pace his admittedly much better cell, wondering what was keeping her from a second visit and when he was going to hear what charges were leveled against him.

The interrogators occupied the warden's office, three men in sober black, minor court officials from the looks of them—Kit did not qualify for the attention of the Queen's ministers. They sat behind the table. Kit was left standing with his hands chained behind his back. The warden stood guard at the door—the only other person trusted to participate in this most secret of proceedings.

"Christopher Turner?" the gentleman sitting in the center asked, not giving any of their names or titles.

"Yes, sir."

"You are a player employed for some years at the Theatre?"

"Yes, sir, since 1580."

"Is it true that you are the illegitimate son of the late Earl of Dorset?"

Thus far everything was public knowledge. "Yes, sir. He main-

tained me until his death. Since then I have earned my own way."
Kit didn't want to make a heavy point about the division from his
family in case it was taken as protesting too much.

"On what terms stand you with your father's family?"

Kit gave a shrug. "No terms. We do not move in the same
circles."

This answer was taken as lacking respect. At a signal from the
man on the right, the warden thumped Kit in the stomach. He
hunched forward, struggling to regain his breath. At least the
terms of this engagement were now clear.

"Know you one Thomas Saxon?"

"Yes, sir, he is also employed at the Theatre."

"You are friends?"

"I go drinking with him." He noticed the finger of the man on
the right move. "Sir," he hastily added.

"What about Anthony Babington, Robert Gage and Charles
Pilney?"

"I've had a drink with them a time or two, nothing more.
Babington's a windy fellow, speaks little sense and I can't stand
him, but still he's not shy to get in the ale." Kit braced himself,
knowing the tack he had decided to take was going to earn him
some more thumps. He gave the gentlemen a smug smile. "Can't
be helped in my line of work. Fame onstage means all sorts of folk
want to be seen with you. What can I do? My public loves me."

This bit of boasting earned him close acquaintance with the
rushes and a kick to the kidneys. Kit breathed through his nose,
mastering the pain, sweat dripping off his brow. They waited for
him to stagger to his feet, making no comment about the rough
treatment that he was receiving before their eyes.

"Do you follow the Catholic heresies, Turner?" snapped the man on the left, who until this point had been silent.

Kit gave a hoarse laugh. "Nay, sir. My local priest will tell you I'm not the most pious of men, certainly no time for heresies, far too serious a matter for a gadfly like me. I struggle to get to church on the Sabbath."

The warden went for the face this time, putting his fist in Kit's blaspheming mouth. He spat the blood from his split lip, hoping he hadn't swallowed any teeth. Running his tongue along his jaw, Kit was relieved to find them all present and accounted for.

"You do not take matters of faith seriously?" asked the third man coldly.

How much longer was this going to go on? "I'll take them much more seriously from here on," Kit promised ironically, watching the warden's fist for signs of where the next blow would fall.

It was a kick to the back of the knees, forcing him down on the floor. The warden administered more blessings to his guest until the second man signaled him to step back. Kit couldn't get up. All he could do was lie with his face pressed to the floor, praying this would end.

"Do you wish to change any of your answers, Turner?" asked the first man.

Kit shook his head.

"You know not your legitimate family. You go drinking with Saxon and the others, but that is all. You are not interested in religious matters."

That about summed it up. "Those are my answers."

The three men rose. "Thank you, warden. We'll return three nights from hence to see the prisoners."

Kit now knew the other man had to be Saxon, as Mercy had said all his family was safe. He wondered if Saxon was holding up under the same treatment. Likely not: Tom had always been a bit of a coward and would sell his grandmother to get free of trouble. That didn't bode well for Kit, but neither could he guess what lies the man was spinning about him, as he truly had no idea what Babington and his crew had been about. The only course for him—one he had to stick to whatever the wind—was to be the idle player more interested in his box-office appeal than politics.

"Return him to his cell. Keep him separate from the other prisoners," the chief interrogator instructed.

And with that the men swept out of the jail.

The warden hauled him up by the back of his grubby doublet and clicked his tongue. "My, my, you don't look so pretty now. Mayhap your lady will prefer me; what you think?"

Kit thought he could burn in hell. "Shog off."

The jailer punched him in the stomach and dragged him back to his cell, leaving him on the floor. "Aye, man, your public just loves you." He banged the door closed and strode off laughing.

It had been four days since she'd last seen Kit, but it had taken her as long to find a place to stay; until then she had no kitchen, however small, to make her bribes, and she guessed only home-cooked food would do for the warden. On the first night with no offers of a roof forthcoming from any of the congregation she approached, she'd had to take a flea-infested room in a tavern on the Bermondsey Road. She'd been too scared to leave it to go in search of pie ingredients, let alone venture into the kitchen to ask to bake it.

The next night had been the same. On the third night, her luck had changed: curiously, Reverend Field had intervened on her behalf—lingering guilt perhaps for the poor behavior of his son, whom he had sent packing back to Antwerp. She now had a room just round the corner from the prison, lodging with Goodman Dodds and his wife, the poorest couple in the congregation. Dodds was a street cleaner and his spouse took in washing; they were thankful for the additional source of income, if grudging of their guest. Their two daughters, Humiliation and Deliverance, shared their chamber with Mercy, but had obviously been told not to talk to her. They acted as if she were a ghost they couldn't see. Mercy was very lonely and not a little depressed in spirit to find herself so reviled by people who had once sought her company.

The Doddses were not rich enough to have their own oven, so Mercy took her chicken pies to the baker. She'd made three: one for the Doddses, one for the jailer and one, she hoped, for Kit. Leaving the first offering in the Doddses' kitchen under cover so the rats wouldn't get it before they returned, she hurried to Marshalsea.

Mercy waited nervously outside the prison for the warder to answer her knock.

"Ah, Mistress Cherry Pie, back again." The jailer's eyes flicked to the basket. "What've you got in there?"

She raised the corner of the cloth to tempt him. "Chicken."

"Made by your own fair hands?"

"Of course."

He beckoned her into the office, dropping the latch as he closed the door behind her. "I'm afraid your Master Turner is a bit out of sorts today." He pulled a long face. "I pray it isn't the fever."

"The fever?" she gasped. "How bad is he?"

The jailer helped himself to the pie, then spotted a second underneath. "This for him?"

"Aye, but should I call a doctor?"

"Nay, my dear, they kill more often than they cure. Give him a day or two and we'll see if he's on the mend." He could see that she had no intention of quitting the subject until she had more reassurance. "I don't think he's that ill. He'll doubtless feel much better for eating this pie of yours." He took the second from the basket. Mercy knew with sinking heart that Kit wasn't going to see a crumb of it. "You know, sweetheart, you don't want to go wasting your time on fellows like that player." He stuck his thumbs in his belt. "No good they are. You need a real man to care for you. Fine girl with your looks, and a cook, to boot"—he gestured to the pies—"you won't have to search far to find such a one." He gave her a wink. "What about it, eh?" He smacked his thick lips, eyes on her breasts rather than her disgusted expression.

"Stanton, Stanton, what you doing in there?" screeched a woman, rattling the door.

"By the Lord of Ludgate, 'tis the wife." He scuttled to the door and flung it open. "What brings you here, woman?"

A small firebrand of a female strode into the place, starched ruff framing a thin face, her gray eyes latching on to each object like a butcher's hook. "I've brought you your dinner, you clay-brained guts, you! What's she doing here?"

"Visiting a prisoner, Mary. See, she's brought him his dinner." He gestured to the pies like a street conjuror producing a brace of doves from under his cloak.

The woman sniffed, not fooled by her goodman's expression

217

of innocence. "Can't you leave the drabs alone, Stanton, for five minutes?"

Mercy saw a way to get the pies to Kit at least, if not obtain leave to visit him herself. She bobbed a curtsy to the woman. "My betrothed is in the next cell along, mistress, but your goodman said he's sick. Would you be so very kind and see that he gets the attention he requires—good food, a doctor if needs be? I'll pay you well for your pains." She flourished two shillings from her pouch.

The woman perked up at the appearance of money, revising her opinion about Mercy in an instant. A woman with that kind of coin at her disposal would have the sense not to dangle after her husband. "I can do that for you, mistress." She bit the coins, then pocketed them with a sniff. "Run along. You don't look like the normal sort that comes round here. I counsel you to stay well away. Place is full of rogues and villains." She thumped her husband in the belly.

"Thank you, mistress." Mercy bobbed another curtsy and made a quick escape. The woman's advice was sound; Mercy's problem was that she had no choice but to return to this place. But if she couldn't even see Kit, what was the point?

That night, Mercy sat sewing a new shift for herself in a corner of the Dobbses' kitchen, by the dull glow of smoking rush light, trying to work out how to outwit the jailer and get both herself and her pies past him again. She couldn't rest until she had seen for herself how serious Kit's fever was and was determined he would have decent food to aid his recovery at the very least.

No one broke the silence in the single room that the family shared. Goodman Dobbs read his Bible, chewing his lip with one of his few remaining teeth; Deliverance and Humiliation sat on the other side of the hearth from Mercy, darning hose with coarse wool thread; Goodwife Dobbs slept in a chair, exhausted by a day at the wash tub, arms reddened by long immersion in water. The whole family was as wrung out as the sheets the goodwife had struggled with all day.

There came a knocking at the door. Dobbs got up with a grunt, protesting at the late hour. Suppressing a troubling cough, he warily opened the door, hand on the club he kept ready by the entrance.

"Open up, Dobbs," called a muffled voice on the other side. "Pray be swift."

"Master Edwin, what brings you here at this time of night?" Dobbs threw the door wide.

Mercy was astonished to see Edwin enter, Faith and Ann Belknap with him, between them supporting Grandmother.

"It's Mistress Isham. She refuses to be quiet until she's seen Mercy," Faith said. She looked exhausted, coif askew, cheeks pale. "I've had to catch her six times today to stop her wandering off on her own to search. Finally, Ann found her on her doorstep asking for Mercy, so we decided we had to bring her here and put her mind at rest."

Mercy rushed forward to help support her grandmother. "Oh, Gran, you shouldn't have worried! See, I'm here, safe with the Dobbses."

"Safe!" spluttered Ann, outraged that her friend had chosen to lodge here rather than at her house. "Is that what you call it? Why ever haven't you come to us, Mercy? I don't care a fig that your father's thrown you out—you must know that."

"It's not about my father—the matter is deeper than that, Ann." Mercy begged her friend with her expression to bear with her until she had a chance to explain.

Ann gave a disgusted sniff, only now realizing what a wretched place they had entered, as far apart from her luxurious home as the north is from the south. "It must be if you've chosen to live here. It's not some silly 'punishing-yourself-to-please-God' idea of yours, is it? For, if it is, you and I will be having some very serious words."

Mercy shook her head, tears sparkling. Ann was right: not so long ago that would have sounded exactly like her. Now she felt that she and God were in this together, putting up with the indignity to protect the innocent.

"This is a fine parcel of trouble," grumbled Dobbs, shaking his wife to wake her. "Give up the chair, wife. Old Mother Isham has come calling. I think we have some fancy piece from the City, as well as the whole suit of Harts here, bar John, and I don't doubt but he'll follow on after."

Rousing herself, the goodwife ushered Grandmother into the chair, pressing her hand to her aching back as she lowered the old lady down.

Gran sat, but refused to let go of Mercy's hand. "Are you well, my sweet darling?"

Mercy nodded, biting her lip. No, she wasn't really, but it was her own choice to put herself through this. And who was she to complain about a little suffering when she had her freedom?

"I tried to take the paddle to John, but he took it from me."

Grandmother fretted at her ancient cloak, hands quivering. "He shouldn't have put you out like that—no shoes, nothing!"

Mercy had spared the Dobbses the details of her departure from her home; she would have preferred that they remain in ignorance, but they were listening avidly. Ann looked close to another outburst.

"No shoes!" she hissed.

"That's no matter. I have new ones. Look." Mercy lifted her skirts to her ankles so her grandmother and Ann could admire her fine red shoes.

Grandmother smiled, her eyes peering in the gloom. "I can't see them so well. What are they like?"

"Scarlet, Gran. With a heel."

The old lady nodded. "Aye, I wager your Kit got you those. He's a fine man. Don't you let him slip away, you hear?"

There was no chance that Kit could go anywhere just at the moment. "I won't. Thank you for calling on me, but had you not better go home? It is very late."

"I'm staying here—with you. I'm going to see your young man with you tomorrow; you can't be going to those bad places on your own." Grandmother huddled in the chair, giving every sign that only bodily force would part her from the Dobbses' kitchen while Mercy still lived there.

Mercy looked to Faith and Edwin for aid, but her sister raised her eyes heavenwards. "I really think she means it, Mercy."

"Goodman Dobbs?" Edwin asked plaintively.

Dobbs threw up his hands, thinking only of what would get them all the best night's sleep. "She can stay in the chair if she wishes. Mercy can bring her home tomorrow, if she's willing then."

Her brother heaved a sigh of relief. "Thank you. Mercy, will you do that?"

Mercy nodded. "I'll sleep by her. See she lacks for nothing. And bring her as far as your door."

Faith grimaced at the reminder that Mercy was not welcome within. She pulled her to one side. "How fare you, sister?"

Mercy noted and appreciated that Faith had not renounced the blood tie as their father had demanded. "I am well, thank you."

Faith hugged her. "And your young man?"

"Not so good. He is ill, I believe." Her voice was not as strong as she would have liked.

"I will pray for him. And you." Faith wiped Mercy's ash-smudged face with her handkerchief, much as she had done when they had been children and Faith had acted the part of mother. "Be careful—I worry for your safety in that vile place."

Mercy sniffed, trying not to cry in front of the Dobbses. "How is Father?"

Faith gave a helpless shrug. "As you would imagine, he's heart-broken."

"I really wish it could be otherwise."

Faith pressed her face to Mercy's. "I know, my dear. We all do. Conscience is a terrible thing."

Edwin kissed Mercy and drew Faith away. "Come, sister, we've disturbed these good people enough for one night. Be well, Mercy."

"And you, Edwin."

Ann embraced her. "My mother is going to demand that you come and stay with us, you know. You'll have Belknaps bothering you until you fold."

Mercy squeezed her back. "Please don't. I can't explain—it's too dangerous. Kit is innocent, but I've discovered that sometimes innocence isn't enough. You can best help us both by staying away just a little longer."

Ann was far from convinced—and why should she be when she did not understand what was really at stake? "I refuse to see Mercy Hart thrown out like yesterday's peelings. Your father has a lot to answer for."

"He thinks—perhaps with reason, when you consider the outward signs—that Kit is bad for me."

"Humph! I think your father thinks too much sometimes."

Mercy gave a gurgling laugh. "Maybe you're right. I've thought for a while now that we could benefit in our family from less worrying about godliness and more loving as God would have us do."

"Wise words, my friend." Ann hugged her in farewell. "Be well."

"I hear and obey, O mistress." With a watery smile, Mercy let her go.

The two Harts and Ann departed, leaving Mercy feeling the full bittersweetness of what it meant to love her family almost as much as she loved Kit.

chapter 17

GRANDMOTHER'S APPEARANCE AT THE DOBBSES' home gave Mercy an unexpected weapon in her battle of wits with Warden Stanton. When she woke up the next day, her mind had cleared and she knew exactly how she was going to defeat the guard: unleash Grandmother on him. After giving the old lady breakfast, she explained the situation to her in terms she could appreciate.

"Gran, there's this horrible man at the prison. He tries to prevent me from seeing Kit."

Grandmother nodded, her eyes as bright as a redbreast's this morning. "I'll deal with him, dear, never you mind."

Mercy wasn't sure she could leave it to Grandmother's devising. "You mustn't threaten to paddle him, understand?"

Grandmother gave an impatient wave. "Of course not. I'm not daft, Mercy, just old. And forgetful." She blinked. "Where are we going?"

Perhaps this wasn't such a brilliant idea. "To see my Kit."

"Ah yes. He's a very handsome boy, that one."

"That's right. But he's in prison."

"Whatever for?" Grandmother protested, as if this were the first time she'd heard the news.

"It's not important. I just need you to help me to get in to see him."

"Yes, yes, I understand."

Mercy gathered up Grandmother and her trailing cloak, thinking it best to make her move while some fragment of the truth lodged in the old lady's remembrance. She placed in her basket the offering of almond tarts she'd thrown together rather hastily the afternoon before, hoping they would appeal to the warden's appetite. She could but try.

The warden was surprised to see Mercy back so soon, and forced out of his usual bullying course when he saw the old lady hanging on her arm.

"My grandmother is weary, sir. Might she rest in your office while we discuss Master Turner's health?" Mercy asked with rather more forthrightness than she had used with him before.

The man could see the old lady was weaving about, soon to tumble in a heap on his very doorstep if he did not act quickly. "Aye, come in." He opened the door with alacrity. "Here, mother, take your ease in my chair." He surrendered his command post to her, letting her sit at the table.

"Thank you, young man," quavered Gran. "You're a fine one, aren't you? You remind me of my cousin Aldus."

Mercy couldn't remember such a relative, but it was never a good idea to interrupt Grandmother when she was reeling in an idea from her past.

The warden preened, shifting his wide belt on his generous stomach. "I try to keep myself in good health for my duties, mother."

"I'm sure you do. Not many men these days make the effort,

you know. They overindulge in pies and so forth and let themselves swell up like tubs of lard—and modern fashions can be so cruel." She patted the stool beside her. "Let me tell you about Aldus—I'm sure you would've got on famously had you met. Mercy, where are those lovely tarts of yours? A little bite of something sweet keeps us all smiling, wouldn't you say, Sir Warden?"

"Aye, mother." His eyes flicked to the cloth that Mercy was unwrapping on the table.

"Run along, child, go see Master Turner. The warden and I are busy."

Mercy left as she heard Grandmother begin on one of her convoluted tales for which she was well known in the family. She had got worse since her infirmity, and to plunge into a story with her was like unraveling the wool after a kitten had got in the yarn bag.

"Yes, Aldus, there was a fine man, till he got taken up for sheep-stealing, of course, and that was in, when was it now, the day when that man ruled us, now what's his name?"

"King Henry?" the warder prompted helpfully.

"Nay, the other one—in the young king's stead. Ah, marry, Somerset, that was the man—or was it Lord Dudley? We seemed to get through our rulers very quickly then, faster than a pair of shoes lasts a tinker."

Leaving the warden caught in the coils of Grandmother's memory, Mercy slipped along the corridor to Kit's door. She didn't have the key, but at least she could peer in at the grate when she stood on an upturned bucket.

"Kit, my love, are you there?"

She heard rustling from the corner. It was horribly dark in the cell, only a little gray light coming in from a barred window high in the wall. Kit came to the door. His face was swollen and he had a blackened eye.

"Oh stars! I thought you had a fever!" She pushed her slim hand through the grate to touch his cheek.

Kit rubbed a palm over his face self-consciously. "Nay. I just had a little disagreement with my kind host."

"The devil! He told me you were too ill to see me."

Kit kissed her fingers. "I'm never too ill to see you, Mercy. But I imagine I must look very bad to you—nothing that won't heal, I promise." It then occurred to him that she was on her own, but not coming in. "But, Mercy, should you even be here? Where's the jailer?"

Mercy blinked back tears, determined not to spoil Kit's brief time with her by crying. "Grandmother is entertaining him for me. He won't get away for several minutes."

Kit gave a dry chuckle, holding his ribs. "I'm glad to be revenged on him. Punishment by Grandmother will make me smile when I next have to encounter him."

"But that can't happen again—I can't let him hurt you." She clenched her fists round the bars. "Do you want me to tell your brothers?" she whispered.

"Nay, this was to be expected." Kit shrugged it off as of no matter. "They can guess what is happening—I'm just thankful it isn't worse."

"Worse!"

"Mercy, what do you think happens in the Tower? I have only blows to battle—a little tenderizing for their questions, they think it. Give that to me any day over the rack."

Mercy really didn't want to know, preferring the false comfort of her previous state of ignorance about the workings of justice in the kingdom, but she forced herself to think of what was happening here. He was right: rough treatment in the Marshalsea was far better than the attention of the trained torturers kept by Walsingham in the Queen's name in the Tower.

"Is this what you meant about it getting worse before it gets better?"

"Aye. Never fear, he's done no permanent damage. I'll be as handsome as ever before you know it." He gave a self-mocking snort.

"I think I'll put poison in his next pie," she said fiercely.

He laughed. "Nay, don't do that. He might feed it to me. The chicken was excellent. I dined off those like a king."

"I haven't got anything for you today, I'm afraid."

"You are a banquet. I will feed off the memories of seeing you all day and all night. I love you, Mercy Hart."

Ah, that reminded her. She gave him a tremulous smile. "Hart no longer. I've left home."

"Oh, darling."

"But it's not so bad. I'm staying with a very kind family—and Grandmother, Faith and Edwin have all called on me. And Ann— I had great trouble fending them all off with their offers of help." None of this was exactly a lie.

"I wish I could shake some sense into your father." Kit wrapped his fingers round hers on the bars.

"He is following his conscience, as I am following mine."

"Then the sooner I can make you a Turner, the better."

"Aye." Mercy pulled out the grass ring to show him she still wore it. Kit's eyes were suspiciously bright as he touched the faded plait. She could hear noises behind her. The warden was stirring from his lair. "I must go. I'll come back when I can."

Kit smiled as she made to get down from the bucket. "Mercy?"

"Kit?"

He stood back so she could see him gesture in step with the words. *"My thoughts are wing'd with hopes."*

She performed the response on her little platform. *"My hopes with love."*

"Remember, love and hope, Mercy!"

Hugging that thought to herself, she hurried to retrieve Grandmother and return her home.

In July, the trap so carefully set by Walsingham snapped shut on the main players in the piece. Since January, Babington had run a scheme to get messages in and out of Mary Queen of Scots's prison in watertight beer barrels, thanks to an obliging brewer. No one in the Catholic conspiracy realized that Walsingham and Lord Burghley, the Queen Elizabeth's chief advisers, were well aware of their every move, intercepting the letters, then sending them on to the intended recipients. The brewer was their man, happily taking bribes from both sides.

Will laid the situation out to his brothers as they took a boat from London to the Queen's summer retreat at Richmond.

"I can't believe that even hotheads could be so foolish," he told them in a low voice, anxious to escape the attention of the oarsmen. "It seems that after one drunken night of treasonous talk"—he gave Tobias a pointed look—"Babington finally lost his patience with the slow creep of the plot to release his captive queen. He decided to cut to the chase, sending Mary a letter in which he proposed a new plan: invasion by friendly foreign powers, a rising of English Catholics, Mary's release—and assassination of Elizabeth by a party of gentlemen, himself included."

"That man has a death wish," commented James.

"Aye, I saw a copy of the letter in Lord Burghley's keeping. But there's more."

"Need there be more?" asked Tobias. "Is that not enough to hang them?"

"Aye, but they were never what this is about. The kernel of the matter is that Mary replied."

"Gads. This . . . this means a queen will be arraigned for treason to her fellow monarch, to whom she swore loyalty," marveled James as he worked out the implications of that fatal step. "I've never heard the like! It is going to set the fox among the hens on the continent, and north of the border."

Will nodded. "But her note was all Walsingham required. Like the cat outside the mouse hole, he swooped to scoop up the London end of the conspiracy. Babington and friends are on the run, very soon to be caught, I would hazard, as the whole realm is against them."

"So there is no connection being made to our friends in the Marshalsea?" Tobias knew that only distance from these events would keep Kit safe.

"I know not. But Babington and his crew face the ultimate penalty for their crimes. We've run out of time: we can't leave Kit in prison if they start passing down verdicts of hanging, drawing and quartering."

·✾·

Will, James and Tobias paced the corridors of Richmond Palace
hoping to pick up on any word concerning their brother's fate.
Lord Burghley and his son, Robert Cecil, issued from the Queen's
privy chambers, heads close together. Both dressed in black robes,
the elder looked like a well-fed mink while the younger had a pale
hawkish face. Friendly to the Laceys, they had helped them on
many occasions before.

Will made the approach. "My lord, Master Cecil." He gave a
practiced bow.

"Dorset—and your brothers!" Lord Burghley gave the three a
bow and rare smile. "What brings you to court in such force?"

"These are troubling times. We are concerned for the safety of
our Queen and those near to her." Will gave a subtle nod to
James—his wife was one of the Queen's ladies and thus in the
front line for any frenzied attack on the monarch. "We came seeking news. Have all those involved in the plot been apprehended,
think you?"

Burghley gestured to them to follow him into a window niche.
"Not yet, but they have quit London and will soon be caught,
for there is no loyal man alive who would shelter them. They will
be behind bars and the head of the conspiracy will soon find her
imprisonment much more confining than of late. You need not
fear for Her Majesty: we have doubled the guard. No one will
get close to her." He patted James's arm. "Or those who attend
upon her."

As agreed on the river, Will now moved into the second part
of their approach and feigned a disgusted expression. "It has come

to my notice, my lord, that one of my late father's by-blows has got mangled up in this business in some distant manner. A low kind of man—a player of all things—but he was taken up well before the recent exchange and now languishes in the Marshalsea. I am convinced of his innocence—he's a fool drinking with such fellows, but not a rebel—but he could be an embarrassment to the family if he comes to more notice in the matter."

Burghley did not look surprised to hear of this—few details escaped the attention of the Queen's chief minister. "A side-shoot of your family, you say?" He glanced at his son, but Cecil made no comment. He had been the source of their original information that Kit had been arrested, but as a good friend to Will at court did not reveal that the earl had been possessed of the knowledge for some weeks. "Well, well, I can see how that might worry you." He shook back the long sleeves of his robe. "Make a note of it, Robert. We'll look into it."

That was as much as the Laceys could hope for at this time. "You have our thanks." Will bowed.

Burghley and son strode away, in a hurry to deal with the far more pressing matters of a rebel queen and the missing conspirators.

James's wife, Lady Jane, emerged from the Queen's apartments. She was sweetly rounded with child and would soon be retiring from the Queen's service to give birth, but not soon enough for Tobias's overprotective brother. Her fickle mistress disliked talk of childbearing in her presence and preferred to ignore the fact, demanding a swift return to duties after the smallest of absences for lying-in.

"My love." She kissed James on the mouth before greeting

Will and Tobias. "How went your interview with my Lord Burghley? I saw you talking so retreated to give you space."

"Burghley will investigate the matter, which is better than putting Walsingham on the trail." James caught his wife in his arms. "But how fare you this day, my little bird? All well?" He placed his hand on her stomach.

Jane wrinkled her nose at him. "My feet hurt."

He lifted her into his arms. "Then you must rest—and I know a quiet corner."

Jane smiled hopefully and kissed his neck. "Indeed, my lord, then I suppose I must be commanded by you in this."

"Aye, marry, you must." Whisking her away with a flash of pink petticoats, James strode off in search of his private retreat.

Tobias gave up any hope of seeing James for the rest of the morning. "Is there anything else we can do here?" he asked Will.

"Nay." Will folded his arms and leant back against the stone wall, closing his eyes in weary thought. "But I think you should go in search of our fair messenger and tell her what's afoot. This plot has come to its crisis and Kit must be even more careful in his response to questioning. If we can get word to him through her good offices, we will be yet more obliged to the damsel."

A very good point. Tobias waved his farewell, already heading for the river. Will straightened up and set his shoulders firm, turning his attention to showing his loyal face about court, an activity he had no stomach for, but one that had to be done. Not for the first time, Tobias was grateful he did not bear the burden of the earldom.

chapter 18

WHAT NONE OF THEM HAD anticipated was that Mercy would be taken up for questioning before she could be warned of the new developments. Tobias arrived at the Dobbses' house to learn that she had not come back from her visit to the Marshalsea the day before. At first, the Dobbses had not been much moved on their lodger's account, assuming she had gone to visit friends or been allowed home, but when Edwin had called to ask after her, they had concluded that something more sinister had occurred. Edwin had gone to the Marshalsea only to be denied entry by the smirking warden.

Tobias knew Edwin as a nodding acquaintance from Porter's fencing school, where he too was a pupil. He took Mercy's brother aside.

"Tell me what the warden said exactly." 'Sbones, he hoped this wasn't spiraling out of control. He would never live with his conscience if the little maiden suffered for doing as they had asked.

Edwin gave a helpless gesture. A pleasant enough fellow, he was not at his best in a crisis, reduced to handwringing. "He said that Mistress Cherry Pie—"

"What?"

"His term for my sister. She takes fresh-baked pies in to your brother, sir. He said that she was wanted for questioning and that he had been ordered to detain her overnight. The officials should be there now. I've no idea what it's all about: Mercy's never done anything to anyone."

Tobias had a fairly shrewd idea exactly what it was about. Now the Babington plot had been foiled, the authorities were dotting their final "i"s by checking any person with the least connection to the business. Mercy had made herself a person of interest by her faithful attendance on Kit. But this was where the Laceys had to draw a line too and come forward to help.

"I'm sending word to my brother, the earl. He'll get her out, I promise."

Edwin shook himself into action. "And I'm going to my father. The City merchants won't like it one bit that one of their daughters has been detained so unfairly."

Aye, that was a good idea: the power of the City fathers was not something even the most aloof of governments could ignore. "Tell him we'll meet at your house as soon as the earl can gain leave from court." It was a fair way to Richmond; Tobias had already spent a good part of the day sailing up and down the Thames. "It may not be until late this evening, but we'll be there, I promise you."

No fool, Edwin blinked his pale-blue eyes, trying to fathom why an earl should show such friendship to a merchant family. "What is afoot, Master Lacey? Is my sister in danger?"

Tobias thought it very likely, knowing how harsh London prisons were on anyone caught on the wrong side of the door.

"Deep business, Hart, but Mercy is clear, I promise you. We will protect her, for after all she is to be our sister."

Edwin choked. "That . . . that man really means to marry her?"

"That man is my brother, and a finer person you will never meet. And, aye, he'll marry her, come hell or high water, so I wouldn't stand in his way if you value your skin. I predict that when he gets out of prison—and he will get out—he's going to quick-march your sister to the altar before you can say Robin Goodfellow."

Mercy was afraid. She had never experienced such bone-shaking terror since the last plague outbreak had swept though the city, taking half the infants with it under its black cloak. But that had been a smoldering fear, an anxious watch over the family to see if any showed signs of the illness; by contrast this was a blaze of emotion that left her cowering in the corner of her cell.

The warden—oh, how she hated that man, God forgive her—had waited for her to unpack her latest offering of gooseberry pies before informing her with relish that she was about to become his newest guest. He'd given her no time to send out a message, but marched her straight past Kit's door to a cell along the corridor. On the watch for a visit, Kit had seen her go by and responded with angry shouts and kicks to his door. He had gone ominously silent after the warden had left her alone.

"Kit?" she whispered into the corridor. That was no use: he'd never hear her. "Kit!"

No reply.

She had passed the night in dark despair, sure that Kit had done something desperate and been punished for it. By morning she was near frantic—and hungry and thirsty to boot.

The jailer came back in the early morning with a plate of food. "Here you are, mistress. I've orders that you can't mingle with the others in the common yard, so you get waited on. Not as good as your baking." He placed it on the pallet bed next to her. Mercy shrank further back against the damp wall, her fist clutching the dried-grass ring tight against her chest.

The jailer scratched his hose. She closed her eyes, resisting his attempt to draw her attention to his manhood as he stood before her. "It makes me sorry to see you in here, Mistress Cherry Pie, but you should make the best of it. It won't go so hard with you if you keep me well disposed towards you." He adjusted his belt, wafting the rank smell of unwashed body in her direction as he posed before her.

Mercy swallowed bile and buried her head in her arms.

A rough hand landed on her head, catching in the hair straggling from her coif. He tugged at a lock. "Such a pretty thing, aren't you, but no denying you are all woman. Would you purr for me if I stroked you, I wonder? I can see why the player keeps you at hand." A coarse palm drifted over her bodice, but retreated when she curled up in a ball, denying him access to any exposed skin.

"I can see you need to think on't. But then you're not going anywhere, are you?" He fiddled with his hose again, chuckled and left to carry on with his rounds.

Seeing where his hands had just been, Mercy left the bread he had brought her to the mice.

Kit had been dumped down in the pit again for his protest at Mercy's arrest. His bones ached. A sharp twinge with every breath gave him cause to suspect that the warden had fractured a rib with his latest beating. Yet that was nothing to the pain of his imaginings as to what his sweet Puritan was going through. If she was hurt, he would murder the jailer—he knew he would not be able to stop himself.

He tore up his shirt and used it to bind his chest, moving awkwardly, as there was not an inch that hadn't been bruised.

The worst was that he could do nothing—send no word to their friends, offer no comfort to Mercy. All he could do was pray.

He went down on his knees in the filthy straw and clasped his hands. "Remember me, Lord?" Not the best start to a desperate prayer, but he wagered that Mercy's faithfulness carried a little credit over to his account. "I pray your pardon for not talking to you of late." For six years, to be precise. "But if you would watch over her and get Mercy free of this place, I will . . ." What could he use to bargain with an all-powerful God? The idea was absurd. But God had to have a special place in his heart for Mercy—He had to or there was no justice in the world. "I will be eternally grateful."

Feeling foolish, but a tiny bit relieved, Kit got to his feet and resumed his pacing.

The warden was back. Oh, God; oh, God. Mercy hunched in a corner, hoping he would not stay long.

"Come, Mistress Cherry Pie, there are some kind gentlemen here to talk to you."

Knowing she had no choice, Mercy rose and smoothed her skirts, feeling with fingertips to make sure that her hair was decently covered.

"You look pretty enough for their lordships. Come with me."

With a firm hand on Mercy's back, he propelled her along the corridor to his office. Three officials robed in black sat behind his table. The warden took his place at the door behind her.

Mercy bobbed a curtsy, not daring to speak first.

"Mercy Hart?"

"Aye, sir." Her voice was a whisper.

"Your father is John Hart, mercer?"

Mercy nodded.

"We need your answer, mistress, for the record." The man in the center gestured to his colleague on his right-hand side, the one who was making notes of the interview.

"Yes, my lords."

"You have come to our attention as you have been visiting a certain prisoner—his only visitor, according to the warden."

"I see, sir. How . . . how may I help you?"

"By answering our questions. What would you say were your beliefs, mistress?"

Mercy remembered the schooling her father had given her in this against the day persecution should return to these shores and turn on the reformers. "I believe, I trust, as our gracious sovereign, the Queen believes."

The men nodded, well satisfied. None could argue with that.

The man on the left gave her an avuncular smile. "This must all be very confusing for you, a decent Christian girl caught up in this sorry business."

"What business is that, sir? Forgive my ignorance, but I do not understand why you wish to speak to me."

The warden shifted on his feet, but the man on the right shook his head. The official in the center looked down at a piece of paper before him.

"You are sixteen?"

"Aye, marry, sir, I am."

"Why do you come to see the prisoner, Christopher Turner?"

Mercy glanced at the more sympathetic of the three men. He was watching her closely. "We are betrothed, sir."

"You wish us to believe that you, a God-fearing maid, is like to be wed to a player?"

She looked down. "We do not have my father's agreement to the match, sir."

The notetaker snorted and muttered something under his breath.

"And you carry no messages for him out of this prison? He has not asked you to communicate with any of his confederates?"

Mercy was relieved she could answer honestly. If the question had been differently phrased she would not have been able to be so forthright. "Nay, my lord, on my honor, I carry nothing out. I know of no such confederates."

The notetaker was somewhat shrewder than his companions. "And what do you carry in, mistress?"

"Mainly pies," she replied. "The warden here likes fruit, but has a taste for savory ones on occasion."

The three men frowned at the jailer.

"Good my lords, I have to test them before handing them on to the prisoner," the jailer protested, "in case she smuggles messages or weapons to the man."

"And has she tried to do so?" snapped the questioner in the middle.

"Nay, sir. Just wholesome cooking, nothing else—or I would have told you."

"Hmm." The official stroked his fingers down the length of a quill lying on the table before him. "Have you ever heard your betrothed mention one Babington?"

Mercy could tell from the alertness in their bearing that they had come to the nub of the matter. "Nay, sir."

"Pilney or Gage?"

"Nay, sir, we don't talk much when we are together." She didn't mean it to sound as it did, but perhaps her misspeaking was for the good. The three gentlemen all looked down and smiled, doubtless filling in for themselves what the two youngsters did to pass their time together. She blushed, letting them think what they liked of her if it would help Kit.

"He's a fine-looking man, some would say. Is he ambitious?" asked the man in the center.

"Aye, sir."

They looked up, interest pricked.

"I think he wishes to take the lead in the next new play to be put on at the Theatre. And marry me, of course." She looked down at her red shoes peeping out from under her skirts.

"Humph!" the notetaker said, clearly dismissing her as empty-headed and Kit for a vain fool.

The man in the center turned to his brethren. "Are we finished here, my lords?"

As they were conferring, there came a pounding on the entry to the prison.

"Open up! Open up!" roared a man. "Stanton, I'll have your guts for my garters if you don't give me back my daughter!"

The official in the center raised his eyebrow at that. "Warden, I think you had best go let the man in before he starts dismantling your defenses with his bare hands."

In a moment, the warder was back with John Hart pacing at his side. Seeing Mercy standing in the center of the chamber, her father pushed past the jailer and seized her in a punishing hug.

"Mercy, you foolish child, what muddle have you got yourself in now?" he asked, giving her a shake. "Are you well?"

Four others clustered into the room behind Hart: Alderman Belknap, Reverend Field, Silas Porter and Edwin.

"Sirs," began the alderman, "I can vouch for Mercy being a good girl. The minister here has known her since a baby and will tell you the same. I think you have the wrong party if you suspect her of anything."

The man in the center tucked his papers away in a leather folder. "I'm happy to tell you that the young lady is not suspected of anything but being too good a cook for the warder to turn away. We were about to let her go. Gentlemen, we are agreed?"

The two men flanking him nodded.

"Aye, marry, let the girl go." The notetaker blotted his copy. "I fear she'll have enough punishment for her foolishness if she marries the man."

"And what of Kit?" Mercy plucked up the courage to ask. "Master Turner, I mean."

Her father huffed impatiently into her hair.

The notetaker drew a letter from a leather wallet. "Now that we've struck you from our enquiries, young lady, thinking you the last possibility of a connection to . . . er . . . another matter, my Lord Burghley has given us instructions to release the fellow. We are satisfied that he is no longer of interest to the Crown and, fortunately for him, being a foolish player is not a hanging offense. He is bound over to keep the peace, but otherwise free to go."

Mercy tugged at her father's doublet. "Please, Father, may we have him fetched and take him with us?"

"It seems that I can't stop you getting your way where that young man is concerned. Warden, will you bring him to us? Here's for your pains." John Hart flipped the man a coin.

Mercy resented any more going into that beast's pocket, but she knew better than to rock the boat at this stage, not when they were so close to getting free.

"I'd best go with him," volunteered Silas, sizing up the man. "In case he forgets his way."

The three officials were showing themselves out as Kit was brought into the room. Hand clasped painfully to his side, he blinked in surprise at the gathering. He made a sorry sight: one blackened eye, a swollen jaw and bruises marring his skin, but to

Mercy he was the most beautiful thing she had ever seen. Easing away from her father, who reluctantly let her go, she flew to him.

"Oof!" Kit gasped as she collided with his midriff. "Easy, love, I'm a bit tender there. Are you well? Not hurt by him?" He flicked a vicious look at the jailer.

She shook her head.

"So why's everyone looking at us like this?"

A quick survey of the room told her that Silas and the alderman appeared amused, Edwin resigned and her father stoic. Mercy leant away to tell him the good news.

"We're free, Kit. Neither of us is the least bit of interest to the Crown." And in case he still didn't understand, she repeated, "We can go."

He whooped with joy, tried to spin her round, but unfortunately his injuries made him drop her after only half a circle. Never mind: they were leaving.

"Then let us bid farewell to this pleasant hostelry before anyone changes their mind." He gathered her to his side, leaning on her shoulder for support.

John Hart didn't agree with Kit on much, but he seconded the player in this. "Aye, we'll go home and get you cleaned up a bit. Looks like you've got some nasty cuts there that need tending."

Mercy raised an eyebrow at her father's change of heart towards Kit.

"Good Samaritan and all that," mumbled her father sheepishly.

"And may I come home too, Father?" she asked.

"Aye. The past few days have fair killed me. I can't seem to stand having you from home, no matter if you deserved it. Come back to the Bolt of Cloth, Mercy."

"And Grandmother will paddle you if you keep me away much longer."

He gave a weary chuckle. "Aye, there is that."

chapter 19

WORD SPREAD QUICKLY THROUGH SOUTHWARK of the imprisonment of the youngest Hart child, bringing Rose hurrying to the bridge house to offer Faith and her mother comfort while they anxiously awaited news of Mercy. Silas went in the opposite direction, heading for the jail to see what aid he could offer there. Ann arrived soon after, telling them that her father had gone to support John Hart in his demand for Mercy's release.

"I doubt they'll keep her, not with the man most likely to be the next Lord Mayor breathing down their necks," Ann said confidently, revealing what Rose had long suspected: Master Belknap was destined for high office.

The women's quiet time together was interrupted by the arrival of no less a person than the Earl of Dorset, accompanied by James and Tobias.

"That's all we need," huffed Rose as Faith stirred herself to get out the best glasses.

"Hush, Aunt, they come to help Mercy," chided her niece.

For once, Rose did not resent Faith's correction, for she could see that she was right. The three noblemen looked ready to saw through the bars of the prison themselves if John's mission proved fruitless. And they were keeping her mother happy: she looked in heaven to have three such fine gentlemen in her presence. Any moment now, Rose predicted, they were going to be importuned for kisses.

Conversation traveled a rocky road over the next half hour; so wide a gulf separated the two families that Ann struggled to bridge the divide, and found that few congenial topics could be mustered. Everyone's mind in any case was on what was happening at the Marshalsea. It was a relief to all when voices were heard outside. Rose could distinguish Silas's deep bass among the lighter tones.

"It's them." She rushed to the door and flung it wide. "Silas, John, what news?"

She had her reply when she saw Mercy supporting a battered Kit. The pair came into the room to the cheers of the Lacey brothers.

"Here she is—the heroine of the hour!" Then the earl astonished the company by kneeling before Mercy's feet and kissing her hand. "You have our deepest thanks, lady."

James elbowed his elder out of the way to offer the same gesture of respect. "Our brother is a lucky man."

Tobias, who now knew Mercy somewhat better after their conspiring on his brother's behalf, risked Kit's wrath by kissing her soundly on the cheek. "Ask me anything in my power to give and it is yours."

"Tell him to go jump in the river," growled Kit.

"I understand your feelings entirely," said Tobias, standing shamefaced in front of the brother that had suffered for him. "But I want to thank you first for your steadfastness, Kit, under what looks like rough handling."

Kit waved it away despite the very clear evidence of his mistreatment. "'Twas nothing, sprout."

"Now for my dip in the Thames." Tobias made as if to run to the window.

Laughing, Mercy pulled him back. "Nay, that won't be necessary. This was a mad business; I've no doubt you have paid for your part in it with sleepless nights."

Tobias winked at Kit. "She's much kinder than you, brother."

Kit smiled down affectionately at his love's head. "Aye, much more merciful than I. There must be something in the name."

John Hart moved to restore some sort of control over his own house. "My lords, as you can see, we have no need of your intervention, but I had not realized quite how closely the matter concerned you."

The earl offered his hand to his brother and shook it warmly. "Welcome back, Kit. Aye, this one here is of our blood, Master Hart—a most worthy sprig of the stock from the evidence of his bearing in the last months. You must understand, sir, that he was always blameless in the business. My younger brother fell in with a bad lot for a few weeks before being rescued by Kit. Sadly, that kind act exploded in his hands like a faulty musket, suspicion falling where it was least warranted."

James folded his arms, surveying the young couple. "I've never seen such a pair of turtledoves cooing and billing over each other, and this the brother who always swore there was no such thing as love."

Mercy turned shocked eyes to Kit. "Did you in sooth?"

He tapped her nose. "I just hadn't met the right maiden. I will burn all my cynical sonnets and from henceforth write only love songs."

"So when are you going to see them wed, sir?" asked the earl as if the matter was clearly settled.

"From the looks of it, the sooner, the better," Ann said as she hugged her father in thanks for his part in the release.

Rose stepped forward. "Yes, John, when are you going to allow Mercy her heart's desire? Or need we change the family name to *Hard*-Hearted?"

John raised his hands in surrender. "Mercy has already made her choice. My coming to her in prison did not change that."

Kit carefully set Mercy aside to turn to her father. "Sir, I may not look the sort of man you would wish for your daughter . . ."

Rose smiled. The poor lad was as battered as a man who had just been rolled down Hampstead Hill in a barrel: not a prepossessing sight.

"But with me, I promise you she will want for nothing. Alderman Belknap here will vouch for me that I have begun investing, I hope wisely."

"I should hope so too," muttered Belknap. "It was my advice he took."

"I intend to continue at the Theatre, not only because it earns me an honest wage, but I also have obligations there that I will not lightly break. Mercy will be marrying a player if she marries me."

"If!" protested Mercy. "I *am* marrying you, Kit Turner, and there's an end to it!"

Tobias nudged James. "I told you she'd produce a landslide when she got rolling."

Kit, however, was not yet fully aware of the character of the girl to whom he had just pledged himself. He put his finger to her lips. "Hush, now, this is between your father and me, Mercy. Let me deal with this."

"Oh, dear, oh, dear," muttered James, shaking his head. "Our brother has a lot to learn about the fairer sex. You never, ever do that."

Kit was suddenly sitting in a chair, a sharp elbow having found a tender spot. Mercy stood before her father, looking defiant, if somewhat bedraggled after her night in prison.

"Father, I know you said you would give me nothing if I married Kit, but I think you are wrong to say so."

Reverend Field raised his eyes to heaven at this show of daughterly forthrightness, but no one else in the room was surprised by the new Mercy.

"I do not want anything from you, but I would be proud to go to my husband as a Hart, not as an outcast, and even prouder if you would give me the dowry you have always said would be mine if I married a man you approved." Mercy put her hands on her hips. "The husband of my heart has borne his imprisonment with Christian fortitude and patience. What more proof do you need that he is worthy of my hand?"

Rose almost felt sorry for her poor brother-in-law. John had been buffeted first by earls, then by players and now by one determined daughter. But, all credit to the man, he stood up to them.

"Mercy, you know what I said about Turner?" John said sternly.

Mercy's expression dimmed, turning to resignation. "Aye, and I'm sorry for it."

His solemn face broke into a smile as he enjoyed the gift he was about to hand her. "But I've decided I was wrong and you are right. Reverend Field, will you wed these two young people as soon as the banns can be read?"

Mercy's expression was radiant with joy, bringing tears to Rose's eyes to see her so deservedly happy.

Reverend Field fumbled the brim of his hat in his long fingers. "Aye, John, that I can. Players, after all, may not be completely beyond redemption if they choose good God-fearing girls for their wives."

"Amen," muttered Kit, pulling Mercy down on his knee and squeezing her in retaliation for her elbow strike.

"Then, my lords, ladies and gentlefolk all," announced John, "there are wounds to tend and empty bellies to fill. I bid you welcome to my house. Pray, make yourself at home while I take my new son-in-law to my chamber to bathe his bruises and find him fresh clothes."

Kit looked unwilling to be parted from Mercy, but she ushered him away.

"Obey my father, Kit. We both could do with a change. The smell of Marshalsea is not one we want to linger about us."

As the two left the room, pausing only to kiss in the doorway, Silas sidled up to Rose. "Mistress Isham, what say you to making it a brace of weddings, hey?"

Rose batted him on the chest. "You've been waiting to spring that on me, haven't you, you rascal?"

"Can't stop an old soldier staging an ambush, my lovely Rosie." He circled her waist. "So, what do you say?"

Her Silas really was a one: he was never happier than when teasing her. Even a proposal could not be done without a laughing spirit. "Not before the Reverend Field. At St. Mary's," she challenged him.

"Aye, I can agree to that. That Field fellow looks a barren pasture, not much joyful fruit to be had there for all his sterling qualities."

"Then I agree." Really she had made her mind up weeks ago; just been waiting for the man to ask. He had the depth and constancy of character that had been sorely lacking in her previous relationship.

"Excellent, i'faith." He scooped her up into a kiss. "Rosie Porter you will be!"

"Oh wonderful!" chirped Rose's mother. "Everyone's kissing. This is quite the most fun I've had since the coronation. I want a kiss too!"

Edwin bent to his grandmother. "It will be my privilege." He kissed her wrinkled hand as if she were the Queen herself.

Grandmother Isham pinched his cheek. "Aye, you'll do, Edwin, you'll do."

Kit and Mercy's wedding day was set for four Saturdays later at the end of August. London was quiet under the long days of summer, talk of rebellion subdued as the main actors in the piece had been caught and now awaited their grisly fate in separate prisons. Tom Saxon had been quietly released from the Marshalsea the day after Kit and Mercy, but chose not to return to the troupe. Rumor had him heading north to try his fortune there. Mercy guessed he was too embarrassed to return to the close-knit community of actors after the lies he had told about Kit.

The impending marriage had proved a fascinating one to organize with nobles and guildsmen vying for the honor of hosting it. The Lacey family had offered to hold the celebration at James Lacey's fine London house on Broad Street, but John Hart had proudly refused.

"It's a merchant's daughter who's getting wed, so the City will look after her," he told the earl.

So Mercy was going to her wedding royally dressed in the finest clothes the merchants could provide, in St. Magnus's near the northern end of the bridge at the entrance to the City, and was having her wedding feast in the Guildhall itself. The entertainment was to be provided by Burbage's company performing a play written by Will Shakespeare—his first for the troupe. Kit had not been allowed to see it—that would spoil the surprise—but Appleyard had let slip it was a first rate comedy full of dazzling wordplay. The company was still a little in shock that something so good could come from rural Stratford.

Mercy spun on the spot, letting her skirts bell out like a flower. Her rogue's princess indeed, and so she felt now that she had put on her finery, a blue satin dress worn over a farthingale, with creamy silk stomacher embroidered with gold, matching sleeves and forepart thickly sewn with seed pearls.

Ann Belknap, who was sharing the attendant's duties with Faith, came into her bedchamber and gasped. "Mercy, you look beautiful!"

Having no mirror in her room, Mercy had been trying to catch her reflection in the window. "You think so?"

"I know so." Ann noted with approval the diamond and gold necklace—a gift from Mercy's father—and the blue satin shoes.

"One would never guess the little maid who first sang with Kit at our supper party was the same girl. I'm green with envy." She giggled, gesturing to her clothes. Ann looked very fine herself, wearing a new grass-green silk gown and pale-green stomacher in honor of her friend's marriage.

Mercy bit her lip, wondering whether the blue silk bonnet and gold net caul on her hair was too daring. It was more suited to Elizabeth's court than to a City church, but her new sisters-in-law, Lady Ellie and Lady Jane, had sent it to her as their gift. She raised her hand to pat it nervously.

"Don't touch it!" Ann skipped across the room. "Faith said she had spent hours arranging it."

Mercy dropped her hands. She had intended to go to Kit like one of the beautiful butterfly court ladies he admired in his poetry and she would not doubt that instinct. She had to show him on this of all days that she could change too and meet him in a happy place between straitlaced Puritan and dissolute player. There was no backing away now for either of them.

Guessing her thoughts, Ann held out her hand. "You are perfect as you are. Come, it is time. Your father waits below and the litter has come for you."

Mercy shivered at yet another extravagance. She was going to be carried through the streets of London like visiting royalty, not plain Mercy Hart.

Seeing her friend's panic-stricken expression, Ann tweaked her skirt. "You goose. You mustn't keep Kit waiting."

No, that was true. They had waited long enough. As a final thought, she tucked the grass ring on its silk thread into her bodice. This was what rested between them—love that had survived prison, not all the glitter of one day.

"For Kit," she whispered, her fine butterfly clothes fluttering down the stairs, wing'd with hope.

In an upstairs room on Silver Street, Kit rummaged through his trunk of clothes, cursing. The picture of indolence, Tobias lounged at the window, while Will and James stood at the door, smirking.

"Where is that damned navy-blue doublet? I'm sure I put it in there last week." Clothes flew into the air like earth as a dog buried a bone.

Tobias tossed his silver-handled knife. "Are you really wearing that tedious thing?"

Kit stood up, his hair sticking up in worried peaks. "I can't shame Mercy at her church by dressing too garishly."

"You're right," Will commented to James. "He's completely sunk." He passed James an angel from his money pouch, outcome of a recent bet on how tamed their brother had become under Mercy's influence.

Kit threw a shoe at them.

"See, he's definitely of our blood. Knows shoes make the best missiles." James chucked the footwear to Tobias.

Kit, meanwhile, had found the blue doublet and began pulling it on. At least it was new and of the best cloth he could afford— that would count with the merchant family he was marrying into. He stuffed a foot into one of his polished black shoes. "'Snails, where's the other one?"

Tobias lobbed it to him, hitting him on the back. "Fifteen–love."

Kit brandished it at him. "Later, sprout, I'll get you later."

Ruff pinned and a comb dragged through his hair, Kit was finally ready for their inspection. He held his arms out. "How do I look?"

James shrugged. "You're dressed."

Will elbowed him. "You look well enough, Kit. We aren't ashamed to be seen with you."

Satisfied with this muted praise, Kit moved to the door. "We'd better hurry: I don't want to be late."

Tobias caught up with him and flicked his ear. "Where's the earring?"

Kit's hand went to the pouch hanging from the gold-linked belt that Will had given him that morning. "I thought it best to leave it off."

Tobias bit his tongue, refraining from further comment. Even he had some mercy for the condemned man on this day of all days.

The arrival of the four brothers at the church caused more than a few female heads to turn. Mercy was peeking out of the curtains of her litter, having got there a few minutes earlier, so had a grand view of their loose striding progress through the crowds gathered to see the spectacle of the Theatre man marrying the City daughter. First, the blond earl in scarlet, at ease with command; dark-haired James in moody black, clearly capable and not a man to cross; mischievous Tobias in forest green, winking at the girls; and her Kit, in midnight blue, holding himself with the player's confidence before an audience.

Her father went to shake hands with them and take the three Laceys inside to their seats of honor, where the female part of their families already awaited them. Kit came over to the litter to help her out.

"Are you ready, my love?"

She stepped down onto the stone path, shaking her skirts self-consciously into perfect folds. Milly Porter and her tailor friend had done her proud with this confection.

He held her at arm's length and whistled. "My stars, Mercy, when the bud blooms, she does so in splendid style!" He turned her to admire her costume, a courtesy approved of by the crowd who whistled and cheered. "You cast me in the shade."

Feeling light-headed with excitement, Mercy drank in the sight of her love. It didn't matter to her what he wore; he could have come in a jester's motley and she still would have wed him. But something was missing.

"You didn't leave off your earring for me, did you, Kit?" she asked, feeling that she must be a terrible influence to make him pluck his plumes like that. On this day of all days, he should be a dazzling peacock, not a sparrow.

"Aye, marry, I did, mistress. Anything to please my lady." He kissed her hand.

"Do you have it with you?"

He gave her a puzzled look. "Yes."

"Put it on—for me."

Grinning, he dug into his pouch and hung a new earring in

his lobe: a large pearl that no one could fail to see. He shrugged sheepishly. "A thank-you present from Tobias. I didn't want to offend the sprout."

Mercy laughed. "*Now* you are ready to make your entrance." She tugged him towards the church.

"Better follow the lady," called a well-wisher. "She can't wait to get her hands on you!"

"I don't blame her!" shouted a stout woman with a child on her hip. "God don't make many like that one."

Unable to resist a friendly crowd, Kit pulled Mercy back. "One last kiss of sweet Mercy Hart." He gave their audience what they wanted, bending her back into a scandalously passionate embrace in the very porch of the church. "*Now* I'm ready."

He swung her up to bow to the crowd. Laughing and blushing, Mercy curtsied as they acknowledged their applause. Making their final exit as a betrothed couple, they disappeared into the church hand in hand.

About the Author

EVE EDWARDS (eve-edwards.com) has a doctorate from Oxford University. She has visited Tudor houses, attended jousts and eaten Elizabethan banquets to get the sights, sounds, and tastes right for this novel. And, yes, she can testify that it is possible to eat neatly Tudor-style, without a fork. She lives in Oxford and is married with three children. The Lacey Chronicles begin with *The Other Countess* and *The Queen's Lady*.